MOM WALKS: GETTING CRUSHED

REBECCA PRENEVOST

Hope you enjoy!
Rebecca
3/24/2021

RP

Mom Walks: Getting Crushed. Copyright © 2021 by Rebecca Prenevost

Cover Illustration by Ginger P. Designs

ISBN 978-1-95-358203-4

WEDNESDAY, JAN 8

The word *Classified* is scribbled across the top. Fifth-graders are so unoriginal these days. I peek my head back out Kayli's door and down the hall. The coast is clear. She must be downstairs eating breakfast. But I can't open this, right? She'd kill me. I hold the folded note up to her bedroom light, searching for any glimpse of the words hidden inside. No such luck. I'm just going to have to ask her about it. I slip the note in my back pocket and toss the rest of the tissues and wrappers scattered across her desk in the trash. How can she get any work done in this mess?

"Hi, Mommy!" Ryn startles me, popping her head through the slightly opened door. But her cheerful face instantly brightens my mood. That, and the fact she's already out of her pajamas and into her favorite purple leggings and teal penguin hoodie. I'm not even bothered by her dripping-wet hair. I actually can't thank her second-grade teacher enough. Since he taught her class about hygiene, she's been showering every morning.

"Morning, sweetie. Don't you look nice today?" I smile,

patting the back of my pants to double-check the note's still there. "You know where Kayli is?"

"Kitchen." She scoots around me to snatch two hair ties from a dish on Kayli's desk. Prancing back out, she looks over her shoulder and playfully blows me a kiss. I can only shake my head as I go downstairs. She's lucky her fun-loving personality makes it easier for her older sister to tolerate an occasional unauthorized borrowing of accessories.

Turning the corner into the kitchen, I slow my pace. Although Kayli's fully dressed and her hair is done, she's madly working on something amidst a sea of papers, folders, and pencils scattered across the island. I brace myself for any impending panic. She doesn't have a ton of time before the bus comes.

"Morning, hon." I play it cool, giving her a quick squeeze before getting my coffee going. "Still finishing up your homework?"

"Nope. All done." She closes her workbook and looks up, sounding oh-so-certain as she adds, "Just wanted to check my math answers one more time."

"Got it...great," I reply. No nagging or reminders are necessary. I don't know what I'm worried about. Kayli hardly ever has an issue with getting her schoolwork done. Waiting for my coffee to finish, I help stack her papers and folders into a pile. I feel my pocket one more time and take a deep breath. Now is as good a time as any.

I take out the note and casually set it in front of her. "Oh, hey, I found this on your desk when I was cleaning up...I didn't open it, though. Promise." I do my best to look exonerated as I retreat back to the coffee maker, fill up my mug, and silently pray this isn't round two of mean girl drama.

"Ugh," she groans, leaning back in her stool. "The boys in my class are so dumb." She unfolds the note, flattening it out on the counter. "Look." She gestures to it with a flick of her hand and then crosses her arms.

Heading back over to the island, I tread lightly. My heart pauses while I pick up the note and read the question across the top. "Does Kayli Have Man Hands?" Below it, there are two checkboxes: the box next to the word *Yes* is checked, and the box next to the word *No* is empty. Man hands? I didn't even know that was a thing. Is this supposed to be mean?

"See?" She tosses her hands up and then crumples the note, grumbling, "They're such idiots. *Man hands*...I mean, why would anyone care what my hands look like?"

I breathe a sigh of relief. Ever since Kayli escaped the clutches of her queen bee classmate this past fall, she's been hanging out more with the boys in her class. They tend to avoid the gossip and cattiness and usually play some game or sport during recess, which is right up Kayli's alley. But a survey about man hands? That doesn't seem right.

"Hmm...that doesn't seem super kind, though. Did this upset you?" I cautiously wade in.

"No." Kayli flippantly brushes it off, giving me one of her signature eye rolls before shoving her papers and folders into her backpack. "It's probably Gavin or Brody. They're so stupid sometimes."

"But still..." I try to get a better view of her face to confirm this doesn't mean anything. She looks okay, though. Maybe I shouldn't press her on it.

"Mom." She glares, then tilts her head back in annoyance. "It's not a big deal. I swear."

"Okay, okay." I hold my hands up in innocence, backing away from her and turning to grab my coffee. *Don't worry*, I want to reassure her. This past fall, I learned my lesson the hard way. I need to be much more careful not to insert myself or swoop in and problem-solve for her. It's better for both of us when I let her navigate this stuff on her own.

Cradling my coffee mug to my chin, I inhale its glorious aroma before I take a sip and follow Kayli to the front door. Mm…I can actually feel those first few drops travel through my body as they work their way into my veins, energizing and calming me at the same time.

As Ryn thunders down the stairs, Kayli starts to layer on her winter gear. She looks so tall and strong lately…so grown up. Such a difference from last fall. She seemed so fragile then, as we took that roller-coaster ride through mean-girl land. I literally wince, thinking back to what that did to her self-esteem, never mind our relationship and my ability to trust her. She's like a different person now. So much more confident. And even though she's starting to incorporate a little more sass, she's a lot more open and honest with me, too.

As Ryn darts past us into the mudroom to grab her coat and backpack, she hollers, "Did you remember to sign my math homework, Mommy?"

"Ugh." I set my coffee down and race back to the kitchen to grab a pen.

I hear Kayli and Ryn giggling before Ryn shouts, "Good thing you have us!"

"Don't I know it." I return to the foyer as Ryn holds out her sheet of paper. I skim over what looks like hieroglyphics, frantically trying to spot any errors. It's not going to be much longer until I won't be able to tell the difference. "What about this one?" I point to a blank question.

She slumps over and whines, "That one's too hard."

"Honey…" I rub my forehead, closing my eyes as she turns to put on her coat. I do my best to make my voice sound calm. "Why didn't you show this to me earlier?"

Kayli takes the sheet from me and quickly scans it. She smirks, then crouches down next to Ryn and patiently explains how to solve it. After Ryn scribbles in the answer, Kayli grins as she hands it back. "Problem solved."

"Thanks, sweetie. You're a lifesaver." I sign my name and slip it into Ryn's backpack. "Everyone's got their snacks and water bottles?"

"Yes," they reply in unison, both happy campers now.

The bus comes barreling down the hill toward our cul-de-sac. "Perfect. Have a good day. Love you." I open the door, then maneuver behind it to protect myself from the cold gusts rushing in.

"Love you!" They both look back, wave, and then shuffle with the tiniest of steps down our driveway. It snowed several inches last night, and even though Ben shoveled before he left this morning, a thin layer of slippery frost remains. They're adorable the way they grab onto each other's arms to steady themselves over the icy spots.

I close the door and watch from the window as they get on the bus. When the door finally shuts behind them, I pick up my coffee and take another sip. Ah…and today, I can get back to my favorite routine of meeting up with my two best mom friends, Meg and Naomi, for our weekly morning walk. I finish my coffee, put on about a million layers, and practically skip out the door.

* * *

I can't help but hum along to the radio on my drive to the trail this morning. It feels like I haven't seen Meg or Naomi in forever. Unfortunately, our walks had to take a back seat for the past few weeks. There was simply way too much going on with family gatherings, hosting, and holiday parties for us to spend any real time together. Of course, there were plenty of text messages and occasional run-ins at school functions, but they aren't the same as catching up on our walks.

I pull in next to Meg's SUV and thank my lucky stars Ben makes me keep a shovel in my trunk. The plows still haven't cleared the streets yet, and if they come through while we're out walking, our cars will get blocked in for sure.

"Hey, guys!" I step out of my car and sink into the snow. "Magical day for a walk."

Meg beams as she holds out her arms and tilts her head back. "Hey, Dawn! I know! It's gorgeous, right?" She looks so excited, I'm almost expecting her to start twirling around.

"Do you think we'll get plowed in?" Naomi looks over to our cars with concern. As she zips up her olive-green puffy jacket and tightens her scarf, her no-makeup face somehow maintains its warm, natural glow—an impressive feat, considering how cold and dry the winter air is here in Minnesota.

"I have a shovel just in case." I look around for where the trail's supposed to be. "And I'm all bundled up, so I'm fine with it."

"Same." Meg smiles, acknowledging her sporty white coat, baby-blue snow pants, and coordinating hat and mittens, all displaying labels typically reserved for the most elite skiers.

"Okay…" Naomi still sounds hesitant. "Since we haven't seen each other in ages, I guess we can try it."

"And we can turn around anytime," I offer as we start traipsing through the snow, quickly realizing it's going to be a much more rigorous trek than usual. "We don't need to make it to our usual spot."

Relying on the lines of trees and shrubs to guide us, we slog through the heavy snow as if ankle weights are attached to our boots. But with the trees all frosted and the ground only sprinkled with a few animal tracks here and there, the untouched beauty is worth the effort.

"So, how was everyone's break?" I ask after we've found a good rhythm. "What'd your family think of Breckenridge, Meg?"

"So, so good." Her cheeks are already rosy from the chill… and the workout. "Our condo was right at the foot of the snow school. Kevin and I could even watch James and Brooklyn's lessons from the living room. Each day, we'd drop them off and then venture out on our own. After a day on the slopes, we'd then round 'em up, grab something to eat, and head back to the condo to play cards or board games before crashing. It was the perfect mix of alone time for Kevin and me and family time with the kids."

"Sounds spectacular," I say. "I swear, you should start a family travel blog or something. You're always finding the best things to do."

"Gosh no." Meg chuckles. "My travel agent's the real wizard behind the curtain. I simply tell her what we're looking for, and she sets it all up. We're very lucky."

"I'll say." I turn toward Naomi. "How about you guys? How was your break?"

"Wonderful." She looks up into the sky and closes her eyes for a moment. "You know, I love it when the kids are off from school. We sleep in, lounge around in our pajamas, and simply unwind. I make a big, healthy breakfast every morning, and the kids read, build things, write stories, or color all day. My parents came over for a few days right in the beginning, but then they left to go visit my sister in Arizona, and we soaked up the quiet family time."

"Perfect." I adjust my hat so less cold air can sneak in. "And Arizona is a great place to have relatives this time of year."

Naomi nods. "My parents love it there in the winter. They usually make it down a few times. Bruce and I are actually considering taking the kids down there over spring break."

"That's huge." Meg's eyes widen as she looks across me to see Naomi better. "Would that be their first flight?"

Naomi shakes her head. "We'll drive if we go. We did it a couple of years ago, and it worked out okay. The only thing that makes it a little more nerve-wracking this time around is Lily's phobia of throwing up. She's been doing so much better, but long car rides are still a little tricky. She worries about getting carsick. We still have plenty of time, though, and Dr. Brinks, her therapist, thinks once we get going, she'll be fine."

"I'm glad to hear Lily's still doing well." I think back to how much she struggled with her anxiety this fall. "What a trouper. And maybe the road trip will be a good challenge for her."

"That's what Dr. Brinks says too," Naomi replies.

Naomi and I are so far behind Meg in terms of family travel. At least Naomi has a few road trips under her belt. Ben and I have yet to take the girls anywhere outside of the state. However, this year is supposed to be *the* year. We made it our New Year's resolution to travel somewhere over spring break. Now we just need to figure out where.

We finally reach my favorite old bridge, which spans the two main bays of the lake, and the display stops me in my tracks. The view from this spot is always gorgeous, but it's even more so today. The flawless snow goes on forever, and the tiny line of snow-covered houses around the lake looks straight out of a scene from a movie. I stop, brush some snow off the railing, and look over the edge. "Isn't this pretty?"

"Yeah," Naomi replies, noticeably out of breath. "Do you think we should turn back?"

I shrug. Although the weight of my legs is much more apparent now that we've stopped, I could go a little longer.

"I can do whatever." Meg playfully leans over the railing, enough so that her feet come off the ground. "This is actually kind of fun."

"Let's go back." Naomi's shift in her stance borders on impatient. "This snow's fun, but I'm not sure I have the same endurance as you. Plus, I'm a little worried our cars will be buried."

"Works for me," I say as Meg returns to the ground and we turn back toward our cars.

"So, how's Kayli doing these days?" Naomi asks as we begin to retrace our tracks. "Is everything good, now that things with Sienna have cooled off?"

"With the girls, yes." I shake off the shiver running up my back. With all the lying, hiding, and manipulation centered around that girl this fall, I don't know if I'll ever stop being triggered by the name Sienna. "But I came across a little note or quiz-like thing from some boys in her class this morning that wasn't super kind. Kayli's also mentioned they've stolen her hat a couple of times at recess and have played keep-away with it. She claims it's all nothing, saying the boys are idiots, have strange senses of humor, or whatever. But I don't know…maybe I'm just uber-sensitized to that stuff now."

Naomi looks over sympathetically. "That's completely understandable with what you and Kayli went through. But, you know, those boys may be starting to form little crushes on her. I've heard notes and teasing like that are a growing trend in their grade."

"Oh my gosh," I sigh, feeling my shoulders relax. "I can't believe that never crossed my mind…" I adjust my jacket. Innocent fifth-grade crushes have to be way easier to deal with than mean girl manipulation, right? I glance over to Meg to get her read. With James and his friends, she must have a good pulse on this. "Although, I'm pretty clueless about boys this age."

Meg keeps her eyes straight ahead, her coat swishing to the rhythm of our steps. "From what I can tell, all the notes have been coming from the girls. I haven't heard a single thing about notes coming from any of the boys. And I'm positive James and his buddies could care less about crushes right now."

"Are you sure?" Naomi sounds unusually patronizing. "I'm almost certain I've heard about it coming from the boys too. Lily's not into it either, but numerous parents have told me stories about finding notes in their kids' backpacks after school."

"Oh, I know all about those little notes," Meg groans with even more irritation. "I've found several of them in James's backpack—from the girls. The girls are miles ahead of the boys at this age. For boys, playing keep-away is something they do, even with each other. I wouldn't read much into it."

The crunching of our boots echoes through the frigid air as I try to read between the lines. Is Meg insinuating that Kayli's the one instigating it? Or is she saying I should still be worried about more girl drama? Looking over and seeing her face all tense, I hesitate. Now doesn't seem like the best time to clarify.

Naomi tilts her chin toward her chest, discreetly making eye contact with me as she lowers her voice. "I still think it's a possibility."

"Well, not with James and his friends," Meg snaps, her volume overcompensating for Naomi's. I never would've guessed this could be such a contentious topic. It's like a snow-ball fight could break out at any minute. "He and his friends are so focused on basketball. Plus their homework. They don't have time to think of anything else. Their team has seven tournaments over the next nine weeks."

"Goodness," Naomi exhales but presumably catches herself before careening into one of their more notorious parental divides on overscheduling. She then takes on a much more compassionate tone. "I thought you were hoping to maintain a better balance after everything that happened with James's schoolwork this fall?"

"Yes…yes, I am." Meg's face softens, bringing her volume back to normal as she moves out of the way to let a cross-country skier pass. "And things have gotten so much better. His tutor has helped a ton, and he's not doing baseball at all anymore. It's been great. And Brooklyn has cut way back on dance too. She's planning to swap it out completely for soccer this spring."

The crush topic appears to fall by the wayside like the snow atop the drifts along our path. Meg fills us in on a mother-daughter baking class she and Brooklyn signed up for. And Naomi informs us Lily's taking a break from theater to explore her new love of coding, enrolling in a web design class.

I try to keep track of all their news, but my mind can't help but wander back to the possibility of a boy having a crush on Kayli. I mean, I knew this would happen at some point. But why on earth do they need to do a dumb survey about man hands? Not a great sign. Even under the warmth of my winter coat, my arm hairs rise. I know this is only fifth grade, but it's tough to shake my uneasiness. Especially since I have a history of misreading these kinds of things. I adjust my hat again and roll out my neck. I'm sure it's fine. "Anything else exciting going on this week?"

"Just the usual for me," Naomi replies as our cars come into view. "I'm still volunteering in Leo's first-grade class on Friday mornings and teaching yoga Monday, Thursday, and Friday afternoons." She reaches for my arm. "I can save you your usual spot tomorrow."

"That'd be great," I say. Although my professional world of online marketing campaign evaluations quickly ramps back up after the holidays, fitting yoga into my life always helps. Besides, I need to take better advantage of my part-time, work-from-home schedule. It's one of the main reasons I've stayed with that role.

"We've started to get back into a routine too." Meg looks over triumphantly. "And it helps that I'm not volunteering with any big projects at school. The only thing I'm on point for is putting together that writers' workshop the kids earned from the book fair this fall, and that'll be easy. Ordering catering and making dinner reservations are my specialty."

"For sure," I say as we get closer. Luckily, the plows still haven't come through. "And thanks for the lovely walk through the snow, ladies. I actually enjoyed the change of pace."

"Same." Meg adds a little pep in her step as she grows more excited. "Hey, would you want to try cross-country skiing next week instead of our normal walk? We could rent boots and skis over at Johnson Park, and there's a bunch of trails to pick from."

"Sounds fun...," Naomi says. "As long as we pick one of the easy trails."

"Perfect." I open my door. "Good luck with James's tournament this weekend."

"You too," Meg says, and we say goodbye.

I turn the key and hold my frozen hands in front of the vents for a few seconds. So what if a boy has a crush on Kayli? She can handle a fifth-grade crush, right? It's just another inevitable part of these kids growing up. Besides, she didn't seem that interested. She even called the boys idiots. It's probably nothing. And even if it isn't, whatever it is, I'm sure she's got this.

SATURDAY, JAN 11

"There they are." Kayli points over to her basketball team-mates at one of the corner tables.

"Okay. Good luck, hon." I barely finish replying before she runs off to meet them while I collect my change and hold out my hand for a rubber stamp.

These gym lobbies are becoming all too familiar. This is the fourth tournament this season I've had to pay my way at a ticket counter, weave through tables covered with team-colored duffels, jackets, and warm-ups, and navigate a sea of parents and players milling around. Kayli loves basketball, though, so I put on my bravest front.

I spot a few of Kayli's teammates' moms—Nikki, Cori, and Jane—peeking into the gym doors as they wait for the current game to finish and some seats to open up. I walk over and tap Nikki's shoulder from behind. "Hey, guys. How are we doing this lovely morning?"

Nikki turns around and beams. "Ready as always. And we even get the rare presence of Cori today." Nikki and Cori are next-door neighbors, but they could pass for sisters. And the two of them—and their daughters—are super close. When I first met them, I struggled to keep them straight. Even though Cori's hair is darker, they each have one of those short wedge haircuts that entails way too much upkeep for me to ever consider. They also dress very similarly. It's a rare day when one of them isn't pairing a silky shell with a cardigan, and I've never seen either one of them without their nails or makeup done.

"Aw, must be a special day," I tease as Cori turns to say hello. Cori's usually matched up with her eighth-grade son since her husband, Brad, is Kayli's coach. I also say hello to Jane. Her long frizzy hair, glasses, and cargo pants make her easy to distinguish.

The buzzer blares, and parents from the other teams filter out as we weave our way through to find seats in the bleachers. I plop down next to Jane, and Nikki and Cori squeeze in behind us. While we're settling in, Kayli leads her team across the gym and has everyone toss their bags and shooting shirts behind a row of folding chairs. She then grabs a ball from Coach Brad and directs her team back onto the court to form two lines for layups.

Kayli was pretty disappointed about missing the cut for the A team this fall. But after the season got going and she realized she's one of the better players among this group, she really stepped up as a leader. Being on the B team may have turned out to be the best thing for her.

After the buzzer blares again, our attention turns to the girls. The game is a real nail-biter, which always makes Coach Brad very animated. And when Brad gets animated, I get nervous. By the time the buzzer sounds again at the half, the girls are down by a couple of points, and my stomach feels like I've done a thousand sit-ups.

As the team huddles around Brad, Nikki pats me on the shoulder from behind. "So, I hear one of the boys in Kayli's class may have a crush on her."

I struggle to keep my posture upright, still focusing on the court as I hesitate for a second. My face isn't quite ready for spectators. Since Kayli hasn't mentioned anything in the past few days, I was thinking—hoping—it was nothing. But if anyone knows what's going on, it's Nikki. Although I love Nikki, she's a key operative of the Valleybrook grapevine, and most rumors pass through her. Playing dumb is probably my best strategy.

Once I'm more collected, I turn to face her. "On Kayli? Really? Who told you that?"

"My lips are sealed," Nikki jokes, zipping her fingers across her lips. "But seriously, I'm pretty sure that's what Mandi said. She wouldn't tell me his name, though."

"Interesting…" I smile, doing my best to portray only inno-cent curiosity as I turn to Jane. Jane's daughter, Poppy, is in Kayli's class. And although my heart aches at the thought of all these moms knowing the news before Kayli's shared it with me herself, I still have to know. But I don't want to make it seem like a big deal if it isn't. "Have you heard anything about this?"

She shakes her head. "Me? No way. I rarely get any infor-mation out of Poppy."

I turn back to Nikki. Now, not only do I want to tamp down the gossip, but I also want to buy myself some time to figure this out with Kayli. "Well, she's mentioned some of them have started teasing her a bit—passing notes around and silly stuff like that. But that's all I've heard." I sit up taller and try to act easygoing—not at all concerned. Nothing to see here, folks.

"Have you heard anything?" Nikki turns to Cori, who substitute teaches at the school and usually has a pretty good sense of what's going on with the kids.

"Sorry," Cori replies. "I've been spending most of my time in the middle school lately. But I can ask Emily if you want. Thinking back to Brandon and his buddies, though, they were a couple of years older before they started getting interested in girls."

"That's okay." I pounce at the chance that it's nothing. Besides, it's probably better to keep downplaying it. "I'm sure whatever it is, Kayli has a good handle on it."

The buzzer indicates halftime is over, so we turn our attention back to the game. It continues to be neck and neck through the second half. All the girls are playing so hard, but the team they're playing isn't letting up. Watching the teams continue to exchange the lead, I have to keep reminding myself to breathe. And Coach Brad's amped-up energy and volume aren't helping. As the clock winds down to a minute left, Kayli steals the ball from their point guard and runs it in for a layup to tie the score at twenty-twenty.

I wipe my palms on my pants as the other team calls a timeout, and the girls run over to their bench. I shift in my seat as Brad scrunches his face, shouting commands at the girls. It's easier to watch when he scribbles on his clipboard. But when he points his finger right in Kayli and Emily's faces, it's hard not to cover my eyes. I don't think I'll ever understand why he needs to talk to them like that. Finally, he backs off. The team puts their hands in a stack and yells, "Together!"

It's the other team's turn to inbound the ball, but after a few passes, it slips through one of the player's hands and lands out of bounds. With fifteen seconds left on the clock and Brad yelling directions from the bench, Emily inbounds the ball to Kayli. Kayli dribbles it up the court. She looks to be going in for another layup, but at the last second, someone from the opposing team jumps in front of her. Fortunately, Kayli sees Emily open under the basket and passes her the ball, and Emily puts it in right before the buzzer.

My arms reflexively shoot up as I jump to my feet and cheer with the other parents. Nikki, Cori, and Jane are going crazy around me. All the girls are jumping and cheering too, as

Brad tries to wrangle them into a line to shake hands with the other team.

After the girls collect their stuff, we meet in the hall to congratulate them. Cori leaves to meet Emily's older brother at his tournament, and Kayli's teammates decide they want to eat and then go watch some of the other teams play until it's their turn again. Jane, Nikki, and I find a nearby table as the girls get settled and unpack their lunches.

"So, do you know which boys are teasing Kayli?" Nikki sits down next to me and unwraps an energy bar. Getting to know Nikki better has actually been one of my favorite parts about this season. Sure, she can be a little gossipy, but her welcoming and outgoing personality makes it impossible not to like her.

"Not really." I keep my expression plain, still figuring it's best to keep things toned-down. "All I know is she plays with this boy Gavin and his friend Brody quite a bit."

"Gavin Donder?" Nikki asks.

I take a sip of my sports drink and then nod. "Do you know him?"

"A little," Nikki replies. "He lives in our neighborhood on the other side of the horseshoe. He has an older brother who plays basketball with Cori's son. His mom's name is Lisa."

"That's him," I say, looking over at Jane, who only shrugs. "I chaperoned the fifth-grade retreat with Lisa this fall. I don't know her super well, but she seems nice."

"So, you think he might be one of the boys teasing Kayli?" Nikki continues to probe.

"He might be." I try skirting the issue again. "Whatever's going on, it doesn't seem to be too big of a deal to Kayli yet. And I have no clue how fifth-grade boys' minds work."

"I bet you know more about fifth-grade boys than you realize," Nikki says. "Think back to when you were younger. It can't be that different."

"Oh gosh," I groan. "I was the worst when it came to boys.

I never understood them, and I was so shy and quiet. I barely had any friends at that age, let alone any friends who were boys. And now having two girls, I'm pretty clueless." I return to my matter-of-fact tone. "Either way, Kayli's handled everything so maturely these past couple of months. I'm sure she'll be able to manage whatever's going on with the boys."

"Definitely." Nikki gestures over to the girls' table. "She has so much confidence. I heard she even stuck up for one of the girls who was getting teased for not playing as much."

I follow Nikki's gaze over to Kayli. She's now directing her teammates to pack up their stuff and head over to a different court to watch another team. It seems she can clearly hold her own. I shake my head as I stand up and stash my drink back into my purse, adding sarcasm to my voice to mask the strange mix of both pride and embarrassment. "Yeah, she's definitely not afraid of taking charge these days."

* * *

As the second game begins, I spot Ben and Ryn in the doorway and wave them over. "Hi, hon." I put my arm around Ryn as she scooches in next to me, and Ben sits on the other side of her.

Ryn leans into me and then spins to see Jane and Nikki. "Where are Ethan and Mollie?"

"Sorry, sweetie," Nikki replies. "Mollie decided to stay home with her dad today, but she'll be here tomorrow. Were you able to see her at the skills session this morning?"

Ryn's eyes light up. "We were the last two left in Lightning and Army-Navy."

Nikki leans forward, lowers her voice, and whispers, "I suppose you won both, right?"

Ryn tips her shoulder up and smirks. "It was close, though."

"Ethan's home today, too," Jane says. "I'm not sure if he'll be here tomorrow, but he's sure excited for you to come to his birthday party next week."

"Me too," Ryn replies. Ethan's in Ryn's class with Mr. Kane. Their friendship had a rough start, but now they're good friends.

I turn my attention back to the game and see we're already losing two to ten. Bummer.

"Come on, Kayli!" Ryn cheers and then flinches, looking disgusted. "That girl traveled."

"It looked a little like it." I look down to the ref, but he doesn't blow his whistle. "I'm not sure, though, hon." Ryn knows way more about basketball than Kayli ever did at her age. I'm sure she's picked up quite a bit sitting through her sister's tournaments. And it probably also doesn't hurt that Ben's frequently running the girls to the Activity Center to shoot hoops.

Unfortunately, the rest of the game is a blowout. Kayli's team plays okay, but the other team is taller, faster, and way more skilled. After the final buzzer sounds and the team gathers for a quick huddle, Kayli grabs her stuff and meets us at the bleachers.

"You'll get 'em next time." Ben pats her back, taking her duffel.

"Yeah." She wipes sweat from her forehead and looks up at me.

"That was a good team," I say. "It was fun to watch you guys play so hard."

"Thanks," Kayli grumbles and then turns back to Ben. "Can we still go out for pizza tonight?" Kayli's favorite pizza place is Randy's, which isn't too far from our house.

"You bet." Ben wraps his arm around her and gives her a playful squeeze. "Let's go."

* * *

The smell of freshly baked dough hits us as soon as Kayli and I pull into Randy's parking lot. It's an old-school parlor where they take your order at the counter, give you a numbered table stand, and then bring your pizza over when it's ready. Ryn and Ben are already in line when Kayli and I race in from the cold.

We're a little early for the dinner rush, so there's only one other couple ahead of us and two tables occupied: one with a family that looks like they just started eating and another in the back corner with a family that looks like they're almost done. Looking closer, I realize it's Lisa Donder among a group of boys. She must be with her sons and a couple of their buddies. Although it's not unusual to run into a family we know in our small suburban town, running into her and Gavin tonight seems a little too coincidental. I catch her eye and give a friendly wave. Then I nudge Kayli. "Honey, isn't that your friend over there?"

She looks over. "Yeah." She gives the boys a cheesy expression, raising her hand in this sort of awkward half-wave motion, and then quickly refocuses her attention back to the ordering counter. Seems normal, nothing too crush-like.

"One large sausage pizza, with half mushrooms and half black olives," Ben says, reciting our usual order. I'm sure this place has all sorts of fabulous pizzas, but we've been ordering the same toppings for ten years, ever since Ben and I discovered the place when we moved to town. The only thing that's changed is we used to order a medium. I glance at Ryn and Kayli again. If only everything could be as simple and predictable.

Ben grabs the numbered table stand, hands Kayli the cups for the soda machine, and starts heading toward our usual booth. After a couple of steps, though, Kayli nearly knocks him over, yanking the back of his shirt and redirecting him to sit at another booth toward the front.

"What?" Ben looks back at her, confused. "Why?"

Kayli mouths, "Please."

Ben presses his lips together as he inhales, but he complies with her request.

"What's that about?" he asks as I scooch in the booth across from him.

"She might be avoiding sitting close to those boys over there." I tip my head in the direction of Lisa's table as the two younger boys grab their cups and start over to the soda fountain. I try to disguise my interest by keeping my eyes on Ben, but I can still get a view of the boys in my peripheral.

"Why? Does she know them?"

"One of them is in her class, but I'm not sure which. The other one must be his friend." I follow Ben's stare, and we watch the larger boy push the smaller boy into Kayli. It's not very hard, but it's enough to spill some of her drink.

"Nice," Ben mutters as he turns back to me, shaking his head.

As Kayli and Ryn start heading back our way, Kayli's face is flushed, and I can tell she's trying hard to keep it straight. Ryn, on the other hand, can't hold back her giggles. Ben shifts in his seat, obviously annoyed, as Ryn slides in next to him and Kayli takes the spot next to me.

Ben leans his head in closer to Ryn's. "What's going on over at the soda fountain?"

"Those boys are in Kayli's class. One of them has a crush on Kayli." Ryn grins until she catches Kayli's glare and then immediately looks remorseful.

"Ryn," Kayli groans as she tilts her head to the side, shooting daggers at her sister.

"He better not," Ben warns. "You're way too young for that."

It's now my turn to tilt my head and glare. I love Ben to death, but saying stuff like that isn't at all helpful. The girls should be able to share what's going on with these kinds of things without feeling like their parents will get mad.

"Which one's Gavin, honey?" I try to ease the tension and ingratiate myself with Kayli. After hearing the leak from Nikki and now finding myself envious of Ryn, I so want her to feel like she can share her news with me. "I met his mom at the retreat this past fall, and she seemed pretty nice."

"The shorter one," she mumbles, her threatening eyes still locked on Ryn. "The blond."

"Oh yeah." I look over, trying not to wince as he and his friend take turns jabbing each other in the arm before getting their coats on. "He looks a lot like his mom."

"Food's here!" Ryn shouts as a waiter heads our way, carrying the large pizza. Ben starts passing out plates and napkins as I give another wave to Lisa. Poor thing. She looks exhausted. As the boys follow her out, I catch Gavin's friend trying to trip him one last time before they get through the door. I totally understand why she looks so tired.

"Seems that Gavin's friend likes messing with him." I shoot for diplomacy in describing their behavior, gently nudging Kayli to see if she'll say any more.

"Brody's so immature." Kayli rolls her eyes, glancing once more at Ben before reaching to grab a slice of pizza. Obviously, I'm not getting any more out of her until Ben's out of earshot.

* * *

After we get home, the girls run upstairs to get pajamas on so we can all watch a movie. I follow Kayli up to her room to test the remote possibility she'll fill me in more on these boys.

"You need anything washed for tomorrow?" I casually ask

from outside her closet. "I'm throwing in some towels and could easily fit in a couple more things."

"That'd be great," she says as I hear her rummaging through her laundry basket. "I'm out of socks." After a couple more seconds, she hands over a wad of nasty, almost crunchy, socks.

I pretend to choke back a gag, joking, "Anything else?"

She looks around her room with her hands on her hips. "That's it."

"Okay..." I linger in her room, scrambling for a way to signal she can bring up Gavin.

"Mom?" Kayli asks and then bites her lip.

"Yeah?" I reply and then try to soften my face as I hold my breath.

"If Gavin *does* have a crush on me..." She plops onto her bed. "Would you be mad?"

"Not at all, honey," I reassure her as I sit down next to her and the hollowness in my gut starts to dissolve. I'm still not quite sure about what she thinks of this kid, but regardless, I don't want her to start lying or hiding things from me again. "You know, Dad gets a little anxious about this stuff. He may need a little more time to get used to it."

She pauses and then a huge smile spreads across her face. "I think Gavin likes me, then."

I can't help but return the smile. It's not only the look on her face, but it's also the fact that she's still willing to be open with me. After overinserting myself in her friendship issues this fall and inadvertently pushing her away, I'll do almost anything to prevent that from happening again. I want us to stay close and be able to communicate honestly. I drop the socks on the floor and put my arm around her. Her smile must mean she likes him back. My daughter's first crush...

My daughter's first crush! Questions start piling up in my head. What is she getting into? What does this mean? And how will this boy even treat her? Isn't he the same kid who wrote the note about man hands? The hollowness in my gut is resurrected as I recall the tripping, drink spilling, arm-jabbing boy.

"But..." She looks me straight in the eye. "I haven't decided if I like him back yet."

"Got it." I nod, trying not to exhale too loudly. Maybe this won't turn into anything.

"Yeah," she sighs, leaning into me. "Too many other girls have crushes on him. I just want to keep being his friend. And the girls who have crushes on boys usually act so annoying, batting their eyelashes at the boys and whatever...I definitely don't want to be like that."

"Sounds good." I give her another squeeze, counting my lucky stars over and over again because she's got her head on so straight. "Sounds really good."

WEDNESDAY, JAN 15

I scan the map posted on the wooden billboard outside the ski chalet. Alternating from the map key to the trails of dotted lines and back, I search for the color that's the shortest. Although Naomi said she wanted an easy one, the map doesn't show terrain. It only shows length, and all the routes appear to be between four and five miles.

"Any preference?" I wipe my brow and turn to Meg, holding my hand up to block the sun. It's chilly this morning, but the adrenaline from my nerves is already making me sweat. I haven't been cross-country skiing in years.

"Oh, oh...let's do this one." Meg grabs my arm and eagerly points to the red line. "It goes right by the lake. It has a couple of hills, but it'll be so pretty."

I can't help but laugh. Who knew she'd be so excited? I check the key. It's the second shortest at 4.3 miles. "Works for me." I give her a thumbs-up and trudge back to the bench where Naomi's sitting to lay out my skis. It takes a couple of tries, but I finally get my boots clipped in. Then I help Naomi to her feet, hold her skis in place while she jams her boots in, and prop her up as she gets her pole straps situated.

"Do you mind leading?" I holler over to Meg, who's off to the side, practicing her glides as if they're arabesques. "My sense of direction is horrible."

"Sure...I'd love to!" Meg replies and then glides back over, keeping her front arm extended and holding her back ski up much longer than required. Clearly, she's enjoying this.

"What about you?" I turn to Naomi. "Would you rather be in the middle or last?"

"Last, please." She finishes tucking her mittens up into her sleeves. "It's been forever since I've skied, so I'm going to be a slowpoke."

"Everybody ready?" Meg calls back, already settled into the ski tracks and slowly moving down the narrow but gradual hill.

Naomi confirms she is, and I slide in behind Meg.

"So, what's new, you guys?" I steady my poles as we enter a woodsy area. "Did you have good weekends?"

"Ours was great." Meg glances back. "Brooklyn had dance on Saturday morning, and James had basketball both days. But Kevin was home, which made it easier. And James's team won their tournament, so we all went out for dinner on Sunday night to celebrate."

"Where'd you guys go?" I try to keep my balance as we loop around a corner and the view starts to open up. Naomi's several lengths behind us, so I motion to Meg to hold up.

"Randy's." Meg slows down. "It was packed, so we had to wait a bit, but our family loves that place."

"We love that place too. They have incredible pizza." I focus on the positive, reticent to mention any of the other details from our last visit there as Naomi catches up to us. "How'd your weekend go, Nay?"

"Definitely more chaotic than I'd like," she huffs. "Lily decided she *had* to redecorate her room since suddenly it's way too babyish. So, we packed up all her stuffed animals and old books, and we tossed out most of her crafts and artwork."

"Whoa," I say as Meg zooms ahead again. "That's a huge change."

"I'm still a little nervous she's going to change her mind, but she was adamant. So, now it's very clean and simple with only her nightstand, bookshelf, and desk. She begged me to get her some new bedding and a different lamp too, but with her attitude this week—let's just say it's been a little on the snarky side—I held off."

"Lily? Snarky? That's strange, isn't it?" I wobble a bit, looking up at the large hill in front of us. There's no way I can stay on the tracks for this. I step off to the side and rotate the front of my skis out, so I can herringbone it.

"Not lately," Naomi grunts. Her skis keep getting tripped up as she follows me over to the side. "We've been battling so much about the screen time she thinks she needs to have for her web design class, so that's part of it. But it's probably hormones, too—I'm sure you're dealing with that type of thing with Kayli. I'm trying to be understanding, but goodness...she puts me to the test. And, with her anxiety always looming, I'm nervous about being too hard on her."

"I can't imagine. I struggle to balance it with Kayli, and that's without her having anxiety issues." I grab Naomi's arm and help pull her to the top of the hill where Meg's waiting. I don't want to rub it in, but I'm loving that Kayli's been so even-keeled lately.

"Isn't this unbelievable?" Meg gestures to the view, holding out her poles.

"Yes." Naomi bends over, resting her hands on her knees. "But I'm out of shape."

"Same." I laugh, propping myself up on my poles.

Meg skis over to us. "We're about halfway around. How about we take a tiny break now, and then I promise to get you guys some hot cocoas when we get back to the chalet."

"That's a trick I'd use on my kids." I smirk, shaking my head.

"I know…same." Meg chuckles. "It works, though, right?"

"Every time." I smile. "So, what's new with the writers' workshop? Is everything set?"

"Yes. However…" Meg looks up, rubbing her forehead in an apparent state of disgrace. "You guys are probably going to give me so much crap, but Principal Jacobson also asked me to help plan the fifth-grade dance."

Naomi and I groan in unison. Here we go again with Meg overcommitting.

"I know, I know." Meg buries her face in her hands.

"You told him no, right?" Naomi stands tall, her hand on her hip, glaring at Meg.

"I couldn't." Meg uncovers her face and looks up. "He was basically begging me. He said the other mom planning it needs help since she isn't as organized as me. And I'm going to make it so cute. I'm sure you already know it's Sadie Hawkins style, but this year, we're also going to make it a barn dance theme. We're going to have hay bales for seating, old barrels for tables, mason jar lights, and a barn door photo booth."

"Oh, Meg," I sigh.

"I know." She straightens up, placing her hand on her hip as she starts to sound more irritated. "But get this: the other mom is Stacy Cooper's mom, Cynthia."

"What?" I can't help but gasp. Of all the things to make matters more complicated. The queen bee's sidekick's mom. "Sienna's best friend's mom is helping you plan the dance?"

"Yep." Meg scoffs, then presses her lips together before adding, "But that's not even the worst of it."

"I'm terrified of what you're going to say next." I hold my poles up like a shield.

"Me too." Naomi pretends to duck behind me.

"So, after we finish meeting with Principal Jacobson yesterday, Cynthia pulls me aside. She tells me she's heard so much about James these past few weeks and how she thinks it's so cute and sweet and blah, blah, blah that Stacy has a crush on him."

"What?" I cringe, remembering Meg's disdain for the girls pestering James last week. "Oh, man."

"Right?" Meg throws up her hands, ratcheting her volume up several notches. "I'm telling you these girls are too much. No, Cynthia! It's not cute! Or sweet. These frigging notes and constant fawning from Stacy are a total distraction! That's what they are. James doesn't need it! His attention needs to be on schoolwork and sports."

Naomi and I are speechless. It always takes a minute to figure out what to do when Meg gets this worked up.

"And he doesn't want it, either," Meg keeps going. "I asked him about it last night, and he was squirming in his seat. He was so uncomfortable. He gets so frustrated when the girls badger him or hang around, squealing by his locker. Ugh! This stuff drives me bonkers."

"Yikes," is all I can think of to say. We should probably get back on the trail so Meg can get rid of some of this pent-up energy.

Naomi seems to read my mind, raising her eyebrows as she glances my way. "Maybe we should start heading back to the chalet. A little exercise might help."

Thankfully, Meg agrees, and we all get back on the trail. After a few strides, though, Meg starts cruising again. Naomi and I try to keep up, but it's impossible. We eventually give up and let her finish on her own. When we finally reach the chalet and return our boots, skis, and poles to the rental counter, Meg's waiting in a booth with three hot cocoas.

"Sorry, guys." She slides our cups over to us as we take off our hats and mittens and scoot in across from her. "Thinking about Stacy's stupid crush on James hit a chord, I guess."

"No worries," I say, but I still wonder why a tiny distraction from sports or homework merits this type of reaction. "What do you think it's about?"

"I don't know," Meg exhales, leaning back in her seat. "Maybe when I was younger—and even through college—I placed too much importance on boys. Whenever I had a boyfriend, I'd ditch my friends and start slacking in school and with sports. My mom was more like Stacy's mom. She basically encouraged it. She thought having a relationship was super important because it upped to your status…and, at least to her, your value."

Naomi blows across her cup of hot cocoa to cool it off. "No wonder it's such a trigger, then." Her voice takes on a more consoling tone as she continues, "Unfortunately, I knew a lot of moms who had that same attitude back then—especially with girls. And, sadly, I know a couple of moms I'd put in that category today."

Meg pushes up her sleeves and tightens her ponytail. "And I totally regret it now. I think about what could've been, you know? I was a pretty good athlete back in the day. Could I have gone further if someone had pushed me to keep my focus and energy in the right place? I don't want James to get sidetracked now. He's worked too hard."

"It's all about balance." Naomi nods and then takes a sip. "But kids also need to know they're valuable enough on their own. If a relationship is preventing them from following their passions, at any age, it's not a good thing."

"That's so true." I unzip my jacket a little further and take a deep breath. I so want to tell them about Gavin's crush on Kayli. I'd love to get their insight on it. If only they didn't seem so opposed to crushes. It's not like it's affecting how Kayli values herself or her passions, though. She doesn't even like him back…yet.

"At least I don't have to be too concerned about it for a

while," Naomi says. "Lily's so quiet and shy. I'm sure worrying about boys is a long way off."

I might as well go for it. Even though I can already imagine Meg's reaction, it's almost impossible for me to keep anything from them. "Unfortunately, I may have to think about it sooner rather than later with Kayli." I look at the foam left on my hot cocoa, dissolving little by little. "I'm pretty sure this boy in her class, Gavin Donder, has a crush on her."

Meg raises her eyebrows. "So, those notes and teasing really were signs? And from Gavin, too?"

"Yeah, it seems that way." My heart rate picks up. What did Meg mean by that? "Kayli's not reciprocating yet...but what do you mean, *Gavin, too*? That doesn't sound good."

Meg glances over at Naomi. "I mean—I don't know—he's definitely not the *politest* boy in their grade. His mom seems really nice, but those boys..." She looks over to Naomi again. "I'd say Lisa has a pretty laissez-faire parenting style. Is that your take, too?"

Naomi tucks her hair behind her ears, cringing. "Yeah... that's a generous way to put it. I've heard Gavin and his coconspirator, Brody, both spend quite a bit of time in the principal's office."

"Oh man. Of course." My hand moves to the back of my neck to help support the increasing weight of my head. Great. The first boy who has a crush on Kayli is a fifth-grade hoodlum. I look back and forth to my friends as my mind struggles to process this. "You guys...now what am I supposed to do? You know I can't get too involved. I can't have a repeat of what happened during that whole mean girl drama with Sienna."

"Well..." Meg doesn't bother hiding her skepticism. "Definitely keep reminding Kayli to concentrate on her own priorities."

"Maybe encourage her to be just friends with him?" Naomi

suggests. I can tell she's trying to look optimistic, but it's not at all believable.

At least Kayli's mentioned she's doing both of those things already. I bring my hand back down as some of the heaviness subsides. "Maybe this isn't as big of a deal as I'm making it. Lately, she seems pretty level-headed. Maybe she'll be able to handle it." I sit up straighter.

"I hope you're right, but I'd still keep an eye on it," Naomi warns.

"No, I will. But from a distance." I try to smile. It's time to change the subject. "Speaking of keeping an eye on things, what do you guys know about second-grade math?"

"Oh no," Meg groans, pushing her hot cocoa to the side. "Is Ryn entering the *new math* phase? Don't you remember being traumatized by it with Kayli?"

"I guess not." My mind races, trying to recall who she even had as a teacher. "I never paid much attention to Kayli's homework when she was that age. She's always been so good at getting all her stuff done on her own. But Ryn's a completely different story. And the math problems she's bringing home, with all these strategies of grouping, breaking numbers apart, making tens...I don't even know what else."

"Yeah...that's *new math*." Meg tilts her head sympathetically. "They teach the kids all these different ways to solve the same problem, and then the kids decide which strategy, or strategies, work best for them."

"What?" I look over to Naomi.

"Don't look at me." Naomi shrugs. "Bruce is the one who helps the kids with math. His electrician mind can make sense of it somehow. And please don't take this the wrong way, but I would've thought it'd be right up your alley. Aren't the evaluations you do for work full of statistics?"

"I know, right?" I feel my cheeks warm. "But computer

programs do most of the work for me, and this—the way she's learning it—is completely different than how I was taught."

Meg leans forward, resting her arms on the table. "Once my kids got it figured out, though, I actually liked it."

"Really?" I raise my eyebrows.

"Definitely," she continues. "Because now the teachers don't simply call on the kid who raises his hand the fastest. Instead, they ask the kids to do this when they figure out a strategy to answer the question." Meg centers her hand over her chest and sticks up her thumb. "And then, they ask the kids to hold another finger out when they figure out a second strategy."

"I like that." Naomi sits up taller. "It gives equal footing to kids who aren't as outspoken. Even if they know the answer, some kids—like Lily—are slower to raise their hands."

"Well, Ryn is struggling with basically every strategy, and so am I." I lean back in the booth, suddenly feeling the weight of all my winter clothes.

"I was exactly the same when James was in second grade," Meg admits. "But once he got in Ms. Beal's class, everything started clicking. Same with Brooklyn. You should definitely request Ms. Beal next year for Ryn."

"Hmm...I've never requested a teacher before. Have you?" I look to Naomi, knowing full well Meg's done it almost every year.

She nods. "I actually did it for the first time this year for Leo. He had so much separation anxiety last year, I wanted someone who would be caring and sensitive to that. The school was great about it. I'm glad I did it."

"Oh shoot, you guys." Meg looks at her watch. "I need to get going. I'm taking my mom to her cardiologist."

"I should go too." I grab my hat and mittens and follow Naomi out of the booth. "I need to prepare a couple of things before a call with my manager this afternoon. Another day, another tedious marketing evaluation."

We toss our cups in the trash, bundle up, and brace ourselves for the chill as we open the door to head back out to our cars. "Brr…" I cuddle into Naomi. "I'm not sure how much longer I can last with this cold, you guys."

"Same," Meg says. "I keep reminding myself about spring break. By the way, did you and Ben figure out where you're going?"

"Yeah," I reply as we reach our cars. "His branch manager is letting us stay in his condo in Scottsdale."

"That's not far from my sister," Naomi says. "Maybe we can meet up down there."

I rub my arms to keep warm. "That'd be fun. Let's chat more once it gets closer."

"Sounds good," Naomi says across our cars. "Enjoy the long weekend."

"You too!" I wave and jump into my car, starting my ignition as fast as my shaking fingers can move. With the sun tucked behind some clouds, it's now way colder than when we first got here.

* * *

"Hi, Mommy," Ryn calls from the mudroom after slamming the door.

I peek my head around the corner to see her and Kayli struggling out of their coats and boots. "Hey." I pull off Ryn's hat, hang her mittens on the drying rack, and follow the girls to the kitchen as they grab their snacks.

"How was school today? Anything exciting happen?" I purposely leave out, *How did Gavin treat you today?* I can't be too obvious.

"Mine was great." Ryn beams, scooching up to the island

with a couple of graham crackers. "Ethan told me about his party. It's going to be the best. There will be pizza, cake, and ice cream, and we're going to play all these cool games. He told me to come at five thirty."

"Got it. Dad's coming home early that night, so he can take you." I turn my attention to Kayli. "What about you? Are your friends ready for Friday?" Since Ryn's going to be gone and there's no basketball, I told Kayli she could have a few friends over. It wasn't supposed to be a sleepover, but after lots of begging and promising me she and her friends wouldn't get crazy, I caved. Maybe it'll give me a better window into what's going on in her life.

"Oh yeah." She grins, munching on some pretzels. "Everyone's super excited."

"That's good to hear." I look back and forth with pride between my two cheerful girls. "Any other reason you look so happy?"

"Nothing too big." Kayli's attention stays on her snack as she coyly tacks on, "But Gavin picked me to be his partner for this math project we're working on."

"Math, yuck," Ryn groans, taking her plate over to the sink before going downstairs.

"That's nice." I force every muscle to keep my face expressionless. Gavin, huh? And her smile...it doesn't look like an *oh we're just friends* smile. But I'll get more information if I pretend it's no big deal. "How'd it go?"

"Really good." She sits up, almost shimmying as her eyes twinkle. "He's so funny. He kept making me laugh, so it was kind of hard to focus. And after I finished all the problems, we talked about basketball."

"Funny, similar interests...both good qualities." I have to try much harder to keep my straight face. Kayli shimmying over a boy...what if she actually likes this hoodlum? And worse, it sounds like she got roped into doing most, if not all, of the work. When in the world has she ever done all the work for a group project and not complained? I can't point this out, though, can I? I don't even know how I would say it.

"Yep." She finishes her snack and slides out of her chair. "He has a lot of good qualities…a lot of good *friend* qualities."

"Ah…" I can finally soften my face as she goes to grab her bag from the mudroom. But when she returns, something is different…her eyes still seem too twinkly. "Are you going to help me with dinner? I'm making Swedish meatballs." Maybe if she hangs out with me a little longer, I'll be able to pinpoint it.

"Sorry, Mom. I have a ton of homework." She sounds sincere. "Tomorrow, though."

"Oh, okay." I do my best to keep my voice light—positive —as she heads upstairs. But as I get out the ingredients for dinner, everything feels heavier. Something about this boy— how he behaved at Randy's, what Meg and Naomi said about him being a troublemaker—even if Kayli says she doesn't like him back, her body language indicates otherwise could be on the horizon.

I keep telling myself it's fifth grade, though. What's the worst that could happen? These young relationships are so trivial. Besides, I shouldn't be complaining. She's finishing her homework with no reminding from me, has a solid group of basketball friends, and has been exuding more confidence than ever. I slice open the package of ground beef and drop it in the bowl. I'm sure I'm worrying about nothing.

FRIDAY, JAN 17

"Hey, guys! Come on in." I hold the door open for Mandi and Emily as Nikki gets out of her car. The girls squeeze through, squealing as they fumble with their bags, pillows, and sleeping bags. Kayli giggles along with them, grabbing some of their stuff and helping them keep their balance as they take off their coats and boots. "You too, Nikki...if you have a minute."

"You're so brave," Nikki teases, stepping inside. "Having these crazy girls for an entire night. I couldn't handle it."

"Nah. It'll be great." It comes out a little sarcastic, but I'm not even lying. I'm actually excited to get to know Kayli's friends better. Having them over will let me see and hear things I usually miss. I might even overhear a conversation about Gavin. "Kayli, why don't you get the girls settled downstairs? Dad should be back with Poppy any minute."

As the girls' whispers and giggles fade, a faint "I'm by Mandi!" is followed by Kayli's "Yeah, sleep wherever."

Once the girls seem to have figured out their sleeping arrangements, I turn back to Nikki. "Ben had to drop Ryn off at Ethan's anyway—hey, do you want to stick around for a little while? I have wine."

"I'd love that, but I should scoot." Her disappointment sounds genuine as she reaches for the door. "Drew has a work event, so Mollie's home by herself, and I told her I'd only be a few minutes." She turns to leave and then glances back over her shoulder. "Good luck. And call if you need anything."

"Will do." I grab the door and wave goodbye as Ben and Poppy pull into the driveway. Ben stops the car to let Poppy out before he pulls into the garage. I help her with her stuff and direct her downstairs, and then I head into the kitchen to check on the pizzas.

The pizzas look good, so I scan the kitchen to see what else needs to be done. Tonight, my goal is to channel Meg's party planning skills. There aren't thematic decorations or anything like that, but at least I'm more organized than usual. I even made a list. The plates, forks, and cups are already set out. All I have left is to make the lemonade and cut up straw-berries.

Ben walks in from the mudroom, glancing around the kitchen as he rubs his hands together. "Hey, hon. How's every-thing going…need any help?"

"I think I'm good." I dump a packet of lemonade into the pitcher and start filling it with water. "How'd things go at Ethan's?"

"Poor Jane." He shakes his head, pulling a beer out of the fridge. "That place was nuts. Boys were bouncing off the walls. I didn't realize Ryn was going to be the only girl."

"Oh?" I reach around him and grab the strawberries. "Me neither. What'd Ryn think?"

"No idea." He shrugs, twisting off the top. "I told her I'd pick her up at eight."

"I guess we'll find out then." I grab a cutting board and start slicing as the girls thunder upstairs. Ben holds his beer over his head, weaving his way through their mob to hunker down in the living room.

"Is the pizza ready?" Kayli leads the way, the three other girls trailing close behind.

"A few more minutes, honey." It's then that I notice Mandi's and Emily's eyeshadow. It's subtle, but there's definitely something purple and shimmery on their lids. I didn't notice it when Nikki dropped them off, but maybe I wasn't paying enough attention. It's probably not a big deal. Both Nikki and Cori are always done up, so it's very possible they're on board with it.

"What kind is it again?"

"Pepperoni." I catch Kayli glancing at Poppy. "I thought it was your favorite."

"It is." Kayli pauses, looking at her friend again. "But Poppy doesn't eat meat."

"Oh my gosh...of course she doesn't." I'm sure my face reddens. Although Poppy doesn't react, Emily nudges Kayli. She looks too cool for school with her eyeshadow and her hair up in a messy bun, wearing an oversized turquoise sweatshirt with these bright tie-dyed leggings Ryn would go crazy for.

But instead of making fun of me, Emily teasingly whispers, "G.D. loves pepperoni too."

G.D? I steal a glance at Kayli, who looks mortified as Mandi stands behind her—dressed in an ensemble that mirrors Emily's almost exactly—covering her mouth. Gavin Donder... G.D. It has to be. I look away, pretending not to hear, and get back to the pizza. If her friends are teasing her, that has to mean Kayli likes him back, right? I refocus on Poppy. "I'm so sorry. Can you take the pepperonis off? Or, I could always make you something else too...a peanut butter sandwich or something?"

"It's okay, Mrs. Munsen. Thank you." She smiles reassuringly at me. Her subtle cream sweatshirt and gray fleece pants make her seem even more polite. "I can pull them off."

"Great." Turning my attention back to the oven, I feign

interest in the final seconds of the cooking process while straining my ears to interpret the continued whispers, giggles, and shushes behind me. It's obvious Kayli doesn't want to be talking about Gavin in front of me. "Okay…pizza's ready."

The girls cheer, putting an end to their whispering as they each find a seat at the island. After I divvy up slices, I get them situated with their fruit and drinks. The room fills with silence as the girls eat, but there's no way I'm leaving now. This is a prime opportunity I don't want to miss, especially since they just referenced the initials of Kayli's potential crush.

I turn on the faucet to wash off the cutting boards—and justify my presence—when my back pocket starts buzzing. It's Jane. "Is everything okay?" I don't even bother with a hello as I take the call into the living room.

"Don't worry. It's nothing serious," she replies. "Ryn isn't feeling well. One of you guys should probably come get her."

"Of course." I look down at Ben, wondering how I didn't notice her feeling off before. Maybe she pushed through since she was so excited. "Ben can be there in a few minutes."

He looks up at me, and I silently mouth, "Ryn."

"I'll have her ready," is what I think Jane says. I can barely hear her over the shouting and thumping in the background.

We say goodbye as Ben gets up from the couch. "So, I'm picking up Ryn right now?"

After I confirm, Ben takes off, and I turn my attention back to the kitchen. Kayli and her friends have demolished the food, and they're chugging down the rest of their drinks. "How's everything, ladies?"

"Really good," Kayli replies, standing up and pushing in her stool. "But we're stuffed."

The girls scramble after Kayli toward the stairs, echoing "Thanks!" and "It was delicious."

"What about ice cream?" I call after them, super bummed I missed out on their chatter.

"Later…much later," Kayli groans, dramatically holding her belly as she and her giggling friends disappear down the stairs.

My balance feels slightly off as I wipe down the counters. While Kayli's friend situation appears much improved from the manipulation she was entangled in this fall, watching them tease her about this boy is still a teensy bit disconcerting. Whatever. I'm sure it's harmless, and Kayli does seem to be enjoying herself. I need to keep staying in my lane and avoid getting too involved.

I finish loading the dishwasher as the garage door opens. Ben and Ryn are back.

"Hi," Ryn mumbles, peeking her head around the corner.

"Oh, honey." I walk over to her and help her with her coat and boots as Ben comes in behind her. "You're not feeling well?"

She shakes her head, and I crouch down to give her a hug. "Let's go cuddle up on the couch." I take her hand and lead her into the living room.

Ryn lies down, and I rest my hand on her forehead. "Is it your tummy?"

She nods her head. Her puppy dog eyes are in full force.

"Do you think you need to throw up?"

She squishes her nose and shakes her head again.

"What'd you guys have for dinner?"

"Pizza." Her face begins to regain some color.

"Hmm…" Ryn's had pizza a million times, and it's never been a problem. She actually looks much better now. Now that she's back home. Suddenly, it dawns on me. All that Naomi went through with Lily…and how Lily's anxiety initially showed up as stomachaches. Is that what this is? I take my hand off her forehead. "How was it with all the boys? Daddy mentioned you were the only girl there."

"I don't know," she sighs and then scooches up on the couch. "Kind of weird."

"Were they nice to you?" I give her more room to sit up.

"Yeah…" She hesitates. "They were being really loud, though, and kind of gross with their food when we were eating."

Bingo. "You know, sometimes when we're uncomfortable or nervous, our tummies hurt."

"Really?"

"Mm-hmm." I brush her hair back. "It's actually super common. And what's so great is that you were able to recognize something was going on and you needed to take a little break. Now, the next time you have that feeling, you know it might be nerves. Some kids feel that way before a big game, an important test or presentation, or when they're with a bunch of unfamiliar people."

The worried crinkles on Ryn's forehead start to disappear.

"And," I continue, "sometimes you can even use that nervous energy to help you do better, like to help you run faster during a basketball game."

"That's cool…" She pauses, looking like she needs a minute to think. "Mommy? I'm feeling better now. Can I go play with Kayli and her friends?"

"Well…maybe." I doubt Kayli's going to agree to it, but I'd love the excuse to check on them again. "I don't know what she'll say, but we can definitely ask."

I take Ryn's hand, and we head downstairs.

"No way!" a voice from below shouts, causing me to hesitate on the landing as it continues, "That's not fair!"

"Calm down…" I hear Kayli giggle and then say. "Emily, you know that's Mandi's."

"Alright, alright…" Another girl laughs. "I was only making sure she's paying attention."

"Yeah, right," someone else huffs. Ryn and I reach the

bottom step just in time to see Mandi stick her tongue out and grab a playing card from Emily. "You always try to pull that." Emily smirks, sticking her tongue out in return. Thankfully, it seems they're kidding around.

"Hey, guys. How's everything?" I glance around the room. The girls have obviously been hard at work. Our large sectional couch and heavy coffee table have been pushed further back from the TV by several feet, their sleeping bags are lined up in front, and two of our ottomans have been moved to the corner with the girls' bags stacked on top.

"Good," they all say at once, looking up from their cards with collective grins.

"I like what you've done with the place." I glance past Kayli, scanning the room again as I try to discern an unfamiliar scent.

"We promise to put it all back." Kayli waves her cards, gesturing over to the sleeping bags. "It's so we can sleep next to each other." And that's when I figure out the scent. It's her nails. Hot pink nail polish. We don't even own nail polish—one of the girls must have brought it. Kayli has never once requested to wear it before, let alone in hot pink.

"No, I like it. Great idea," I say as Ryn starts tugging on my arm. My eyes dart to Mandi's hands. Yep. And Emily's too. All matching. Even Poppy's.

"Mommy," Ryn quietly begs.

"Oh, right. So…" I turn back to the girls. "We're wondering if you could use an extra person to maybe help with your game."

"Umm…" Kayli looks horrified as she glances at her friends, who all start staring extra intently at their cards. "Well, this is a four-person card game, so I don't think it's a great idea. Sorry, Ryn. Maybe you and I can play it with Mom and Dad another time."

"No problem," I reply as Ryn scooches behind me. "We'll find something else to do."

As Ryn starts pulling me upstairs, I look back over my shoulder. "Have fun, girls."

"But what can I do?" Ryn whimpers after a few steps, right as another round of hushed whispers and a burst of laughter commence.

As my brain tries to reconcile whether I actually heard the word *Gavin* or if it was my imagination, I negotiate that Ryn can have a little ice cream sundae, get her pajamas on, and watch a movie with Ben…one that Kayli has suddenly become too cool for.

Once Ryn is settled in with Ben, I prep the kitchen for round two of Kayli and her friends. I don't want to miss this time around. After getting out the bowls, spoons, and toppings, I plop down at the island with a magazine and wait. And wait. Over an hour goes by, Ryn's movie ends, and the girls still haven't come up.

"Mommy?" Ryn wanders over with her blanket. "Can you put me to bed tonight?"

"Sure, hon." I mean, how can I say no to that face? "Let's hurry, though, in case Kayli and her friends need help with anything."

We head upstairs, and I try my best to speed her along through her teeth brushing, going to the bathroom, and picking out a story. But, of course, she takes her own sweet time. Finally, after four rounds of hugs, I'm able to shut off the light, turn on the fan, and close the door. I race back downstairs to see if I can catch the girls, but all that's left is a stack of dirty ice cream bowls next to the sink.

"I missed them?" I pout, grabbing the glass of wine Ben has set out for me and slumping down next to him on the couch. "You couldn't stall them at all?"

"Sorry, hon…," he replies, patting my leg. "It's like controlling a level four hurricane. I believe watching a movie was next on their agenda."

"Bummer." I take a sip of wine and offer up the partial truth. "I wanted to use this night to get to know Kayli's friends better. I wanted to make sure they were getting along okay."

"Well, I definitely don't think you have anything to worry about with these girls." He rubs my back. "They seem to get along great."

"Yeah," I sigh, scooching further down in my seat and tucking my face behind my wineglass as I succumb to divulging the full truth. "I suppose I also wanted to see if they said any more about this boy having a crush on Kayli."

"Oh, God." He throws his head back. "Please don't encourage that. She's way too young."

"I'm not encouraging it." I sit back up. Definitely not with this boy. "I only want to be aware of what's going on. I don't want her to hide this kind of stuff from me. Besides, she's not too young. Think about it. When was your first crush or kiss?"

"Well…" He thinks for a minute, scratching his head. "Come to think of it, my very first kiss was in fourth grade. But it was a peck. It didn't mean anything."

"See?" I nudge him. "And this stuff probably won't mean anything to these girls in thirty years either. But I want Kayli and Ryn to feel like they can talk about it and not have to hide stuff from us because they think they'll get in trouble or we'll look down on them."

"Fine. I get it," he replies. "What about you, though? When was your first kiss?"

My neck instantly feels ten degrees hotter. Of course he'd turn the question back at me. I've never told Ben the story about the kiss that occurred when I worked at the golf course, and now is definitely not the time. Talk about missing signs… I'm mortified thinking back to it. I take a little sip, and then another, quickly blocking the resurgence of any more memories as I figure out a way to cover my tracks. "I'm embarrassed to admit this, but honestly, I think it was you."

"Come on!" He throws his head back again. "Not true."

"No, really. I never had boyfriends when I was younger or in high school. I was so quiet and shy. None of them would ever look twice at me." I crack a smile, finally able to make eye contact again. At least this part was true.

"Well, then, they missed out." He winks, resting his hand on my leg.

"Sure did," I exhale. Sticking to facts going forward is so much easier. "But seriously, when you started pursuing me, it was quite a shock. I had no clue what you saw in me."

"You can't be serious."

"What?"

"Honey…" He glares at me, dipping his chin in disbelief.

"Well, what?" I shift in my seat, genuinely wondering now. "What did you think when you first noticed me?"

"I actually remember the night." His eyes take on a slight twinkle before he settles back into the couch. "We were at the house on Fifth…Mackie's. It was homecoming, and the place was packed. The music was blasting, and everyone was dancing and jumping around. But you…not you. You were over in the corner chatting with some dude for a crazy amount of time. Had to be over fifteen minutes. I kept looking over at you and thinking what in the world could you be talking about. It must have been really interesting."

"Yeah, I guess I did that sometimes. I was never the dancing type at parties. Usually, I'd hide off in some corner with some of the guys from my data science classes. But I don't remember meeting you that night."

"No, you're right. I waited."

"What do you mean you waited? You've never told me that."

"I didn't want you to think I was some sort of stalker," he

teases. "But yeah, and after that, I kept spotting you around campus. You were never in large groups, but you always looked like you were in deep conversation with someone. I started thinking you had to be the most interesting person at school."

"Funny. And then you finally cornered me in the coffee shop. That's what I remember."

"I didn't corner you." He tosses his head back with a laugh. "I only asked you for a recommendation. You looked like you knew way more than I did about ordering coffee."

"And the rest is history." I smile and set down my empty wineglass.

"Yep." He puts his arm around me. "Except, you took forever in letting me kiss you. What was that all about anyway?"

"I only wanted to be sure," I kid. But really, I want to move on from this topic and the explanation I'd like to avoid. I lean into him and close my eyes, wanting to make him think I'm tired. Luckily, it works, and he turns his attention back to his hockey game. I snuggle in next to him until the second period ends. Then I notice the clock. "It's getting late. I should check on the girls." I get up from the couch and tiptoe downstairs, hesitating on the landing once I hear the girls talking.

"It's so cute that he likes you," someone whispers and then the others giggle.

"Yeah…," Kayli says. "But we're just friends."

I gulp down the lump that just formed in the back of my throat and continue down the last few steps. "Hey, girls. Everything going okay?"

"Yes." More giggles.

"What's so funny?" *Keep it casual*, I remind myself as I consciously relax my brow.

"Nothing." Kayli purses her lips, her eyes darting down to the floor.

"We're discussing an interesting survey that was done at

school today." Emily's voice is very matter-of-fact, but she looks a little too coy, briefly stealing a glance at Kayli before sitting up straighter.

"Oh?" I look at Kayli, who has buried her face in her hands.

"Yep." Emily keeps going. Sharing her news is apparently a much higher priority than any embarrassment she's creating for my daughter. "Brody surveyed all his friends to see who should marry Kayli."

"Hmm…" I continue to act as if it's no big deal. "So, who won?"

"Gavin!" Emily, Mandi, and Poppy all squeal as they toss their pillows at Kayli.

"I swear, we're only friends." Kayli shakes her head, keeping her face concealed.

"But you should give him a chance," Emily says. "He's funny, he's cute, and he does all these nice things for you. Don't you think she should like him back, Mrs. Munsen?"

"That's up to Kayli." I coerce a smile, restraining myself from telling these girls to stop pressuring her. I turn it back to myself for added measure. "I stay out of those decisions." I shift in my stance as I look around the now-silent room, resisting the urge for a quick exit. "But I definitely think it's time for you guys to get some sleep. I don't want you all to be zombies tomorrow. Your parents won't let you sleep over here ever again."

"We know, we know." Kayli finally lifts her face from her hands.

"Okay." I shut off the TV and turn down the lights before heading back upstairs. "Night."

"Thanks, Mom." I hear a hint of relief from Kayli as the girls get into their sleeping bags.

I roll my shoulders, heading upstairs. Teasing about a boy and wearing matching nail polish is one thing. But encouraging her to like a boy when she just wants to be friends with him? If Kayli isn't interested, why are her friends pushing this? Kayli can decide if she wants to be with a boy all by herself. She doesn't need to be rushed into it by any means. She knows this, though, doesn't she? She'll figure it out. She simply needs a little more time and space.

WEDNESDAY, JAN 22

"He-ey there…" My wobbly cadence mirrors my balance. Steadying myself with extended arms, I make my way over a large snowdrift toward my friends. Deep in conversation, neither Meg nor Naomi immediately acknowledges me. Waiting for them to finish, I glance down at the dirty snow and then up to the coordinating gloomy sky. Winter can be so ugly. I lose patience searching for anything of beauty and start to wonder whether I should try to catch up with what they're saying.

"Hi…sorry." Meg finally looks over and smiles as she and Naomi uncross their arms, and we get started on the trail.

"Looks like I interrupted something important." I look at Meg, hoping she'll fill me in.

"Nothing too serious," she says. "We're talking about the proposed later start times for the middle and high schoolers next year. You've heard about that, right?"

"Not a ton. Have they decided yet?" I ask, relieved their discussion doesn't have anything to do with more kid drama—especially crushes. I raid my memory for the last thing I remember hearing about start times. The school board's been debating this issue for several years, but they've struggled to come to a consensus. I get it since there are several levers at play…busing, parents' work hours, activity schedules…I'm sure they're hearing it from all angles.

"It seems so," Naomi replies, shaking her head. "Next year, the elementary is going to start at eight, and the middle and high school will start at nine."

"So, they're flipping them?" I clarify. "I knew I'd be in for two different schedules with the girls anyway. It was only a matter of who's early and who's late. Are you guys okay with it?"

"It works out great for us," Meg says. "Brooklyn's always up at the crack of dawn, and I know James will love being able to continue sleeping in."

I look over to Naomi.

"It's not the most ideal." Her eyes remain straight ahead, but her tone insinuates they want to roll. "Leo's already super challenging to wake up in the morning, so I have no clue how getting up an hour earlier is going to work. But Lily will likely be grateful. Especially now that she's spending so much time getting ready for things, she'll love the extra time to primp."

"Lily's into primping?" I tease, trying to lighten the mood. "That's hard to envision."

Naomi closes her eyes as she inhales and brings her hands to heart center. It's a move I've seen her do at least a thousand times in the yoga studio. Never on the trail. "I'm trying to be so patient, you guys, but I'm not going to lie. It's such a trigger. I want her to look inward for beauty and understand her appearance isn't for someone else's approval. She's doing her hair every morning and even wears lip gloss now. She asked if she could wear mascara too, but of course, I said no. I hate that she's spending so much time caring about what she looks like."

Naomi and I move over to let a couple of other walkers

pass. I'm so relieved Kayli's more like me. Other than her sleepover manicure, it's definitely been function over fashion. Even her outfits are simple. Her typical attire of leggings and a sweatshirt rarely waver from black, navy, or some shade of gray. More than anything, she has a little athletic flair.

As we get back on the trail, Naomi continues, "And we're already on shaky ground because she thinks I limit her screen time too much. I'm trying to be understanding and let her explore new interests, but I also need to be the parent, you know?"

I nod, thinking of my own parenting tightrope. It's a lot harder than I thought it'd be to be supportive while letting Kayli find her own way.

"I'm trying not to let it drive me too crazy." Naomi stops, raises her arms up, and brings her closed palms back down to her chest again. This time, she's even more dramatic.

"I hear you. And I need you to share some of that Zen with me." Meg shakes her head as Naomi starts walking again. "I'm having a tough time keeping my sanity too. This stuff with Stacy's crush on James is killing me."

"What's going on now?" A pit forms in the bottom of my stomach. Great—more crush trouble. What happened to things being innocent nothings at this age?

"It just doesn't stop." Meg's voice is heavy with irritation. "She follows James and his friends around at recess, giggling, and doing all these silly little things to try to catch his attention. And the notes…I mean, it's constant. I find at least three notes from her in his backpack every day."

Naomi cringes, looking over. "That is a little sad, isn't it? Girls wasting all that time chasing after a boy. How's James handling it?"

"He tries to ignore her," she replies. "But it's hard when she pesters him every single day. I so want to say something to Stacy's mom, but James would kill me. Thank goodness they're not in the same class. I can't imagine how awful that would be."

The pit in my stomach grows as I realize how this might come into play with Kayli and Gavin, but I push through it. I'm sure that wasn't Meg's intention. Besides, none of this is even close to a five-alarm fire yet. "I think you're doing the right thing. I learned my lesson with Kayli this fall. The kids can usually figure this stuff out by themselves if you give them enough time."

"I hope you're right," Meg says as we reach my favorite bridge. The snow on the lake is much cleaner here, so even with the murky sky, the view is still spectacular. It's also fun to see all the animal tracks weaving in and out across the lake. I start to imagine what these little creatures do when no one else is around. Kind of like our kids' school days.

"What about Brooklyn? Did you guys start that baking class yet?" I ask. It's probably a good idea to switch topics.

"It actually started last night," Meg says, noticeably cheering up. "It was super fun. There were six other little girls, one little boy, and their moms. The class description said mother-daughter, but the teacher must have made an exception for the boy."

"Too bad the description wasn't broader," Naomi says. "They could have said parent-child, or something like that. I'm sure other boys would enjoy baking too."

"Definitely," Meg replies. "The instructor promised to change it for the next session."

"So, how'd he do as the only boy?" I think back to Ryn's trouble at Ethan's.

"Totally fine." Meg shrugs it off. "Brooklyn and I actually shared a table with him and his mom. He was such a character and a great baker too. He was helping out Brooklyn quite a bit since, as you know, I don't know my way around a kitchen very well. Brooklyn had a blast."

"That's a relief," I say. "On Friday, Ryn went to a birthday party where she was the only girl, and she really struggled. She was so uncomfortable and nervous, she started feeling sick. Ben had to pick her up early."

"Uh-oh," Naomi sighs. "That sounds a little too familiar."

"I know, right?" I say as we hit our turnaround mark. "But you should be proud of me. I thought of Lily's anxiety almost immediately. Then Ryn and I had a great conversation about how you can have stomachaches when you're nervous, and it doesn't mean you're sick."

Naomi grins, clapping her mittens together. "Yay, momma! That makes me feel so good. That reminds me, though, did I tell you about this mom who called me the other day about Leo's STEM club?"

I glance at Meg, and we shake our heads. "What happened?"

"I don't know the whole story, but she's been trying to get her daughter in STEM club for months now. She's apparently gotten quite the runaround. I feel horrible for not realizing this until she called, but the club is only made up of first-grade boys. You should've heard her. She was so upset. She claimed it was like trying to break her daughter into a secret society."

"Why can't she be added?" I ask. Isn't anything simple anymore?

As Meg and I move off to the side to let a dogwalker pass, Naomi explains, "The competition rules limit the number of team members, and the boys have already been working on their projects for several months—Leo's put in at least a hundred hours creating these blueprints, or plans, for building stuff with household items. Anyway, I assured the other mom I'd connect her with Leo's teacher, but it doesn't sound very promising." As we move back onto the trail, Naomi turns her focus to me. "How are things going with Kayli?"

"Okay…" I start off slowly, but then my words come out

more quickly once I get going. "She had some friends over for a slumber party on Friday. It was fun to see them interact, but then they started encouraging her to like Gavin back. I just want her to make up her own mind about this crush, you know?"

The only feedback I get from Meg and Naomi is some cautious nodding. With their known opposition to crushes, maybe they're holding back to be polite. So, I steer the conversation in a different direction. "The only other blip Kayli's mentioned is her teacher changed their seating arrangement. Now she's sitting next to this kid, Brody, who she doesn't seem to be too thrilled with."

"Brody Callum?" The way Meg asks it clearly signals this is not a good thing.

I try to keep up my pace as I shake my head. "I'm not sure about his last name. I only know he's buddies with Gavin. Kayli sometimes hangs out with him at recess because he plays with the same boys she likes to play with. But it seems he's usually the one instigating the teasing or most of the other trouble."

"It has to be Brody Callum, then." Meg cringes. "Remember? Last week, we mentioned he was Gavin's coconspirator."

I look over at Naomi. My stomach feels like it's caving in on itself as she concurs. I know Kayli's mentioned the name Brody several times. How on earth did I forget Meg and Naomi bringing up his name? I've been putting all my focus on Gavin. I try to swallow the knot in my throat, but it doesn't budge. I can't believe I didn't make the connection.

Meg continues, "He plays basketball with Gavin. I don't know either of them super well, since James has been playing up for the past few years, but he and Gavin are both known to stir up trouble. Brody may even be worse. He's an only child, and his parents travel a ton for work. I think he's left on his own a lot and spends a bunch of time with Gavin's family."

Naomi adjusts her scarf as she offers a look of sympathy. "Has Kayli said why she doesn't like sitting by him?"

"Nothing too specific," I sigh, massaging my neck as Meg's comment carries me back to how the boys were acting at Randy's. Of course, the boy who has a crush on Kayli is a troublemaker, and his best friend is even more of a problem. At least it's not Brody who has a crush on Kayli. And regardless, what can these boys even do? Kayli doesn't even like Gavin back…yet. And, even if she did, what would that have to do with Brody? "Mostly, she complains Brody sits too close or keeps pestering her about dumb stuff."

"Sounds like he may need to learn a little more about boundaries," Naomi says as we reach the parking lot and climb over the snowdrift to our cars. "Kayli needs to stand up for herself if he's making her uncomfortable. And tell her to be firm. Boys don't take it seriously when girls are wishy-washy."

"Or maybe he needs to shower more often," Meg jokes, negating any of the seriousness in Naomi's warning. "I know James absolutely reeks these days if he doesn't take a shower in the morning. I can't believe it, you guys. It's like he turned into an old gym sock filled with decaying onions overnight."

"Or, that could be it too." Naomi laughs. "These kids are certainly getting to be *that* age."

"I'm sure Kayli can figure it out." I compel myself back to optimism and then join in their sarcasm. "I might have to buy her some nose plugs until he gets the hint." Even though I'm starting to feel the tiniest bit of hesitation on whether Kayli can truly handle this, it's better not to blow anything out of proportion now.

"Oh gosh…" Naomi keeps it light, reaching for her door. "She'll probably start a trend."

We're all laughing now as Meg gives a little wave and slides into her car. "Thanks, you guys. I needed this. See you next week."

As I'm about to get in my car, Meg opens her door back up and calls, "Hey, Dawn. Are you going to Cori's wine party on Friday night?"

I grin, recalling how Nikki and Cori came up with the idea while we were waiting for the girls after practice last week. "Yes. You know I love my wine. Are you?"

"Yep. She invited me yesterday when I was volunteering in the library and she was there subbing. I don't know her super well, but I run into her at school every so often. You want Kevin and me to pick you up? That way, we don't all have to drive."

"That'd be awesome. Thanks." I wave goodbye before getting into my car. I can't help but think of Gavin and Brody as I cup my hands over my nose, waiting for my car to warm up. It'd be so much easier if their body odor was the only problem. I check behind me as I pull out of the parking lot. The sun is still buried by clouds. A dark, dirty...stinky day. At least it's good for hunkering down in my office and getting some work done.

* * *

"We're home!" Ryn shouts from the mudroom over the clunking of boots and bags.

"Hey, girls." Walking from my office into the kitchen, I raise my arms and stretch out my back. I lost track of time and sat at my desk way too long.

Ryn stumbles around the corner and heads straight to the snack drawer. I peek into the mudroom to make sure she's hung up everything and find Kayli rummaging through her backpack. "Hi, hon."

"Hi." She looks up, beaming.

"Good day?" Something must have happened. She's rarely this happy after a school day.

"Really good." She pulls a piece of paper out of her backpack, walks past me, and sets it facedown on the island while she grabs something out of the snack drawer.

"Does it have anything to do with that piece of paper?"

"Kind of." She unwraps her granola bar and hops onto a stool. "That's the math project Gavin and I worked on."

"Ugh, math," Ryn groans, shaking her head as she takes a bite of her graham cracker.

"My math's not *ugh*...it's fun." Kayli's eyes twinkle with excitement as she slides her paper toward me.

As I flip it over, my eyes are immediately drawn to the jagged black words in the upper right-hand corner. Scrawled in penmanship not at all resembling Kayli's, it says, "Kayli loves Gavin." This is what she wants me to see? Kayli...Kayli loves Gavin? It takes every ounce of concentration I have to prevent my face from contorting. I thought it was the other way around...and I thought she hadn't decided yet. This can't be how she's breaking the news to me.

Feeling my chest tighten, I discreetly count to five as I inhale. Whatever happens, I don't want to overreact. I exhale, counting to five again as I do my best to relax my forehead. I have to remember she's trusting me with this sacred piece of information. She wants me to see it. But I have no clue how to respond...what voice do I even use? It should sound happy, shouldn't it?

"Honey, did you write this?"

"No way." She looks almost offended, snatching the paper back from me and holding it against her chest as Ryn tries to peek at it. "Gavin wrote it on there after the teacher handed it back."

"I see..." My voice trails off as I focus on keeping my breath steady, hoping it also slows down my heart. I pull out a stool. I don't get this at all. This boy wrote on Kayli's paper that *she* loves *him*. What the heck? Who does that? I'm so confused. Every hair on my arms is triggered to attention while Kayli's taking this as some sort of compliment.

I return my attention back to her. She's literally humming, seeming to savor each bite of her granola bar as she daydreams of who knows what that's allegedly magical about this boy. I have to be making too much out of it—this is fifth grade. I mean, there *are* repercussions if a note like that falls into the wrong hands...although they're probably minimal. But for him to write it like that rather than the other way around. It's like he wants her to take the bullet if there is one. I have to ask, "What do you think about that messa—?"

"Is Gavin the same boy we saw at Randy's?" Ryn interrupts. "What'd he write?"

"Something really nice." Kayli smiles, folding the piece of paper up again.

Really nice? How is writing that *she* loves *him* really nice? But I hold my tongue. I don't want to sound upset. And it's probably not a great idea to discuss this in front of Ryn anyway. I don't want to embarrass Kayli or make her completely clam up. I let it go...for now. "Does anyone have homework?"

"Just math..." Ryn's lips curl in disgust before she whines, "I don't want to do it now, though. Can I work on it with Daddy after dinner?"

"We can try that," I reply, actually relieved by this solution. Battling with Ryn over math problems is something I'd do almost anything to avoid. "I like for you to finish your homework before dinner, but if you think you'll still have the energy and focus to do it after, we can see how that goes."

"Oh yeah." Ryn reaches her arm up as she crosses one leg over the other and then pirouettes for emphasis. "I'll have tons of energy."

As Ryn dances over to the stairs, I try to collect my thoughts. I need to proceed with caution. I don't want to make too big a deal out of this, but I also want Kayli to be more aware. This may be super innocent, but what if it's not? I want her to at least start thinking about it.

"So, what do you think?" Kayli unfolds the paper again to admire the note.

"What do *I* think? Hmm…" I try to buy more time as a million thoughts and questions race through my mind. There's no way I can bombard her with those now. I have to do this in a way that will result in her continuing to ask and care about what I think. And if my experience from this past fall taught me anything, it's that I have the best shot at that if I follow her lead. "I'm not sure." I turn it back to her, trying my best to let her set the tone. "What do *you* think?"

"Well…" She smiles slyly, shifting in her chair. "He's fun."

"Mm-hmm." My heart starts to beat a tad bit faster. I take it we're not talking about the note anymore. We're talking about Gavin.

"And we have a lot of things in common." She keeps her eyes on the paper.

"Yep." I wipe my palms on my pant legs. They like basketball, and they're in the same class. I guess that could count as *a lot of things in common* to a fifth-grader.

"And he's super funny. And all my friends think he's really nice to me." Her eyes light up as she looks up at me.

"They *have* said that." My words come out slowly. Although, she also thinks this note is really nice, so I'm a little wary of their current definition of *really nice*. Do I say this, though?

"Mom?" Her eyes return to the piece of paper as she fiddles with the note.

"Yeah?" I brace myself. I can only guess where this is going.

"I think I might have a tiny crush on Gavin." She shirks off to the side like she's waiting for a jack-in-the-box to pop out.

"Okay." My voice sounds plain, probably too plain. I try to smile, but I'm sure it looks forced—phony. Why is this so hard? So, Kayli has a crush on a troublemaker. Girls can be drawn to bad boys, right? I tell myself she can handle it, but this time it's not sinking in. Can she handle it? All of a sudden, I don't know. The questions tumble out. "So, you guys both like each other? What does that mean? What happens now? Is this, like, a relationship?"

"Mo-om…," Kayli groans, closing her eyes as her head falls back.

"Honey…I'm only trying to understand." I loosen my grip on the countertop. I need to relax.

"Well, you don't have to freak out. It's not like we're getting married."

I take a deep breath as her head returns to its normal position. I've learned *freaking out* is the worst thing I can do when it comes to Kayli. It escalates any situation to the nth degree. "So, this is nothing serious?"

"No. We're just…you know…*crushing*." Kayli grins, looking elated to be freed from the weight of her confession as she jumps off her chair and blurts, "I'm going to do my homework."

"Hey, wait a second, sweetie." I can't help myself as I watch her walk away. Maybe this little *crushing* thing she has going on isn't supposed to be serious, but it's still with a boy who comes with a warning label. I can't leave her blissfully unaware. I need her to be able to notice any blinking red light this boy might set off. "Don't you think it's a little strange that Gavin wrote 'Kayli loves Gavin' on your paper, rather than the other way around?"

"Mo-om…" Her groan is even more exasperated this time as she turns around, slumping over with her arms drooping at her sides. "You promised you wouldn't get mad if I liked a boy."

"No, no, no. I'm not mad…" I wipe any expression from my face. Dang it. I need to keep my composure. "It's just something I wouldn't have expected, that's all." In real time, that's the nicest way I can think to put it. Now I check her face. Seeing it ease a bit as her posture straightens, I feel my heart slow back to normal.

"Okay…?" she half-states, half-questions, giving me one last curious look before leaving.

"Okay." I force another cheese-grin smile until she's out of sight. The minute she's up the stairs, my face collapses in my hands. Ugh…this isn't good. I feel it in my core. She's entered la-la land with this boy, and her level-headedness is getting shaky. I don't know if she'd recognize a warning if it were plastered on a billboard right in front of her. But what do I do? This is simply one of those things kids go through, isn't it? No matter how cringe-worthy it is, I can't get overly involved. And I can't tell her what to do. I'm only supposed to help her think through things. I take another deep breath. I can do this.

FRIDAY, JAN 24

"You're up early," I say as Ryn lugs her backpack into the kitchen.

"I forgot to do my homework last night," she grumbles, pulling out a folder and pencil and scooching herself up to the island.

"Homework?" I sit down next to her and rub her back. "You hardly ever have homework. And didn't you just have homework on Wednesday?"

"Mr. Kane's so mean." She grabs a math worksheet out of her folder. "When I don't get my assignments finished in class, he says they're homework."

I remember back to this fall, when Ryn was having trouble getting her work completed in class. "Are the kids in your class being distracting again with their devices?"

"No," she sighs, shaking her head. "Everyone's fine. I'm just horrible at math."

"Sweetie…" My heart crumbles at the despair in her voice. I grasp to recall what Naomi once told me parents are supposed to say to develop a growth mindset in kids. But all I can think to say is, "That's not true."

"It is too true." She leans into me, whimpering, "Ethan finished this in like two seconds."

Of course he did. Ethan's a brainiac and finishes everything in two seconds, but agreeing with Ryn isn't going to help her feel any better. "Maybe Ethan has done this kind of math before. You haven't. Things always take longer and are harder when you're first learning them. It takes practice and more practice. Eventually, you'll get better at it."

She doesn't look convinced and instead slides her worksheet over to me. Oh great. This will be interesting. I glance down at the paper. Each question has four boxes, one of which is filled in. The first question has the Base 10 Drawing box filled in with four squares, eight lines, and three dots. The other three empty boxes are labeled "Standard Form," "Expanded Form," and "Word Form." What in the world is this stuff?

"See…" I throw my hands up after staring at it for a minute. "I have no clue what this is or how to do it." Sadly, I don't even have to lie.

Fortunately, she giggles.

"But you know what?" I continue, finally remembering something else Naomi said. "I forgot to add one word to what I said."

"What?" She looks up at me.

"*Yet.*" I smile. "I have no clue what this is or how to do it, *yet.*"

She grins and grabs the paper. "I can show you." She writes in the boxes 483, 400+80+3, and four hundred eighty-three.

"See? Amazing." I rub her back again, feeling pretty dang proud of myself. "And the more you practice, the easier it'll get. How about you work on a few more, and I'll get your breakfast going? Peanut butter and honey toast?"

"Thanks." Ryn scooches up in her seat and moves to the next problem. "And juice?"

"No problem." I grab the bread and other supplies from the pantry as Kayli walks in.

"Can I have some too?" She slides onto a stool next to Ryn.

"Sure thing," I say, careful to make my voice extra cheerful as I pour two glasses, pop four slices of bread in the toaster, and get out a couple of plates. "How are you this morning?"

"Good." As she reaches for her drink, I spot something written on her wrist.

"Did you write something on yourself?" My antenna soars higher when she reacts by pushing her sleeve down.

"Maybe," she says coyly, putting her arm behind her back as Ryn tries to see what it is.

"What is it?" The fact that she's hiding it makes me want to know even more. I walk over and make her flip her hand over to show me.

"It's just the letter *G*." She covers it back up with her sleeve. "It's no big deal."

I turn my back to her, retreating to finish making their breakfast. This way, I don't have to have to worry about my expression. "Interesting…" I keep my response brief, with-holding any emotion as I take out the toasted pieces of bread. Branding herself with a boy's initial? What's next? Something more permanent? Naomi's words rush through my head: *Girls tend to forget all about what's good for them and focus way too much on getting their crush to like them.* I'm sure Gavin isn't doing the same. "And then Gavin writes your initial on his wrist too?"

"No way," she gasps as if my question is the dumbest thing she's ever heard. "Only the girls do it. It's like wearing a bracelet, but not as tacky."

Since when does Kayli use the word tacky? I make sure to set my knife down gently before handing over their breakfasts. But I can't let this slide. The thought of Kayli turning into this kid's minion is revolting. I need to be stealthy in planting my seed, though. "Well, I sure hope this was your idea and he finds a way to show his appreciation for you."

"Kayli has a boyfriend...," Ryn taunts, sticking her tongue out as she sways in her chair.

"We're just hanging out." Kayli turns to her matter-of-factly. "He's not my boyfriend."

"Does your *not-boyfriend* know anything about the *mystery* spray that's being set off all over school?" Ryn claps back. "It's making the whole school reek!"

"You don't know what you're talking about." Kayli rolls her eyes.

"Yes, I do!" Ryn huffs, crossing her arms as she swings into her infamous pout mode.

"You guys...please." My head spins playing catch-up. "What's this about?"

Ryn sneers at Kayli, sassing, "I don't know what I'm talking about, so..."

Kayli shakes her head and rolls her eyes again as she shoves the last bite of toast in her mouth and drops her plate off at the sink. "Some idiot keeps spraying boys' body spray in the hallways and bathrooms. The teachers can't figure out who's doing it."

"And it stinks!" Ryn follows Kayli into the mudroom to grab her stuff. "Everyone at school knows it's a fifth-grade boy. They're the only ones who use that stuff."

I close my eyes and focus on breathing in through my nose, then out through my mouth. During her yoga classes, Naomi says to visualize a color coming into my body and then watch it leave as I breathe out. Although only a swirled mess of colors comes to mind, I try it anyway.

Making my way over to the foyer, I try to think of a way to bring up the initial again as the girls scramble to get on their stuff. I know my comment about equivalent appreciation didn't sink in one bit. First Gavin writes "Kayli loves Gavin," then he gets her to tag herself with his initial...what's he going to get her to do next? Out the window, the top of the bus peeks over the hill. Any more discussion will have to come later. I give the girls hugs and then hold open the door for them as they hurry out to the bus. "Love you!" I yell. I so want to include, *Stand up for yourself*, but I don't.

* * *

"Meg's here," Ben yells up the stairs as I finish applying mascara.

"Thanks!" I take one last look in the mirror. I have no clue what to wear to a wine night. Cori seems somewhat stylish, but since the event is at her home, it's probably not super fancy. Hopefully my chunky black sweater and dark skinny jeans are okay. I hurry downstairs, grab a bottle of cabernet and my coat, and kiss Ben and the girls goodbye.

"Where's Kevin?" I slide into Meg's front seat. "I thought you said he could drive."

"He's too tired," Meg sighs. "His flight got changed, so he didn't get home until this afternoon. He wasn't sure he'd be able to stay awake long enough to give us a ride home. It's okay. James has an early basketball game tomorrow anyway."

"Got it." I'm grateful Ben doesn't travel very much. He plays golf a little more than I'd like in the summer, but other than that, I have it pretty good. No hunting, fishing, or work trips.

She motions down at my wine on the floor before backing out of my driveway. "I thought I was supposed to bring an appetizer. Did I mess up?"

I shake my head. "Cori said there'll be eight of us. Half are bringing wine, and the others are bringing apps."

"Ah...okay, fun." She perks up. "So, do you know who else is going?"

"All I know is Nikki and Jane. You've met Jane, Poppy's mom, right?"

"Oh yeah," Meg replies. "She usually signs up to volunteer for stuff with Naomi, so I've met her a few times. She's usually pretty quiet around me, but she seems nice."

"She is," I say as Meg turns into Cori's neighborhood. Marsh View is a notoriously gorgeous part of our community. It has about twenty-five houses peppered along a private wooded horseshoe drive. Each house sits on a lot of at least an acre, and most have meticulous lawns, outdoor sport courts, and swimming pools. And there are all these private nature trails winding through the marshlands in the center. The neighborhood's only a mile down the road from my house, but I've never been inside any of the homes.

As we pull to a stop in Cori's driveway, I take a deep breath to calm the butterflies in my stomach and grab my bottle of wine. Meg gets out and retrieves a tray of chocolate-covered strawberries from the back. Walking up to Cori's massive front door, I'm relieved to be arriving with her. She's so much better than I am with these social situations, and she usually knows everyone.

"Hey, guys!" Cori welcomes us, throwing open the door. "Thanks so much for coming."

"Thanks for having us." I follow Meg in, set my wine on the entry table in the two-story foyer, and take off my coat. The formalness of the dark wood paneling, the iron staircase winding off to the side, and the massive chandelier hanging from above is more than intimidating. I discreetly wipe my palms on the back of my jeans. Suddenly, I feel extremely underdressed. "Your home's absolutely stunning."

Of course, Meg's faux fur vest over a silky navy-blue dress and several layered necklaces fits right in. And Cori is equally stylish in her belted black shirt dress, perfectly accessorized with a gold pendant necklace and matching earrings. Evidently her usual silky shell and cardigan sweater didn't make the cut tonight. I try to forget what I look like as I grab my bottle of wine and follow them into the great room where a couple of clusters of moms are chatting.

"Hello!" Nikki waves us over to her and Jane as Cori takes our items into the kitchen.

Even though they're both in dresses, too, I exhale seeing their familiar faces. "Hey, Nikki. Have you met Meg before?"

"I don't think so." She smiles at Meg. "Nikki Carter."

"Nikki lives next door." I point through the kitchen window as Nikki nods. "Her daughter, Mollie, plays basketball with Ryn, and Mandi's in Ms. Andreen's class and plays basketball with Kayli." I turn back to Nikki. "Meg has James, who's in Mr. Slater's class, and Brooklyn, who's in third grade."

Meg smiles, but I sense irritation in her voice as she says, "No, we've definitely met before…a couple of times, even. Didn't you volunteer during the book fair set up?"

"That's right." Nikki lights up. "I volunteered with Cori… oh yeah, now I remember. You were in charge of that whole thing, weren't you? That's why you look so familiar."

"That's me." Meg's voice still sounds a bit off, but I can't tell what's wrong. "Hopefully I look a little less stressed tonight—"

Cori clinks her wineglass to get everyone's attention. "Since everyone's here, we should get started," she says as we quiet down and gather a little bit closer. "Why don't you all grab a plate of snacks, and we can head over to the dining room, where I'll give a few more details on how this will work."

Cori motions for Nikki to grab a plate and start the line, and the rest of us fall in behind. The only mom I don't recognize is right behind Nikki. She's followed by Natalie Shafer, a mom of one of Kayli's tennis friends, and Lisa Donder, Gavin's mom. Great. My stomach tightens as my body instinctively resists taking the spot behind her. I have no clue what she knows or thinks of the whole Gavin-Kayli situation, and I don't want things to turn awkward here. I discreetly maneuver behind Meg, using her as my buffer.

I can't ignore Lisa completely, though. I just have to keep the topic neutral. I hide my fidgety hands behind my back as I lean across Meg and get Lisa's attention. "Good to see you again. Sorry we didn't get a chance to chat at Randy's a few weeks ago." I'm talking way too fast and straining to maintain eye contact. I need to slow down. "Oh, hey, have you met Meg?"

"I'm sure I have. You look so familiar." Lisa smiles. "Lisa Donder."

"Meg Foster." Meg smiles back. This time it seems genuine. "I think we met this past fall. I helped get things ready for the retreat, but I couldn't chaperone since my mom got sick."

"That's right. You're James's mom!" Lisa reaches for Meg's shoulder at this newfound connection. "Oh my gosh, you did so much work. We would've been lost without you. Everything was so well organized—seamless—thanks to you."

"Thanks." Meg grins as she grabs a plate. Lisa's clearly won her over. "I'm glad it worked out. You know, I think James and Gavin played basketball together a few years ago too."

"Of course they did." Lisa grins back, and then she and Meg continue to catch up on how their boys' teams are doing as we move through the line, removing all pressure from me.

Once we grab our food, we filter into the formal dining room. Every place setting has four wineglasses, each filled with a different cabernet as well as a small notebook and pen.

"The food looks delicious." Lisa sets her plate down next to her notebook.

"Definitely." Meg smiles at the woman I don't know sitting on the other side of Lisa. "Cori's very lucky to have one of the best caterers in town as a good friend."

"I don't think we've met." I try to appear confident. "Dawn Munsen. I'm Kayli's mom."

"Nice to meet you," she replies. "I'm Cynthia Cooper. Stacy's mom."

"Ah, okay," I barely get out before my mouth suddenly turns to cotton. Stacy, Sienna's best friend, who helped make Kayli's life miserable this past fall. I try to smile and think calm thoughts as my cheeks warm. Of course she's Stacy's mom. She looks exactly like her. How did I not figure that out earlier?

"I also have a son, who plays basketball with Cori's and Lisa's older boys." Her chin gestures to Lisa. "So I've known those two forever."

"That's great," is all I can think of to say as Cori clinks her wineglass again. I would have guessed Kayli's name would've rung some sort of bell with Cynthia. Thank goodness I'm wrong.

"As you can see, we have four different bottles of cabernet," Cori begins. "Each bottle is numbered and corresponds to one of the glasses in front of you. The person who brought the bottle will tell us about their wine. After each presentation, we'll try the wine and write down any defining notes or qualities. Once we go through all four wines, we'll mix up the order of the glasses, do a blind tasting, and try to guess which wine is which. Sound fun?"

Everyone nods as I pull an index card from my pocket that has my presentation notes on it. I cross my fingers I'm not first. I'd rather have a little more wine in me before it's my turn.

"Bottle number one," Cori announces, holding up a bottle I don't recognize.

"That's mine." Natalie jumps up, beaming like a pageant contestant as she eagerly presents where it's from, a short history of the vineyard, and a little about the owners. After we've tasted her wine and written down our notes, the next mom goes. As we continue, I'm surprised how different the wines taste even though they're all cabernets. Their uniqueness stands out so much more when they're tasted alongside one another like this. And it's helpful to hear what the others taste, smell, or notice. There are a lot of details I wouldn't normally pay attention to.

My presentation is last. It's short and sweet, and no one has any questions or complaints. By this point, everyone's ready to simply enjoy the wine, relax, and chitchat. We cruise through the blind tasting, with Cynthia being the only one to get all the wines correct.

As everyone congratulates her, Natalie loudly teases, "Too bad your expertise can't be leveraged at the fifth-grade dance."

"Right?" Cynthia laughs. "Maybe I can at least add some value with the food."

"For sure." Natalie keeps grinning. "How are the preparations going, by the way?"

"Pretty well, wouldn't you say?" Cynthia looks across the table to Meg.

"Absolutely." Meg sets down her glass. "It's going to be great. The only thing I'm a little hesitant about is keeping it a Sadie Hawkins theme. I want James to be able to go, but I don't want him to feel like he has to be invited by a girl. He simply isn't into that right now."

I sit back and take another sip of Natalie's wine—my favorite of the bunch—while secretly admiring how sly Meg is at sliding that comment in...directly in front of Cynthia no less. I have no clue if she and Cynthia have discussed the issue before. But now, in front of a crowd, Meg isn't playing any games. There are witnesses here.

"That's such a good point," Lisa says. "I agree completely. These fifth-grade boys aren't there yet. I know Gavin's not. Girls are the furthest thing from his mind right now."

Wait, what? I fight the urge to sit up, bumping my foot on the table leg. Did I hear her right? Gavin has no interest in girls? That doesn't make any sense. I swirl my glass, hold it up to my nose to sniff, and take another sip. I hope that it looks natural. Ugh…and of course I can't say anything now, not with this group. But what the heck? I mean, I know some kids don't open up to their moms as much—maybe he hasn't told her? Or maybe he has told her, but he's described it as the exact opposite of what Kayli's told me? Oh man. What if Lisa thinks of me the same way Meg thinks of Cynthia? I take another sip…I mean gulp.

"Aw, really?" Cynthia says, glancing over to Meg. "I think Stacy's pretty excited about it. I know she has a certain boy she's thinking of asking and wants to get a special outfit and everything. What about the rest of you? What do your daughters think?"

Jane scratches the back of her neck, shaking her head. "Yeah, it's probably not great."

Nikki scooches up in her chair, glancing around the table. "I agree. It's probably better to take some of the relationship pressure off at this age. Their little notes have become such a distraction, and now some kids are writing the initials of their crush on their wrists. All this coupling up is even starting to create some friction between friends."

"I'm on board with that." Cori folds her arms, leaning on the table. "Anything we can do to diminish the hype around these little crushes, or whatever they are, would be good."

I can only nod, feeling my cheeks flush as I look around the table. How is it that all these moms are against crushes? And why didn't I know this before—especially from Nikki and Cori? Why didn't they mention it when they were fishing for information about Kayli at the girls' basketball tournament? It could have been useful to know. I take another sip. Whatever…I'm not even sure it would've changed how I handled things. Would I have let Gavin's initial on Kayli's wrist slide if I knew these moms were so opposed? I don't know, maybe not. Maybe, though…since I still don't think it's the best idea to jump in and intervene.

I look down at my empty glass. Dang it. I'll have to switch to the wine I brought. I roll the tension out of my neck as I pick up my other glass and take a sip. Crap. I knew it. It tastes horrible now.

"See? That's huge," Meg says, looking back at Cynthia. "I definitely think we should bring it up with Principal Jacobson next week."

"It's tradition, though…" Cynthia's sigh borders on whimpering.

"But some traditions have to change." Meg sounds relaxed, but the look she's giving Cynthia is anything but.

"I guess," Cynthia concedes. The pressure of this group must be getting to her too.

After Cynthia's apparent surrender, everyone settles in to enjoy their wine, chatting about more benign things, like updates on basketball and spring break plans. The topic of the body spray comes up briefly, but no one seems to have any clues as to who could be doing it, and the mood stays light. As the night winds down, Meg signals me to see if it's okay that we get going, and we excuse ourselves.

"So, what'd you think?" Meg asks as we back out of the driveway.

"Fun," I manage to say, shivering as the car warms up. "What about you?"

"It was nice getting to know Cori better. I've met Brad a few times since he's on the basketball board. He seems so intense. I didn't know what to expect from her…" Meg pauses, keeping her eyes on the road. "I was a little surprised by her comments on crushes, though. It doesn't exactly line up with what I've heard about Emily."

"Really? Emily? Emily has a crush?"

"Yep." Meg raises her eyebrows, tipping her chin down as

she glances over. "I don't know who her boy of the month is, but she's definitely known as one of the more boy-crazy girls in their grade. I've heard she likes that it riles her dad up...as if that needs to happen more."

Goodness. Meg knows everything about these kids. I'm betting she already knows about Kayli and Gavin too. I do my best to ease into it, paying close attention to her reaction as she pulls into my driveway. "Wow...as if figuring out how to handle these crushes isn't challenging enough. I found out Kayli likes Gavin back a couple of days ago..." She doesn't flinch, confirming my hunch, but I still feel the need to keep going. "I'm trying to let her problem-solve these friend issues on her own, but knowing he's such a troublemaker and seeing glimpses of Kayli making concessions—like the initial on her wrist and such—isn't making it easy."

When the car comes to a stop, Meg looks over, tilting her chin again as she gives me the slightest side-eye. "And Nikki's, Cori's, or those *other* moms' opinions aren't swaying you?"

My stomach lurches. Ouch. "No, I get it. It's..." I hesitate. I know Meg's comfortable voicing her opposition to crushes with James, but that's her style. I need to be more careful. I don't want to overstep with Kayli again. Besides, I want her to figure this stuff out. I don't want to become some sort of heli-copter, snowplow, or whatever the jargon of the month is for an overly involved parent. "I need to find a way to help her see the negatives without specifically telling her what to do."

"Well..." Meg has skepticism written all over her face. "At least Kayli's still open with you. Not all the moms at Cori's can say that. But you also need to be super careful. Gavin's history —he can be pretty vindictive. I don't know how he is with girls, but when it comes to the boys in their grade, he's all about self-preservation. If some kid does something that isn't benefiting him or Brody, or if it makes either of them look bad, they cut that kid out. And fast."

"Wow. Thanks for the heads-up." I offer Meg a weak smile as I open my door and get out of the car. But I struggle to find any other words, so I simply say goodbye. I mean, what else can I do? She pulls out of the driveway as I heave the front door open, its weight feeling heavier tonight. Obviously, this boy isn't good news. I just need to figure out how to warn Kayli.

WEDNESDAY, JAN 29

Hearing footsteps, I grab my coffee from my desk and go see who's in the kitchen first this morning. Kayli's got her hair pulled back in two French braids and is wearing her black-and-purple striped leggings, a black long-sleeved tee, and a jean vest I forgot she even had. The only time I've ever see her dress this nice for school is on picture day. Something's up for sure. "Morning, hon. You're pretty dolled up today. Is something special happening at school?"

"Nope. Just a regular day." She opens the pantry door and assessing her options.

"You're even wearing a necklace…" I get a whiff of something very flowery as she moves to the fridge. Is she wearing perfume…what the heck? If it was any other girl, I wouldn't think twice—she looks cute, smells nice—it simply isn't Kayli. My toes curl, resisting the trigger to overreact. I keep my voice steady, but curious. "And you smell good. What is that?"

"Just lotion." She shrugs, acting like it's her everyday scent as she returns to the pantry.

"Got it." I play along, taking a sip of coffee that's suddenly grown bitter…this has to be because of Gavin. Since Cori's wine night, I've been discreetly trying to probe how things have been going with their relationship, or *crushing*, or whatever. Each time, she's deflected the question or said it's no big deal. I thought—hoped—things were maybe fizzling out. "How about some hot chocolate and toast? It's pretty chilly today."

"That'd be awesome." She pulls out a stool and hops up.

I set down my coffee and get to work, popping the bread in the toaster and heating up the water in the microwave. I need to get her to open up more. Starting with an indirect line of questioning is usually the most effective. "What else is going on? How's basketball?"

She scooches up in her seat and starts gabbing away about the new play they're learning, how she made a three-pointer during yesterday's practice and this rebounding drill she loves. "Oh, and did I tell you there's a team lasagna dinner at Emily's house next Friday?"

"The seventh?" I pull the hot water out of the microwave and bring it over to Kayli, so she can stir in the hot chocolate while I finish up her toast.

"Yeah. Coach Brad will tell you more about it at pickup tomorrow. Parents and siblings can come too." She stops stirring and looks up. "And I need to ask you about Saturday."

"What's Saturday?"

"Emily's brother's team is playing in a basketball tournament at the high school. Her dad is letting her bring Mandi, but she said I could sit with them if I find a way to go."

Kayli wants to go to an eighth-grade boys' basketball tournament? That's kind of strange. I know her friends are going, but it's definitely a first. Wait a second...doesn't Gavin's older brother play with Emily's brother? I close my eyes. That has to be it. She's acting oh-so-casual, too. I need to test my theory, but discreetly. "Sounds fun. Is anyone else you know going to be there?"

"Maybe..." She scratches the back of her reddening neck

before taking a quick sip of her hot chocolate. "Gavin's probably going since his brother plays on the same team."

"Ah." I probably exhale a little too loudly. At least she's not lying about it. Obviously, I'd prefer it if she wasn't so interested in this kid. But if she is, I don't want her to start hiding things about him from me. And, really, how big of a deal can it be? A dressier outfit, some perfume, and going to a random basketball game…it's pretty harmless. Although the branding on the wrist still irks me, and Meg and Naomi's warnings still linger, it doesn't seem like he's being mean to her. And I can't think of an excuse not to let her go. "Well, you don't have basketball, so I don't see why not. When Dad gets home tonight, let's ask him if he can take you."

"Cool." She nods, noticeably relaxing her posture as she dunks her toast in her drink.

But as soon as I see her relax, I start having second thoughts. I mean, this is the kid Meg and Naomi cautioned me about. I wonder if I'll feel better if I learn more about what's going on with him. "So, how are things with Gavin these days? Is he still being nice?"

"Oh yeah." She finishes swallowing. "Yesterday, Brody was being so annoying. He kept telling me I dressed like a boy. Gavin was super nice about it, though. He totally stuck up for me. And later, he told me it might help if I dressed more like Mandi and Emily."

I'm speechless, watching her proudly look down at her outfit.

"Good, right?" She looks up and smiles.

I can't think of anything else to say, and I can't smile back —I actually have no clue what my face is doing right now. I try focusing on my coffee, racking my brain for how to respond as Naomi's voice haunts me. *Her appearance is not for someone else's approval.* Why is it Brody's business what she looks like—and now, she needs Gavin to save the day? But then he sucks at it. It makes zero sense. I literally feel my coffee making its way back up my throat. I have to say…something. I need to get her to start seeing this stuff—but carefully. "Well, I love that you wear clothes that allow you to run around and be active. As long as you like it and you're comfortable, you don't need anyone's blessing on your outfit, right?"

"No, I know." Her voice softens as she looks down at her clothes again. "But Gavin thought…which reminds me—" She jumps off her stool, darts into the mudroom, and then comes back a few seconds later with a notebook and pen. "I was going to tell him something." She climbs back on her stool and starts writing furiously. When she's done, she quickly rereads it and adds a heart-laced pattern around the edge. Then she tears it out, folds it up into a square, and doodles "Gavin" in bubble letters on the front with one more heart to dot the *i*.

Oh my God. Just the sight of this note makes my skin crawl. Not only is it a distraction I now know the other moms detest, but it's also physical proof of their relationship floating around, which can easily fall into the hands of someone who might not have her best interest at heart.

"Kayli—" I stall, hearing Ryn thunder down the stairs. The bus will be here any minute. "Can't you tell him in person?"

"Mom…" She draws out the word, sounding borderline condescending as she rolls her eyes and gathers her things. "That ruins it. When you're with someone, you write them cute little notes. It brightens their day."

"Ah…" My hand instinctively moves to my brow, trying to knead the worry away as she heads to the mudroom to grab her coat. She looks so excited as she goes out of her way for this boy. All she seems to care about is what he and her friends think, even if trying to fit in puts her at risk. All this seems so normal to her. And, unfortunately, it probably is. But it doesn't mean it's right.

* * *

With the slippery roads, I give myself plenty of room to slow down and make the final turn into the parking lot. My car still hasn't warmed up, so even moving the steering wheel takes effort. And after I'm parked, there's a discernable degree of disgust in my breath as I blow on my hands, trying to warm them up. I need to get out of this funk. I hoist myself out of the car and trudge over to Meg and Naomi, moving like a tin man in my fifteen thousand layers. As I get closer, though, the steps get easier. Seeing them huddling together, each pushing their frozen cheek muscles out to smile, I know I'll be able to get through this. "Morning, ladies."

"Brr..." Meg rubs her mittens together and then cups them over her nose as we get on our way. "I almost bailed today, it's so cold."

"Me too," Naomi says. "But this is my only time to catch up with you guys, so I hate to miss it. Let's walk fast. And maybe we can turn back early."

Meg nods as we pick up the pace. "Besides, I have to share my great news." She pauses, clasping her hands together as if she's listening to her own drumroll. "So, Cynthia and I spoke with Principal Jacobson, and he agreed to change the format of the dance, so it doesn't have to be Sadie Hawkins style anymore."

"Impressive." I tease with tiny applause, not thinking for a second that Meg wouldn't eventually get her way, but also using the clapping to boost my own mood. "Good work."

"Wonderful," Naomi chimes in. "I honestly can't believe it wasn't changed before."

Meg beams. "I know, right? Principal Jacobson said the same thing. But now, any fifth-grader can come. Girls can invite boys, boys can invite girls, or anyone can come with their friends, by themselves, or whatever. All are welcome."

"Maybe Lily will even want to go now," Naomi says as I check my zipper to make sure it's pulled all the way up and adjust my neck gaiter. "I'm guessing a lot of kids will reconsider after having this pressure point removed."

"And..." Meg leans forward. "I'm hoping it'll alleviate some of the drama that's going on with the girls."

"Uh-oh," I get out through my chattering teeth. Please, for the love of loves, don't have this be anything to do with Kayli. "More drama?"

"You haven't heard?" Naomi grabs a tissue from her pocket to wipe her nose. "Things between Stacy and Sienna have gotten very rocky. I can't believe Kayli hasn't said anything."

"Same." Meg basically looks at me like I'm from outer space. "It's pretty big news."

Shivers race up my spine. *Sienna.* Triggers me every time. At least it doesn't involve Kayli this time around. "She's been in her own little world lately. What's the scoop?"

"Ugh..." Meg pauses as she covers her face with her mittens. "The word on the street, aka Cynthia, is that Sienna has a crush on James now too. And she's been getting super mad at Stacy for liking him, even though Stacy was the one who said she liked James first."

"Oh, Meg, I'm so sorry," I reply. "More crush drama with James? And especially with those two—sounds like a disaster."

"I know, right?" Meg's breath flares as her volume increases, making me immediately regret my words. I should've said something more calming. Even the swishing of her coat seems louder. "I mean, it's like a soap opera. What is it with these girls? The whole thing's ridiculous. They're basically ruining their friendship over an eleven-year-old boy. What a waste! And James isn't interested in either one. He wants to be left alone."

I shake my head, but a tiny part of me also wonders if James really is the innocent victim Meg's making him out to be.

What if Meg's in the dark, like Lisa is? Hold on—what am I even saying? That's impossible. Meg hears everything about everyone.

"But crazy enough," Meg continues as I maneuver around an ice patch in the middle of the trail, "I'm getting a taste of what it's like to be on the other side. Yesterday, Brooklyn made a huge deal about wanting to wear this cute new outfit to our baking class, even though I told her she'd probably spill something on it. And she wanted to do her hair in a French braid."

"Sounds exactly like Lily," Naomi sighs, rejoining the conversation. "Her recent preoccupation with clothes and how she looks is testing my whole being. Are you worried she's starting to place too much emphasis on her appearance?"

Meg shakes her head. "I'm thinking she has a crush on Elliot, the boy in our baking class. Right as we walked in, she yanked on my arm, so we could get the open seats at his table."

I can't help but cover my mouth. Seems like Kayli's not the only one who's dressing to impress a boy. At least Brooklyn isn't doing it because someone's teasing her about it, though. But when I drop my hand, I wipe any trace of a smile from my expression. Even though Brooklyn's only in third grade, I'm guessing Meg's taking this seriously, so I want to treat it as such. "So, what are you going to do?"

Meg groans as she runs her mitten over her hat and then to the back of her neck. "I don't know. You should've seen her in class, though. All giggly and batting her eyelashes to catch his attention. She kept pestering him for help and laughing at everything he did. I was so embarrassed. I'm sure Elliot's mom thought it was ridiculous."

A bluster of wind nearly knocks us over as we start crossing the bridge. The cold air makes my eyes water so much, there's no way I'm able to take in any sort of view. We don't even make it halfway across before we decide to turn back.

It's only after we're back under the cover of trees that I can finally talk. "Kayli was pretty dressed up this morning, too. She did her hair, wore some sort of scented lotion—the works." I rub my arms to calm some of the shivering. "Apparently, Brody teased her about dressing like a boy. She said Gavin defended her. But there she was, standing in front of me, as girly-girl as could be. Must have been *some* defense."

Naomi looks back and forth to Meg and me. I pray she has some sort of wise piece of insight that will help. But then she asks, "Do you guys think Lily has a crush on a boy?"

"Wha—I don't know…" I finally realize Naomi's been interpreting our stories through a very different lens.

"It didn't cross my mind until what you said about Brooklyn and Kayli," Naomi continues. "But Lily's been dressing differently too, and she's doing her hair and wearing lip gloss. I assumed it was a vanity thing. But what if she's doing all this because of a boy?"

"I suppose it's a possibility." Meg adjusts her jacket while she pauses. "Or, it could be what you said…she's starting to care more about what she looks like in general. Has she ever mentioned anything to you about any boys?"

"Not really." Naomi shakes her head and uses her tissue again. "In the past, she's been pretty open with me. But with all our disagreements lately, maybe she's holding back. I know her coding class is full of boys, but other than that, she hasn't really mentioned anything about any of them. I don't even know any of their names."

"Maybe you're still in the clear, then," I say, although part of me secretly hopes I'm wrong. If Lily does have a crush, I could see how Naomi navigates it.

"Maybe," Naomi says. "These days, we spend most of our time disagreeing about screen time, what she wants to wear, or how much makeup she can use. The only time she brings up boys is to complain about them." Naomi reaches for my arm as she stops in her tracks. "Hey, that reminds me. Have either of you heard anything about their gym teacher only picking boys to be the examples? Lily noticed it a month or so ago, and then she actually started keeping track. Mr. Klaven hasn't asked a single girl to serve as the example in gym class for over three weeks."

"That's a little hard to believe," Meg sighs, crouching into her coat as a gust of wind whips through. "Are the girls simply not raising their hands?"

As Naomi goes on to describe more of what she's heard from Lily, my head gets stuck on the clothes discussion, and how I once started dressing differently for someone.

Back in the day, I thought my manager at the golf course was being helpful when he recommended I wear shorter shorts and more fitted tank tops. It wasn't like he asked me to walk around naked—he once suggested a bikini, but I assumed he was kidding. Besides, all the other girls who drove the beer cart dressed like that. God, I thought that job was the best…out in the sun, everyone always in the mood for a good time, and the tips were phenomenal. He promised they'd be even better with a "more salacious" wardrobe. And he *was* right.

"I'll talk to James about it." Meg brings me back to reality as we approach our cars. "We haven't had a ton of time to chat lately. I've been so busy getting everything set up for the writers' workshop on Monday. I think the kids are going to love it."

"Who's the author again?" Naomi asks as I try to straighten my posture. Every muscle in my body feels frozen. I can barely turn my head toward Naomi, my neck is so tight.

"Her name's K.T. Wakefield," Meg replies. "She writes this amazing fantasy series with all these lessons for kids about standing up for themselves and what they believe in."

"Oh! She'll be great," Naomi says. "Lily has several of her books. And I love how she makes her stories accessible and relatable to both boys and girls."

"I think so too." Meg stands up taller. "She's going to read a couple of excerpts to the younger kids and tell them about how she became a writer. With the fifth-graders, she's also going to help them get started on a short story of their own."

Naomi cups her hands, bringing them to her chin. "Lily's going to love that."

Trying to smile, I mumble some sort of goodbye and escape into the sanctuary of my car. My hands are shaking, so I have to use both of them to turn my key in the ignition. Seriously, why on earth did I just remember my stint at the golf course again? What is it with those years and my memory lately?

Beads of sweat dot my brow, even though the rest of my body is like an ice cube. I rub my hands together, waiting for my car to warm up. I started working at the golf course after high school. The money was phenomenal—the tips alone nearly paid my college tuition—and everyone was all about having fun. The cocktails flowed freely, but I focused on working hard to earn the money I needed to pay for school. They were long, hard days, but I tried to be friendly and help get people what they needed.

I kept busy—maybe too busy to notice the signs. Like when my manager complimented how great my legs looked. Or when he ran his finger across my tank top strap. I probably should've looked more offended, brushed his hand off, or stepped away. But I was nervous, awkward, tongue-tied. I didn't want to make *him* uncomfortable. And I needed that job.

My hands finally warm up enough to unclench, and I check behind me one more time before pulling out. The coast is clear. This is absurd. Kayli's changing outfits is a completely different thing than what I experienced back then. I need to forget about it and move on.

* * *

Dusting off his hands as he struts into the living room, Ben looks like he's accomplished something big—something much bigger than simply putting the girls to bed. "Another day. Another bedtime. Done." He smiles, picks up his beer, and sits down next to me. Partially hiding his face behind his drink, he asks, "Don't you think we should've figured out how to get these girls to put themselves to bed by now?"

"Probably." I chuckle, recalling how many times I've had that same thought. "But Kayli insists her friends' parents still tuck them in, and she's not ready to give it up. When I ask the other moms about it, they warn we'll never get this time back, so we should do it as long as the girls let us."

"I guess…" He takes a swig and leans back. "Oh, and I hear I'm taking Kayli to this basketball tournament on Saturday? Anything special I should know?"

Now, it's my turn to duck behind my glass. Unfortunately for me, my wineglass isn't as big of a shield. "Yeah…I should probably warn you that this boy Kayli likes is going to be there. Gavin—remember him? He was one of the boys we ran into at Randy's."

Right on cue, Ben's whole chest deflates as he tosses his head back, stares up at the ceiling, and groans, "Are you serious?"

I could have predicted his response down to the exact muscle twitch. I don't know if it's a daddy-daughter issue, a fear of future drama or heartbreak, or what. "Honey, I'm sure it will be fine." I do my best to sound reassuring, resting my hand on his leg until he angles his face to look at me. I'm obviously not thrilled about it either, but I'm not ready to divulge that to Ben. It'll only make things worse. Besides, how bad can it be? To lighten the mood, I add, "There is going to be a crowd of people there, so it's not like they'll be making out in front of you."

There's not even the tiniest shift in his facial expression.

I go back to trying to be reassuring. "I doubt anything will happen. Worst case, they may want to sit together, or she might want to chat with him for a while." I set my glass down and scooch back next to him. I tilt my head to match his, waiting for him to turn his face, so I can fix my eyes on his. "But, honey…please, please don't give her a hard time about this. She'll start shutting us out."

"Fine," he grumbles, leaning forward to snatch up the remote. "But there better not be any teenybopper drama or commotion at the game, or she'll be coming home very early."

"Aye-aye, Mr. Tough Guy." I smirk and teasingly salute him. For now, I'll take what I can get. I think with a little more time, both he and Kayli will be able to figure this out.

SATURDAY, FEB 1

"Kayli and I are going to take off," Ben hollers up the stairs.

"Just a minute!" I call back, grabbing my sweatshirt off the bed and rushing downstairs. I want one last look before they leave. I hurry past Ryn, who's finishing up her lunch in the kitchen and meet Ben and Kayli in the mudroom right as Ben opens the door to the garage.

"Have fun, honey, and be good." I fix Kayli's coat collar, inhaling a whiff of her floral scent and noticing the shimmer on her lips. Knowing Gavin's going to be there, I'm way more nervous than I thought I'd be having Ben take her. My hands linger on her shoulders as her eyes sparkle with excitement. Feeling her bounce on the balls of her feet, I now want to trade places with Ben. How will Kayli act when she sees this boy? Will she sit by him? How close will Ben be? Oh man, what if Gavin does something mean…will Ben stay his easygoing self?

"I will." She beams and follows Ben out the door.

I grab the door before it closes and pop my head into the garage, suddenly not ready to let her go. Deep breath. It'll be fine. Ben can sit with the dads, and it's my turn to take Ryn to basketball anyway. I push aside any worry. "What time are you thinking you'll be home?"

Ben looks to Kayli, who shrugs. "Not sure. We'll play it by ear. Before dinner, though." He gives a final wave before I close the door and head into the kitchen.

"You almost ready?" I ask Ryn, hoping her skills session will keep my mind off Kayli.

"Yep." She scooches off her stool. "Just need to fill up my water bottle."

"What are you guys working on today?" I load her dishes into the dishwasher, wipe the crumbs off the counter, put the milk and cheese slices back into the fridge.

"Probably the same things we always do," Ryn says, heading into the mudroom to put on her coat. "Dribbling, passing, shooting, and defense. But we might get to scrimmage...that's my favorite! I can't wait to play a real basketball game."

Ryn continues chattering about their practices and who she thinks is the best at all the skills on our way to the Activity Center. Accurate or not, it amazes me how she puts her own name at the top of nearly every list. I wish she were this confident with her math.

At the gym, Ryn hands over her coat and water bottle and dribbles over to her friends, Mollie and Josie, who are shooting at one of the side hoops. I hesitate for a second, seeing Nikki on the bleachers by herself. There's no way I can avoid her here. But I have to try to keep the conversation on basketball. That's much safer than crushes. I go over and plop down. "How's Mollie enjoying the season so far?"

"Loves it." She smiles. "And she loves playing with Ryn."

I nod and smile back. It's nearly impossible to talk over the thirty second- and third-graders dribbling and shooting. Thankfully, the second-grade portion is only for the first hour.

After Coach T blows his whistle to gather the girls, it's quiet enough to talk again.

Nikki tips her head toward mine. "Did you have a good time at Cori's wine night?"

"Absolutely." Crap. I was supposed to keep our conversation on basketball. I try to keep my response diplomatic. "It was fun to have time to get to know everyone a little better. Usually, when I'm around other moms, I'm with my kids or only have a few minutes."

"For sure." Nikki leans closer, giving my leg a playful tap. "What'd you think about Lisa saying Gavin wasn't interested in girls yet? I mean, Mandi's repeatedly mentioned that he and Kayli have quite the crushes on each other. And she's meeting him at the game today, right?"

"Mm-hmm," I sigh. Of course she steers us onto gossip. And now, knowing she isn't a fan of these crushes, I need to be even more careful with how I talk about it with her. I don't want to lie, but I want to minimize its importance as much as I can. "I don't know Lisa super well, so I didn't want to start anything. Besides, I don't think it's anything too serious. Maybe Gavin hasn't even brought it up. Girls seem a lot more open with their moms at this age from what I can tell."

"Totally agree." She turns to face me, tucking her hair behind her ear. "And Lisa's been so busy lately. I'm sure she's not in the loop as much. You did the right thing by not fanning the flames. Cynthia's going through some rough spots with Stacy and her crush, too."

Stacy and her crush. It's funny Nikki doesn't mention James by name. She has to know what good friends Meg and I are. Maybe she's also being cautious.

The whistle blows again, and I turn my attention to see what's next, pretending to be extra interested in what's happening on the court. The girls appear to be doing contests, which makes my interest much more plausible. It also helps that Ryn is winning most of them.

Coach T blows his whistle again to call the girls over, so he can hand out sports drinks to the girls who displayed the best team spirit and sportsmanship.

"I love that he focuses on sportsmanship," I say, preempting any topic other than basketball.

"Yeah, he does a nice job. And everyone's improving so much. Especially Ryn. And it looks like she's picking up on some of Kayli's confidence too." Nikki nudges me and motions over to Ryn, who's raising her sports drink up in the air like she won a national championship.

"Goodness." I shake my head, grabbing Ryn's coat and standing up. "I wish some of her confidence with basketball would translate to her schoolwork."

Nikki grabs Mollie's coat as she climbs off the bleachers. "Oh, she's struggling?"

"With math, definitely." My body starts to unclench as a clear and safe ending for my time with Nikki comes into sight. "I know teaching all these strategies to these kids is supposed to be helpful, but right now, it seems a little overwhelming for her…and me. And because she doesn't get what they're teaching instantaneously, she deems herself officially bad at math. She barely even wants to try now. Even the word *math* makes her cringe."

"We went through something similar when Mandi was in second grade," Nikki says as we wait for the girls to round up their balls. "Playing dice games seemed to help. There are a few that use a ton of adding and subtracting. After a while, Mandi started realizing how quickly she could tally, put together, and take apart numbers. Her confidence with math soared."

"What a great idea," I reply as Ryn and Mollie walk over, with one of the third-grade coaches not far behind.

"I'll text you the details on one of our favorites." Nikki waves goodbye as she and Mollie take off, while Ryn and the third-grade coach wait patiently next to me.

"Hey, Dawn." He smiles once Nikki's out of earshot. "Patrick."

"Hi." I can't recall if this is the same guy who asked me about Ryn playing up with the third-graders when the season first started. Neither Ben nor I were super excited about it, wanting Ryn to have a fun, more low-key season with her friends instead.

"So, I know I asked you about this before, and you weren't completely on board, but we're short on girls for this weekend's tournament. We could really use Ryn's help."

"Oh?" I look down at Ryn, who's bouncing up and down, grinning ear to ear. "It seems like Ryn's interested, but I'll have to run it by my husband, Ben. Where's the tournament?"

"It's at one of the middle schools in Cantondale. It's a one-day pool play tournament on Saturday. The games are at ten, noon, and two." He glances over to the other girls on the court and then turns back to me. "If it's okay with you, it'd be great if Ryn could stay and play with us for this session and then join us at Thursday's practice at six."

"You'd like her to stay and play right now?"

"That'd be great." He smiles, looking at his watch. The third-graders are still shooting around, but he probably needs to get practice going. I need to decide quickly.

"Please, Mommy," Ryn begs, holding her hand up in prayer position.

"I suppose." I give in for now. "But I can't promise anything about next weekend until I talk to Ben."

"Understood." Patrick puts his arm around Ryn as he leads her over to the other girls for introductions. I head back to the stands to warm the bleachers for another hour.

* * *

Ryn's mixing the chocolate chips into the cookie dough when I hear the garage door open. Ben and Kayli are home right on time. I hold myself back from meeting them at the door. Instead, I pretend to act like a normal person, pulling the rolls out of the oven, giving the beef stew a quick stir, and then helping Ryn scoop the dough onto the cookie sheets.

"Hello?" I call out when I hear footsteps stomp into the mudroom.

"Hi, hon." Ben comes into the kitchen, gives me a kiss, and walks over to the counter to peek in the crockpot. "What are we having tonight?"

"I made stew since I wasn't sure when you guys would be home." I shift my focus from him to Kayli as she darts past us without even saying hello. "What's up with Kayli?"

"She may need a little break from me." He grimaces as if he feels bad, but I'm not buying it. I swear there's a smile hiding underneath.

As I slide the cookie sheets into the oven, a million possibilities race through my mind. And all of them have something to do with Gavin. I take a deep breath. "What happened?"

Ben hesitates, looking over at Ryn. "Hey, Ryn, will you please go wash up for dinner?"

I nod at Ryn, and she scampers out of the room as I take her place on one of the stools. My stomach starts to turn as I watch her head upstairs. I tell myself to be patient and wait to see where this goes.

"It went okay for the most part." Ben's chest heaves as he runs his hand through his hair. "She was sitting with Emily and Mandi, not too far from where I was with Brad and a couple of other dads. But there was a group of boys a few rows above them on the bleachers, and towards the end of the second half, they started acting rude and doing some pretty dumb stuff."

"Like what?" I get up, returning to the stew for an unnecessary stir. I feel a sudden need to move around.

"Like idiot things boys do. You know, things like throwing down a kid's hat or glove."

"Ah…" I leave the spoon dangling in the pot and start getting the bowls and silverware out of the cupboards.

"Yeah, so then one of these jerks has to go down by the girls to grab his stuff. And when he does, he says something pretty upsetting to Kayli."

"What'd he say?" It takes all the discipline I have to set the dishes on the counter gently.

"I didn't actually hear it. I only saw her face. She seemed happy to see him at first, but after he spoke to her, she looked pretty upset. And right at the end, one of the boys shouts out, 'Kayli loves Gavin!'" He shakes his head. "The whole gym heard it. And then, of course, the boy who spoke to Kayli earlier starts pounding on the kid who yelled it out."

"Oh my gosh," I groan, unable to keep my head from falling forward. Each word grows less steady coming out. These boys. No wonder she's so upset. "How'd she handle it?"

He shrugs as he sits down, running his hands through his hair again.

"Did you talk to her about it after?" I can't even guess how he dealt with this. Ben hates confrontation, but he also despises crushes. I've never seen him handle a collision of the two.

"I tried. But I may have messed it up," he says sheepishly, shaking his head. "I was so embarrassed she was even involved…I may have asked her a little too angrily who the boys were and what she did to provoke them."

"Oh man…" I tilt my head back. I can't even look at him. He blamed her. This is what I was afraid of. Ben's usually so cool, calm, and collected. But there's something about being involved with conflict or drama—I'm sure it has something to do with how his parents fought when he was growing up—it turns him into a different person.

"Yeah. She got pretty defensive, telling me it wasn't her fault, the boys are in her class at school, and that Brody is the biggest idiot."

"Hmm…" I continue to hold my tongue. Of course she did, but I don't say that to Ben. I can even picture Kayli's scowling face in the back of his car—I know it all too well. It's the same look I received through my rearview mirror way too many times this fall.

"So, what do we do?"

"I don't think anything, now." If Ben's going to blame Kayli, it's better if he stays out of it. "Except maybe give Kayli more time to cool off."

"Really? So, all we do is wait?"

"Really. I'll talk to her about it later tonight." I pull the cookies out of the oven and downplay the issue. "For now, will you tell the girls that dinner's ready?"

"Okay, yeah, sure." Ben sounds relieved as he gives me one last curious look before sliding off of his stool and going to get the girls from upstairs.

A few minutes later, I hear Ryn telling him about basketball as the three of them come back down. Shoot. I totally forgot to mention that.

"So, you stayed late and practiced with the third-graders today?" Ben asks Ryn, but he keeps his eyes on me as everyone sits down.

"Mm-hmm." Ryn beams before biting off a huge chunk of her roll.

"Sorry." I cringe at Ben. "I was planning to tell you—and so you know, nothing's final. The third-grade coach came over after Ryn finished with her session this afternoon and said they were short on numbers for this upcoming weekend. Ryn seemed so excit—"

"That's awesome!" Kayli cheers, standing up and high-fiving Ryn across the table.

"Can I do it, Daddy? Please?" Ryn clenches her hands, holding them up to her chin.

"The tournament's only on Saturday," I reason. "It's in Cantondale, so it's super close. You'd need to bring her, though, since Kayli has a tournament that weekend too."

Ben presses his lips together as he looks back and forth between Ryn and me. Little by little, his forehead relaxes, and he finally relents. "Fine. I suppose we can try it."

"Yay!" Kayli and Ryn's hands shoot up in victory.

"And," I say, hoping to leverage the positive mood in the air, "Mollie's mom was telling me about this great dice game we can try tonight after dinner."

"What dice game?" Ryn halts her cheering and shoots me a suspicious side-eye.

"It's called Seventeen. Nikki says it's super fun. Each person takes a turn rolling the dice to see how many times it takes to get to seventeen. When your total's less than seventeen, you add the dice to the total. When the total's greater than seventeen, you subtract from the total."

"Sounds like math," Ryn pouts, crossing her arms.

"Nikki says Mollie and Mandi love it, so I think we should try it."

"Fine," Ryn huffs, uncrossing her arms. "It's a good thing you made cookies tonight."

After dinner, Ryn and Ben go down to the toy closet to see if they can find the dice while Kayli helps me clean up. I try to figure out a way to bring up the Gavin situation.

"So, how'd the tournament go today?" I load the plates into the dishwasher as Kayli brings over everyone's glasses.

"I suppose Dad told you," she mutters.

"Not really." If I pretend not to know too much, I can get her version of the story.

She pulls out a stool and sits down. "You know that note I wrote Gavin on Wednesday?"

Of course. The note. I knew it'd come back to haunt me.

"So, Brody found it, and he started teasing Gavin about it. And now, he won't stop. Brody keeps making a big deal if Gavin wants to sit next to me or work with me on a project."

"Oh, hon." I try to be sympathetic. "I'm guessing Brody's a little jealous of the time Gavin's spending with you."

Kayli rests her arm on the counter, propping her face up with her fist, her smooshed cheek further emphasizing her despair. "And then yesterday at school, Gavin said he doesn't want me to play with him and Brody at recess anymore. He thinks it's better if we pretend we don't like each other for a little while."

Wait, what? Hold on—pretend they don't like each other? What does that even mean? Is Gavin asking her to lie to protect him? That's so not right. Actually, it's completely insane. I restrain myself from tilting my head back. I need to stay calm and help her see what's happening—help her think through this.

I try to keep my tone even. "Wow. That's an…unusual request. How does that make you feel?"

"I don't know," she moans, slouching down into her stool. "I get it, I guess. I'm just annoyed Brody's so mean."

My mind races for something else to say. Obviously, I'd be elated if this crush thing were over, but *pretend* over is not *actually* over. Pretend over is super shady. She needs to see that.

Suddenly, she sits up straighter, folding her arms on the counter as she begins to rant. "Then, when Brody started throwing Gavin's things down during the game, Gavin got mad at *me*. I wasn't even doing anything!" She throws her hands up. "It was all Brody! Mandi, Emily, and I were just sitting there… well, Mandi and I were sitting there."

She slouches back down, but now it's my turn to straighten

up. Gavin getting mad at her and making her feel bad is idiotic. Why doesn't she end it for real? "Honey, I'm not sure I understand how Gavin's idea about pretending not to like each other is a good idea. I mean, how does that benefit you?"

She flippantly shrugs. "I'll still get to be with Gavin."

She can't be serious. What does *being with Gavin* even mean? "Maybe you could go back to simply being friends with him? Then you wouldn't have to lie."

"I knew that's what you'd say," she snaps, shaking her head as she slides off the stool.

No, no, no. We're not going back to those days again. I overstepped. I need to stick to getting her to think about stuff. I can't tell her what to do. I have to keep reminding myself Kayli shuts me out when I don't give her enough space or start telling her how to handle things.

"I'm sorry, hon. I don't know. What do *you* think you should do?"

"I guess I'll try it Gavin's way for now." She still seems way too unfazed as Ryn and Ben come back upstairs. "I mean, there's no doubt he likes me." Her eyes start to light up as she stares off at the wall. "He's always leaving notes in my locker, saying how cute I look or telling me a funny story about something someone in class said or did. I like having inside jokes with him. And it sounds dumb, but I like it when I catch him looking at me." She turns back to me, looking oh-so-certain now. "We just have to be more careful around Brody."

Although this is not at all what I was hoping to hear, I actually get what she's saying. Those things do feel good, but it doesn't make the pretending not to like each other right.

"Found 'em!" Ryn holds up the dice at the top of the stairs, with Ben right behind her.

"Great," I say to Ryn, thinking the exact opposite about Kayli's ordeal.

As they get set up at the table, my stomach churns with a

renewed sense of unease. Everything's been going so smoothly with Kayli these last few months. She and I have gotten closer again, and I love how much she's sharing with me. I have to be so careful not to hinder our bond by overstepping or getting too involved in her friendship decisions. But pretending not to be in a relationship with someone, even as a fifth-grader, feels wrong on so many levels.

As Ryn takes her turn, I can't shake how I'm feeling. This could be bad. Really bad. "A five and a six," she squeals. "Is that good?"

"It's eleven," Ben says. "Roll again."

Ryn rolls. "Four and two."

"Seventeen!" Ben writes her score down. "In only two tries. Good job, buddy."

What the heck? Ben's not supposed to be helping her. She's never going to learn from that. "Let's try to have everyone figure out their own score." I try to be subtle with my intentions in front of Ryn, wishing I could think of a similar kind of hint I could give Kayli.

"It's your turn to roll the dice, Mommy," Ryn says.

My thoughts exactly.

WEDNESDAY, FEB 5

I bring Ryn's dishes over to the sink as she slides off her stool and heads back upstairs to finish getting ready for school. Glancing at the clock for the fifth time in as many minutes, I feel the dread roiling in my gut grow. Ten after eight, and still no Kayli. Only thirty more minutes until the bus comes. I wipe up Ryn's crumbs and then brace myself as I begin the gauntlet upstairs.

My chest tightens with each step. I feel like I'm climbing up the side of a volcano, and Kayli's mood is the unpredictable lava simmering inside. "Kay?" I lightly tap on her door a few times before nudging it open. She's not in her bed, but her closet light is on. I say her name one more time before going over to peek in. Seeing her sitting crisscross on the floor in there, unshowered, and with only a T-shirt and undies on, I know it's not good. "What's going on?"

"I don't know," she wails, burying her face in her hands.

"Are you sick?" It's a long shot but worth a try.

"No." She looks up at me with tears starting to stream down her face.

I crouch down and rub her back. "What is it?" I really

don't need to ask. This has to be about Gavin. These past couple of days, I've been walking around on eggshells trying to figure out the right things to say or do. This little pretending arrangement he devised has really taken a toll on her...and completely exhausted me.

I've repeatedly told her it's not good when people feel like they have to hide who they are, and I've tried to remind her how a boy should treat a person he cares about. But she either brushes it off or gets defensive. And if I go so far as to offer any sort of advice, forget it. Smoke starts coming out of her ears before I can get more than three words out.

"It's just so hard."

"What is?"

"Gavin."

Inhale, exhale. Be patient. Calm face. No judging. "What's going on, honey?"

"He's being so mean to me lately." She wipes her nose on her sleeve. "I know he's pretending because of Brody, but nobody else at school knows that's why. All they see is him treating me like dirt, and me taking it."

"That's awful." I coerce my voice to remain steady and my expression to stay plain. But my stomach is literally eating away at itself as I watch Kayli shrink into this meek, voiceless being. For the love, why is she allowing him to treat her like this? This is not the confident daughter I witness every other weekend on the basketball court. It makes me want to throw up. I'm fighting every impulse I have to demand she break up with this kid—I know that'd only blow up in my face. And besides, she has to learn to see this stuff herself. I have to find some way to get her to recognize that what this kid is doing isn't right.

She sighs, starting to collect herself. "It's the only thing we can do now, though."

Huh? "Why do you think that's the only thing?" I ask as

gently as I can. There have to be at least a million other much better alternatives.

"What else can I do?" She stands up and starts digging through her drawers.

"Uh…," I stammer. Come on, think…this is my chance, and I'm blowing it. I can't tell her to end it, but I need to tell her something to get her to see that she needs to end it. All I can think of, though, is a repeat of something I've already said numerous times. "Think about the type of boy you want to be with and how they should treat you. If Gavin isn't doing that, you should end your relationship with him."

"But Gavin *is* the type of boy I want." She puts her hand on her hip as she looks back at me. "He's cute, smart, super funny, and he has lots of friends."

Ah, of course. He has all the uber-important superficial qualities girls her age want. My case isn't looking good. "But how does he treat *you*? How does he make *you* feel?" I ask, searching every inch of her face to see if it connects.

But her face is stone cold. Is she mad? Is she still thinking about it? At least she's stopped crying. Then her chin dips down for a fraction of a second. Wait…was that a nod?

"I have a math quiz this morning. I can't miss it." Her voice quivers, but at least she wants to keep moving forward. This is good. It doesn't solve anything, but her possible nod makes me feel like I made a tiny bit of progress.

"You've got this." I look at my watch. She doesn't have a ton of time to finish getting ready. "You just need to get dressed and grab something to eat. What can I do to help?"

"Will you make me cinnamon toast, please?" Her demeanor seems to shift as she pulls out a pair of leggings. It's somehow stronger…more confident. "And set out some graham crackers for my snack?"

"No problem." I pause before turning to leave, resting my hand on her back. "Love you."

"Love you too." She looks back and smiles before fishing some socks out of her drawer.

My steps are lighter as I hurry back downstairs. And I breathe even easier when Kayli comes down a few minutes later, fully dressed, with hair braided and smelling of a hint of flowers. I put a container of graham crackers in her backpack as she gets on her coat and boots. I hand her the toast in a paper towel as Ryn stares out the window.

"Bus's here!" She whips open the door.

I give the girls a quick hug and then out the door they go. As the bus door closes after them, my heart rate finally returns to normal. Boy, do I need my walk with Meg and Naomi this morning.

* * *

I almost miss my turn into the parking lot as thoughts of Kayli and Gavin continue to gnaw at me. The conversation with Kayli this morning was a start, but I need to do more to get her to see the seriousness of what's going on.

I pull in next to Meg's SUV. Everything looks so ugly. The snow's all brown and muddy. Even the sky has a tan hue to it. I hope we get another couple of inches of snow soon, so this filth gets covered up. If it has to be this cold, it should at least be pretty.

"Hey, guys." I leap over the dirty snowbank to meet Meg and Naomi on the trail and get on our way. Their faces are the only two bright spots around. "How's it going today?"

"Really good," Meg says. "I was updating Naomi on the writers' workshop."

"That's right. How'd it go?" At least it gets my focus off Kayli for a while.

"Amazing." Meg beams as she goes on to describe how invested the kids were and how everyone was so excited to learn about the new writing contest the author is going to judge. I always love how Meg gets so into this stuff. She's practically prancing down the trail.

"I was wondering how the writing contest part worked," Naomi says as a squirrel crosses in front of us. "I've been hearing conflicting things from different parents, and Lily wasn't sure about it either."

"Okay..." Meg bounces with giddiness. She's about two seconds away from giving spirit fingers. "So, more information will be coming home on Friday. It's totally optional, but if the fifth-graders want, they can write stories using some of the tips and tricks they learned. The stories are due at the end of the month. Then two fifth-grade teachers, Ms. Andreen and Ms. Thayer, will select the top ten stories and submit them to the author, who will then determine the final winner. Lily should totally do it. With her writing talent, she'd have a great shot at winning."

"Yeah...maybe." Naomi's quiet for a minute, focusing on fixing the snap on her cuff before she looks up and says, "Ugh...you guys, recently things have been so upside down with her. One day, we can't agree on screen time, and the next, we're arguing over makeup. And now I'm worried she's starting to diet. A few days ago, she asked me if she was the right size. And last night, when I checked her browsing history...it seems like she's been on a couple of sites that have tips on how to lose weight. I'm telling you, my worrying never stops with her."

"You *spy* on her browsing history?" Meg looks over with raised eyebrows.

"Without a doubt." Naomi doesn't miss a beat. "When Lily and I initially negotiated her screen time, I warned her I'd periodically make sure she wasn't stumbling onto inappropriate sites. She's probably forgotten all about our *deal* now, but I still check. I'm not simply letting her go off into the wild west of the internet to do whatever she wants."

I look back and forth at the two of them. This could turn into a whole new debate, but I want to finish our current conversation first. "So, what are you going to do?"

"I have a call in to Dr. Brinks," Naomi replies. "I haven't confronted Lily yet, but with her history of anxiety about food and getting sick, I don't want it to spiral into something worse. I want to make sure it's handled the right way from the start."

Gosh, she's good. How does Naomi always think of everything? "That's smart."

"But it's also so defeating." Naomi tilts her head back and rolls her neck before looking back over. "I've always focused on eating for health with the kids, how it's okay for bodies to be different sizes, and it's what's on the inside that matters. Now, it all feels like it was for nothing."

Meg adjusts her hat and turns to us. "Speaking of defeated, did I tell you about all the texts I got the other day?"

Naomi and I shake our heads. I search alongside the trail for any glimmer of white snow.

"Oh my gosh," Meg groans, hiding her face with her mittens for a minute, all her joy and excitement now drained. "So, Sunday morning, I wake up to twelve text messages from a number I don't recognize. And they weren't even intended for me. They were for James. Twelve! From the same number! Some *friend* of his thought my number was his number."

"See?" Naomi looks up to the sky, shaking her head. "Reason number five million and fifty-nine Lily will not be getting a phone anytime soon. What'd they say?"

"Other than ten million emojis? Pointless, silly things like James is so cute doing XYZ at recess and blah, blah, blah, he's so good at basketball. Totally useless distractions. When I asked James about it, he got super defensive, claiming he had no clue who would do that."

Naomi nods, her voice growing more exasperated as she continues, "When I talk to other moms, they think it's all so innocent. 'Oh, it's just emojis, what's so harmful about that?' Well, when you're added to a group chat with eight kids pinging you with hundreds of emojis at all hours of the night, it becomes a problem."

Naomi stops at our turnaround mark, lifts her arms up to the sky, and then folds over and hangs for a moment. I'm seriously expecting her to go full-on downward dog next. Finally, she stands up and sighs, "Sorry. I guess we all have our buttons."

Our boots crunch over the brown snow for several yards uninterrupted.

Naomi finally breaks the silence. "How are things going with Kayli?"

I keep putting one foot in front of the other, but it's hard not to let the weight of her words slow me down. I know she's asking out of genuine concern, but for some reason, it still feels like a punch to the gut. I guess we do all have our buttons. I'm suddenly brought back to Kayli's tears this morning and how I didn't make as much progress as I probably should have. I push my parenting insecurities aside, knowing Meg and Naomi only want to help. "I'm not going to lie. It's been a little rough."

"Does it have anything to do with how Gavin's been treating her?" Meg looks over cringing. "I've heard he hasn't been super nice to her lately."

"Same." Naomi can't hide the dismay from her eyes or her tone.

"You have?" All the air exits my body as I fight to keep it together. Of course, they've heard all about it. I don't know why I'd be surprised. They probably learned of it days ago. "Where'd you hear that?"

"Stacy's mom, mostly," Meg replies. "She's nonstop chatter during our dance planning meetings. I think she was trying to get some hint across to me pertaining to James or something, so she was using Gavin as an example."

"Ouch." I force my legs to keep moving. "I didn't realize how widespread the news was."

"How's Kayli feeling about it?" Naomi asks.

"I think she's confused." I stare straight ahead. Brown and more brown is all I see. "I am too, actually. Gavin's been giving her quite the mixed messages, telling her he likes her when no one else is around, but not acting nice to her when they are. It doesn't feel right. I keep trying to point out what he's doing, but I don't think I've figured out the perfect way to handle it yet."

"So, wait...," Meg says. "Gavin's still telling Kayli he likes her, but then when he's around others, he acts like he doesn't?"

"Pretty much," I reply. "Kayli thinks when Gavin spends time with her or gives her any sort of attention, his friend Brody gets upset. So, to *fix* this, Gavin suggested keeping things more on the down-low. But now, it sounds like it's gone to a whole other level."

"That's awful..." Meg draws it out as if it's one long word. "And such a head game for Kayli."

"I hear you..." My voice trails off. I can't even think straight anymore as I remember back to the head game I was once entangled in.

Everything with my manager at the golf course seemed so innocent. I was so naïve. And then out of the blue—or so I thought—that kiss. My imagination didn't have enough to draw from. Before it happened, I couldn't even conceive of the possibility. Is that how it is for Kayli too? "I'm trying to get her to see what's going on. But maybe I'm not saying the right things, or saying them in the right way."

Naomi grabs hold of my arm, slowing both of us to a stop. "Listen, I know you think it's better to give Kayli her space to problem-solve and avoid swooping in and rescuing, but this scenario's pretty risky. With how Gavin's treating her, you may want to reconsider."

"No, I will—I'm…I'm working on it." I quickly avert my eyes and start walking again, a little faster this time. I'd do almost anything to be back at our cars. I look around for something to help shake the golf course memory. My eyes land on two squirrels playing chase off to the side. The situation with my manager was so different. We were so much older. The stakes were so much higher. Kayli's in fifth grade. It's not the same. "I wish I had more experience with how to handle crushes at this age. My first real relationship was basically Ben, and that wasn't until college."

"Really? I was almost never single," Meg jumps in. I'm actually grateful she hijacks the conversation this time. "Kevin and I met in college too, but there were *several* guys before him. In fifth grade, it was all about Tad Westphal. So many girls liked him, and I felt so lucky when he finally settled on me. We stuck together for a while too…well into sixth grade. We called it *going out* back then."

"How about you, Nay?" I ask, preferring to keep the focus off Kayli and my sorry state of parenting. "When was your first boyfriend or crush?"

"Good question." She looks up to think. "Maybe ninth grade? It was this boy I sat next to in Spanish. He had gone to a different school before that year and didn't know a ton of people at first. We didn't even hang out that much, though. My parents were always so strict."

"So, when did you meet Bruce?" I ask. Hearing these stories is so much easier than rehashing my parenting shortcomings.

"I'd known Bruce forever…probably since fourth or fifth grade, but we didn't start dating until Junior year. My parents knew his family and that he was a good kid, so they were always okay with him."

"Isn't that funny?" I ask as we near the finish line of our trek. "I mean, you married someone you knew in fifth grade. What if that happens with one of our kids…ending up with someone they know right now, too?" As soon as the words leave my mouth, my stomach lurches. Gavin Donder seriously can *not* be my son-in-law.

"I can't imagine that," Meg replies. Then she quickly adds, "No offense, Nay."

Naomi laughs. "No, I get what you're saying. It's strange to think of it that way."

"I also wonder how these dating apps will affect it," Meg says. "None of that was around when we were dating."

"That reminds me." Naomi reaches for Meg's arm as we arrive at the parking lot. "I was going to ask what you've heard about the school's new video app the kids are starting to use."

Meg smirks, rubbing her forehead before she sighs, "Yeah. I figured you weren't going to be in love what that idea."

"Wait, what's going on?" I ask, feeling like I'm the last to know once again. But not even two seconds later, I'm almost sorry I asked. I'm inches away from covering my eyes, watching Meg and Naomi duke out the pros and cons of this video app and its ability to hone the kids' presentation skills.

Of course, Meg's in favor because she thinks it will help the kids with public speaking, increase their engagement in their work, and help them see where improvements could be made. She also likes that the kids can share the videos with their parents. And, of course, Naomi's opposed because she's basically against all technology and nervous the kids are going to misuse it. Oh, how I love my friends. At least they give me the full picture.

Naomi piles on, "It's only a matter of time before something inappropriate gets shared."

Meg counters, "The teachers are well aware of that potential. There are a ton of security features to monitor and prevent it. But, if something does happen, it could be a good learning opportunity too."

Naomi rallies, "Well, I sure hope Lily isn't involved in that *learning opportunity.*"

And, I'm done. My head's officially full. "It's always something, isn't it?" I say.

"Never ends," Meg proudly states before sauntering off to her car.

As I slide into my car, I lean my head back. *Learning opportunity.* That's how my coworker told me to view the kiss with my golf course manager. She was trying to make me feel better. My guilt was immeasurable. I didn't think I'd done anything to make him think I was interested, but maybe I did...

He'd worked at the golf course for years. He was always looking to have fun. And he loved to tell jokes. Sometimes they got dirtier than I'd like, but I'd still politely laugh. He was like a big brother or a young uncle. I didn't want him to think I couldn't handle it. I thought we were friends—buddies. I definitely missed something, though. That kiss came out of nowhere.

FRIDAY, FEB 7

Hearing rustling noises from the mudroom, I glance up at my computer clock. Seven twenty, and Ben's already left this morning—one of the girls must be up early. I get up from my desk and find Ryn on the mudroom floor, digging through her backpack, surrounded by a mess of scattered papers. "Honey, what are you doing?"

"Finding my math." She yanks out two sheets of paper before standing up.

"Homework again?" I follow her back into the kitchen, where she sets her math worksheets on the counter, grips a pencil in her mouth, and hoists herself onto a stool. "Didn't Mr. Kane give you enough time to finish these in class?"

She slumps over, whining, "I'm too slow, and Daddy couldn't help me last night."

"Oh, hon." I search my brain for the right thing to say. "It's totally okay to take your time. I'm just proud that you're trying so hard to understand this stuff."

"But it's so hard," she moans, scowling down at her paper.

Peeking over her shoulder as I rub her back, I glance down at a couple of the problems. All I see is a bunch of nonsensical circled or crossed-out lines and dots, intermixed among plus, minus, and equal signs. What kind of math is this? I have absolutely zero clue how to help her. "Um...well...you did great with that dice game we played a few nights ago. That had a ton of adding and subtracting, and you were able to figure it out."

"That game's for babies, though. Anyone can add and subtract those numbers. I'm horrible at second-grade math." She shoves the papers across the counter. "I hate it."

My heart starts cracking apart. I have to get her to change this habit of negative thinking. "You are *not* horrible at second-grade math." I grab the papers and sit down next to her. "Look at this." I hold up the sheet she was working on. Thank goodness, it's almost finished. "You totally know how to do this. You only have one question left on this whole page. And you have only a few more on the second page. I know you can do it. Who cares how long it takes? How about I make some pancakes? I bet you'll be all finished by the time they're ready."

"I guess." She's still frowning, but she takes the paper back from me.

"Perfect." I jump up, elated I'm off the hook from my short-term math tutoring duties, and start pulling ingredients from the pantry. Longer-term, though, I need to get her out of this funk. I grab the milk and eggs from the refrigerator, mix everything together, and pour four circles into the pan. I know she can do the work—she usually gets the answers right. It simply takes her longer. The real problem's her confidence, but how do I fix that?

"Done!" she shouts as I'm putting a couple of pancakes on a plate.

"See. I knew you could do it." I push her homework off to the side and hand over her plate. "How about some blueberries too?"

"Fine," she mumbles, shoveling a huge bite of pancake into her mouth.

"And you have such a fun day to look forward to. Remember? We're going to Emily's house tonight, and Mollie and Ethan are going to be there."

"Oh yeah." She sits up straighter as she starts to perk back up to her usual self.

"And I'm pretty sure they have a sport court in their basement, so you can get a little more practice in before your tournament tomorrow."

"Do I smell pancakes?" Kayli strolls into the kitchen. Her hair is curled, and she's wearing the sparkly black pants and chunky cream sweater I got her a couple of months ago for our annual holiday dinner with Ben's parents. The last time she had it on, she had to be bribed.

"You do." I make up a plate for her as she sits down. "And don't you look nice. Is something special happening at school today?"

"No…I just wanted to look nice."

"Ah…" Obviously, this is another attempt to impress Gavin. Only heaven knows why she wants to keep doing this, though, when he's essentially treating her like crap.

"And maybe I'll keep it on for the team dinner tonight."

"No, you can't." Ryn pushes her empty plate toward me, grabs her worksheets, and hops off her stool. "What if we play basketball?"

"Fine…" Kayli drags the word out but then quickly recovers. "Whatever. I'll change when I get home."

Ryn puffs out her chest a bit as she heads off to the mudroom, taking her schoolwork with her. Once I hear her head back upstairs, there's a heightened sense of urgency to take advantage of my alone time with Kayli. Even though I know it's not the best practice to seek out trouble—and it's only an outfit—I need to keep steering her in a better direction with Gavin.

I start off playing it casual. "So, how are things with Gavin these days?"

"Okay." She shrugs as I clear away Ryn's dishes and retrieve my mug.

I take a sip of my coffee, hoping if I give her time, she'll say more.

"He does some pretty dumb stuff sometimes. Usually during recess. But when he thinks no one else is looking, he looks at me, passes a note, or whatever." She catches herself smiling and suddenly covers her face with her hands. "I don't know why, but I like when he pays attention to me. It makes me feel good or tingly or something."

"Hmm…" I'm astonished how in tune she is with these feelings but then so oblivious to others. But this is good. She's talking and being open. "But what about when he does the dumb stuff? How does that make you feel?"

"Not great, I guess," she sighs, rolling her eyes. "It's all so stupid, though. Just little things to make sure Brody doesn't think he likes me."

And here's my opening. "Don't those stupid things ever remind you of what Sienna used to do and how she made you feel?"

Kayli locks her eyes into mine, but it's only for a second until they lower to the counter. "I don't know…maybe. But it's different."

"Is it?" *Please, please connect the dots,* I telepath to her.

Silence. She avoids my eyes, only opening her mouth a tiny bit and then shutting it.

"Kayli!" Ryn shouts from the foyer. "Bus!"

Kayli jumps off her stool and hurries to the mudroom.

"Hug?" Ryn reaches her arms up towards me as I walk into the foyer.

I give her a big squeeze and then wave her off as Kayli

stomps in, shoving her boots on a little further with each step with her coat and backpack dangling off one shoulder.

"Love you, hon." I hold the door open, so wishing I knew a few more perfect words to squeeze in that would keep her thinking about how Gavin's manipulating her. I don't, though, so I leave it at that.

* * *

Cori smiles, welcoming us into her grand foyer. "Come on in. You can hang your coats here, and then all the kids are downstairs playing basketball."

Ryn's feet shuffle with giddiness as she grabs onto the back of Kayli's shirt and follows her around the corner. I can only imagine how excited she is to play with the big kids. "Thanks so much for hosting this." I hand Cori my tray of cookies and move the girls' boots off to the side.

"Of course." Cori leads Ben and me into the kitchen, where the parents are hanging out. "It's been a long time coming. Emily's brother has had his team over several times now, and Emily's been begging for quite a while to have her turn. You guys know everyone, right?"

I scan the kitchen and nod. The dads are all off to the side by the wine bar. A couple of the moms are at the other end of the island, nibbling off of a ginormous charcuterie board. And Nikki's chatting with Jane at the end of the island closest to us, where the trays of bruschetta, stuffed mushrooms, and some sort of antipasto skewers are.

Cori and I grab glasses of wine, leave Ben with the guys, and head over to Nikki and Jane. "Hey guys, good to see you. Is everyone ready for tomorrow?"

"Hey…yeah." Nikki's smile quickly fades as she rests her hand on my arm but then steps away, glancing around. Then she tilts her chin down, raising her eyebrows as she lowers her voice. "But seriously, how are *you* doing?"

As Cori and Jane look more concerned, I grow more confused. "What do you mean?"

Nikki trades looks with Cori and then Jane. "I mean, with Kayli. Wasn't she super upset when she got home this afternoon?"

My mind races as I try to recall Kayli's face when she got off the bus today. Come to think of it, I was busy getting the cookies out of the oven when they got home. And then, Ryn and I got in another conversation about her math. I assumed Kayli was upstairs, changing. "I don't know." I try to cover my parenting lapse. "Things were a bit of a scramble today with getting everything ready to come over here. Oh my gosh, you guys, what'd I miss?"

No one says anything for a few seconds. Each of them avoiding my eyes as I search their faces. "You guys—Nikki—please tell me."

"If Kayli didn't say anything, maybe it's not a big deal," she finally says, shifting in her stance. "All I know is what Mandi told me, so it might not be totally accurate."

"But what is it?" My words come out more quickly and louder than I intend. I'm finding it harder and harder to hide my impatience.

Nikki takes a deep breath. "Apparently, Kayli wore a bit dressier of an outfit today, and some of the boys started teasing her about trying to impress Gavin. But then, it turned into this weird chanting thing, where the boys—including Gavin—started shouting *butterface* over and over. The recess monitors put an end to it pretty quickly, but Mandi said Kayli was mortified."

"Butterface? I don't get it," I say as everyone's eyes go straight for the floor. "What does that mean?"

Silence. Zero eye contact.

I swear it's been over a minute.

I look across to Nikki again. "Nikki, please, tell me."

"Everything looks good about her, *but her face*," she mutters, lifting her eyes only for a second. Her face is as red as I've ever seen. "I'm so sorry, Dawn."

My throat is physically frozen, and there's an iceberg the size of Antarctica stuck inside. I can't speak. I can only imagine Kayli in the middle of the blacktop surrounded by a bunch of kids chanting this horrendous insult. She must have felt humiliated. And I was too busy to console her after school. Trying to think of something—anything—to say, I finally force sound out of my vocal cords, "That's horrible. I know she's struggling a bit in figuring out what she should do about Gavin. Hopefully this tips her decision."

Nikki cringes, glancing back and forth from Jane to Cori to me. "I hope so. From what Mandi says, Gavin hasn't been super nice to her in recent days."

Cori reaches over to rub my back. "I'm so sorry, Dawn. I've heard it's gotten pretty bad."

"Poppy actually mentioned it too." Jane grimaces.

Poppy. The girl who never says anything to her mom. It's gotten so bad that Poppy's even talking about it. This is way worse than I thought. My daughter's now known around school for liking a boy who's treating her like crap.

My brain weighs a million pounds while my stomach's doing backflips. Even though I command myself to stay calm and act like it's no big deal, these moms know me too well, and their faces clearly show they sense my distress.

After what seems like forever, Cori starts talking again. "You know, with Lisa gone so much recently, I think Gavin's starting to stray a bit from his normal self."

"That's right!" Nikki's voice borders on a gasp as her hand goes to her forehead with this reminder. Then she and Cori take turns doling out mundane details of Lisa's dad being ill.

Apparently, with her out of the picture, Brody's had a more negative influence on Gavin.

I can't even respond. I don't understand why Kayli's letting Gavin treat her like this. It doesn't make any sense.

Cori looks at her watch. "We should probably get the kids up here for some lasagna. Their game's pretty early tomorrow, so I want everyone to get home at a decent time."

"What can we do to help?" I barely get out, but grateful beyond words for the change in topic. My stomach's a disaster right now.

Cori gestures to Nikki. "How about you and Jane round up the kids, and Dawn can help me get all the food set out."

"Perfect," I say as Nikki and Jane head towards the stairs, and Cori directs me to pull two huge salads out of the refrigerator while she retrieves the pans of lasagna and garlic bread from the oven. We finish setting up everything on the island right as the kids are coming in.

Kayli appears to be her normal self, leading the way through the buffet line and joking around as she and her teammates then squeeze in around the breakfast nook. Whatever happened at school today doesn't seem to be top of mind. Ryn, Ethan, and Mollie follow the older kids through the line and take their food to a card table a few feet away.

Once all the kids have gone through, the adults take their turn. While I wait at the end of the line, I watch Brad go over to say a few things to the girls.

Brad's voice booms. "Thanks again for coming, girls. Even though our season's not over yet, I want to say how much I've enjoyed coaching you this year. You've all done a fantastic job and have improved so much. You've been great teammates to each other, you work hard, and I look forward to finishing out our season strong." He raises his glass to the girls. "Together!"

The girls cheer and clap and then all lift their glasses and shout, "Together!"

"That was nice of you." I turn to Brad as he gets in line behind me. I discreetly wipe my palms on my pants as I try to get past the news about Kayli and Gavin and figure out why I feel so nervous in Brad's company. He's only Emily's dad...and Kayli's coach...and the one who's always screaming at her games. This is silly. I need to act normal. It's not like he'll start yelling at anyone here. "And thanks for coaching this year. I'm sure it's a ton of work."

"It's been fun," he replies. "And Kayli's having a great season."

"Thanks." I continue to fake my laid-back act. I take a plate and start filling it with salad and lasagna, even though I know there's no way I'm going to be able to eat any of it.

"And thanks for letting Ryn help out with the third-graders." He follows my lead. "Another board member told me she's quite the player."

I try to move through the line more quickly. "I'm a little nervous, but she's excited."

"Oh, don't be. From what I've heard, she'll be able to keep up no problem."

"I guess we'll find out tomorrow." I give him my most real-istic smile and then indicate I'm going to go join the moms in the dining room. Although it feels more like I'm moving from one pressure cooker to the next.

"This looks amazing, Cori. Thanks again for doing this." I'll do anything to steer clear of more talk about Kayli and Gavin until I can talk to Kayli. "The girls look like they're having a blast too. I love that they've gotten to be such good friends this season."

"Me too," says Nikki. "I was actually a little worried in the beginning. Emily and Mandi have been so close—like sisters really—and in the past, they haven't been the most open to other girls. Being on this team has helped them see it's okay to have lots of different friends."

"Agree," Cori says. "It's been great. And I'm so glad most of them aren't wrapped up with boys yet. I can't imagine them going through what Stacy, Sienna, and Liz are battling."

Here it comes. More crush talk. *Most of them…*yikes. She has to be referring to Kayli. But then, what did she say about Liz? I know Sienna and Stacy have been clashing over James, but Meg hasn't mentioned anything about Kayli's tennis friend, Liz.

Nikki shakes her head. "Wouldn't that be awful? I pray that doesn't happen. I had a boy come between a friend and me once, and it was horrible. We were such close friends, too. But then without doing anything, my friend's crush started liking me instead of her. Even though I didn't like him back, she still blamed me. And she never got over it."

I so want to get off this topic, but I can't let it go. I have to find out more details for Meg. "I'm sorry, but did you say that Liz likes James now too?"

Nikki's eyes widen as she leans forward. "You haven't heard? It's a complete disaster. Even before Liz came into the picture, it was a debacle. Sienna and Stacy were totally throwing each other under the bus as they vied for James's attention. Now, the roof's completely blown off since James chose Liz as the person to go with him to see the nurse when he got hurt at recess."

Cori nods as she finishes off her last bite of lasagna. Then she stands up and starts taking everyone's empty plates. "Just another reminder why I'm so grateful Emily isn't into boys."

My mind swirls as we start to help Cori clean up while the kids finish their cookies. Emily isn't into boys, huh? Interesting. That's not what Meg says. But how does Cori not know? I mean, Nikki's her best friend after all, and Nikki practically knows everything. Whatever. I have my own rabbit hole to get out of. We quickly finish cleaning up, say our goodbyes, and get on our way. I can't remember a time I've been more anxious to tuck Kayli in at night.

* * *

It's eight forty-five by the time we get home, and with both of the girls needing to get up early tomorrow, it's time for bed. I follow them up as Ryn chats excitedly with Kayli about the game they were playing. After the girls get their PJs on and brush their teeth, I tuck Ryn in first.

"So, you had a good time?" I ask as she crawls in under her covers.

"The best! I guarded Poppy, and I kept stealing the ball from her."

I shake my head and smile. I have no idea what to make of this. Poppy isn't one of the strongest players, so it may not be saying a whole lot that Ryn can steal a ball from her, but hopefully, it's a sign she'll do okay tomorrow. I'm so glad Ben's taking her. My nerves would be through the roof. "You better get to sleep soon, so you can keep up the good work tomorrow."

She throws her arms around me as I lean down to give her a quick kiss. "Love you."

"Love you too, sweetie." I get up and turn off her light. "See you tomorrow."

My feet feel like they're on pins and needles, heading over to Kayli's room. I come in right as she's tucking her journal away and climbing into bed. I can only imagine what she wrote about today.

"I feel like I barely had a chance to talk to you about your day." I plop down next to her. She looks like she could fall asleep any minute, but I have to know more about what happened at recess.

"I know," she yawns, rubbing her eyes.

"Did your day go okay? Any compliments on your outfit?" I get straight to the point.

Her eyes stare down at her blanket. "From the girls," she grumbles. "But the boys were kind of mean about it. They actually made fun of it at recess. Even Gavin."

"Made fun of it? How?" I ask as she yawns again and turns over. Does this really not bother her? Or is she trying to hide from me?

"I don't know…," she groans. "I don't even care. The paras made them stop."

"Oh, hon…that had to have been so hard." I have to get her to see what's going on. Everyone else can see it. Her friends, their parents…enough is enough. "Especially when it seems like Gavin acts one way with you sometimes, and a totally different way when he's around his friends."

She rolls back over to face me. "Kind of like Coach Brad."

"Huh?" Where is this coming from…how is what Gavin's doing like Coach Brad? This doesn't make any sense.

"Yeah, like tonight he's all nice and says all these nice things, but then during games or practices, he can be screaming his head off at us."

Whoa…my mind's officially blown. What do I even say? "Uh…I don't think it's quite the same thing, sweetie," is all I come up with. She's right in a way, though. Brad blows up at the girls for sure, but he's her coach. Not her boyfriend, or crush, or whatever. "But the relationship you have with your coach is so different than a relationship with a boy. You'd never want a boy you're with to yell at you like Coach Brad does. They should treat you kindly and make you feel good about yourself. I don't think Gavin's doing that, do you?"

"Ugh…you never listen," she groans again, this time pulling her pillow over her face for a second. "I've told you a thousand times about all the nice things Gavin does. Now you're going to start being all negative on him?"

"What do you mean?" I sit up straighter. "I listen. I just heard you say he was one of the kids who was making fun of you at recess."

"You don't get it," she huffs, rolling over, so her back is to me again.

"Honey…" Here we go again. She's shutting me out.

"I don't want to talk about it anymore. I want to go to bed."

"What about hugs?" Our tradition. It's a bad sign whenever this goes out the window.

"Goodnight, Mom." She doesn't roll back over.

Ouch. It's like a knife through the heart. I slowly get up off her bed and walk toward the door. As I take one last look, she rolls over again to make it so she's not facing me from this side now. I turn her light off and close the door behind me.

I sit down on the top of the steps, holding my head in my hands. I seriously can't believe we're here again. Her shutting me out and thinking we're on different sides. I've done everything to let her figure this out on her own. Then one tiny little misstep—I push a little too hard or insert myself a little too much—and I'm on the outs. But I can't have my daughter accepting this kind of treatment as par for the course. Not only will it demolish her confidence, it will also affect her perception of how she should be treated in a relationship. But where the heck do I go from here?

WEDNESDAY, FEB 12

Using the side of my car to steady myself, I carefully make my way across the sheet of ice blanketing the parking lot. Last night, there was a brief period of sleet that preceded the snow, and it's made the side streets and other less-used areas more than a little tricky to navigate. Fortunately, as I get closer to Meg and Naomi, the ground isn't as slick. "How's the trail? Do you think it's going to be too slippery?"

"It seems okay," Meg replies. "There's still a tiny bit of snow on top to keep your grip."

Naomi agrees and we get on our way. I'm just grateful I can use our walk as a distraction from what's going on with Kayli. It's not like things between us have been outright horrible, just excruciatingly distant. Since Friday, she's gone back to spending most of her free time in her room and keeping her lips sealed. I try to push these thoughts aside, though. I want to enjoy my time with my friends. "How's everyone?"

"Better than yesterday, that's for sure," Meg sighs, pumping her arms more vigorously this morning. "Brooklyn had a play-date after school with Elliot, and it did not go well."

"Wait, who's Elliot again?" Still coming out of my fog, I've forgotten where Meg's mentioned that name before. At the same time, I remember I need to talk to Meg about James and Liz. Not right now, though. She already seems too upset.

"The little boy in her baking class," Meg says. "The one she gets all dolled up for. He and Brooklyn were having such a good time in class on Monday night, his mom asked if Brooklyn wanted to come over yesterday for a couple of hours after school. Brooklyn was elated, of course, but after I dropped her off..." Meg stops walking and covers her face. "Oh, you guys, I'm so embarrassed."

I stop and look over at Naomi, who shrugs. A stream of possibilities run through my head...Brooklyn got sick, maybe wet her pants...at her age, nothing could be too bad.

Meg finally peeks through her hands before saying, "I'm just going to say it. Brooklyn tried to kiss Elliot." She puts her arms down and starts walking again as I check my mouth to make sure it's not hanging wide open. Her stride, and the speed at which her words come out, begin to pick up the pace. "I don't know what she was thinking. I'm sure it made Elliot super uncomfortable. His mom called me about an hour into their playdate and asked me to pick her up early. It was one of the most awkward phone calls I've ever had."

As Meg describes her conversation about Brooklyn, more fog clouds my mind. The unwanted kiss—although this one so much more innocent—unexpectedly pulls me back to that night at the golf course. I was trying to be helpful. It was late. Everyone wanted to go home, so we were all pitching in. I went to the walk-in cooler to grab some mayo or dressing—one of those economy-sized vats used to refill smaller containers. I had just pulled it off the shelf when I felt the warmth on the back of my neck. Someone's breath. Then the hand on my shoulder pulling me around. I barely saw who it was before their lips were on mine. I tried to say no, but the pressure on my lips made it difficult—I dropped the dressing and ran out of there.

All of a sudden, my feet slip beneath me. Startled by the icy spot on the trail, I grab onto Naomi for security as I catch my balance. "Oh gosh, sorry!"

Naomi smiles and she and Meg help stabilize me before Meg returns to her story. "I told her I knew she was trying to show Elliot she cared about him, but at her age, kissing a friend isn't appropriate. Then I said something like, she could high-five or do a special handshake."

I nod, trying to keep my focus on their conversation as we cross my favorite bridge.

"We also talked about how she has so much going on and worrying about boys could take her away from other things she cares about."

It's astonishing how steadfast Meg is on these kids' relation-ships. I get that they're young, and they don't need to be made into a big deal, but discouraging kids to avoid them altogether seems unrealistic. And now, how am I supposed to tell her what I've heard about James? I can't imagine how she's going to take it. "Isn't it crazy all these things that come up that we never guessed we'd have to think about?"

"Yes." Naomi extends her arms above her head, stretching out for a couple of seconds before she continues, "Yesterday, I had something come up out of the blue too. When I picked up Lily from her coding class, she was talking to a boy. And I could tell from a mile away she wasn't simply talking to him, she was flirting with him."

"Wait, what? Lily? Flirting?" I hold my gaze on Naomi, trying to gauge how she's feeling about this. Surprisingly, she doesn't seem that upset. "So those signs, caring more about what she looked like and such, were about a boy?"

"It seems so." She looks over at us without an ounce of distress on her face—she actually looks happy. "The whole ride home, Lily gushed about him. She said he told her she's so pretty already, she doesn't need to wear makeup. And he's always complimenting her, telling her how smart and talented she is. She was beaming. It was pretty cute, actually."

Of course, Lily's crush is perfect. But when I glance over at Meg, she's shaking her head. Regardless of how nice this boy seems, a crush is a crush, and she clearly disapproves. "So, who is he? Does he go to Valleybrook?"

"He's a fifth-grader at Park Academy, and he's a computer wiz. He actually wants to help Leo create a website so he can start selling his STEM building plans online."

"He sounds like a dream," I tease, totally envious, but also hoping to prevent Meg from sounding off. Not only is she anti-dating for kids this age, she's also not a fan of the nearby private school.

"I can't believe *you're* not worried about this!" Meg erupts, tossing her arms up as she whirls around at our turnaround mark. "Aren't you concerned Lily's too young for this?"

I want to duck my head into my scarf and cover my ears. Here we go...

"No...you're right," Naomi says, surprisingly taking a solid step towards a peaceful resolution. "I suppose I'm a little worried, but for now, things seem pretty simple. They sit next to each other in class, talk during breaks, and that's about it. And I like that he encourages her to be who she is. There's a huge benefit to having that kind of relationship standard set early on."

I hear a truck off in the distance as our boots crunch over the trail. Encouraging her to be who she is? It's basically the exact opposite of what Gavin's doing with Kayli—the standard he's setting...I can't help but bow my head in shame.

"I don't know." Meg shakes her head again, appearing to struggle to stay calm. "I'm not convinced. I mean, look at what Kayli's going through..."

Ouch. Do I even bother trying to lift my head?

"How *are* things with Kayli lately?" Naomi's voice is soft, consoling. At least she's trying to be sympathetic. "I heard she had a pretty rough time last week."

"Unfortunately, I'm not quite sure." My voice wavers as my posture weakens. "We got in an argument about it on Friday night, and since then, she's been avoiding me."

"Oh no." Naomi looks over, her eyes full of pity. "Things with you two are off again?"

"It seems I can't win." I take a deep breath. The cold air is almost paralyzing as I look around for a source of strength. All the trees and shrubs are covered with a shell of tiny ice crystals. I imagine myself wearing a similar layer of armor the next time I'm with Kayli. "Whenever she thinks I overstep or give her advice she doesn't want to hear, she shuts me out. I'm at a loss for what to do—other than waiting it out. It reminds me so much of what she and I went through with Sienna. Hopefully there's a limit on what she'll put up with from Gavin too."

"I sure hope she hits it soon." Naomi lowers her head. "That poor girl. This year has provided quite the learning opportunities for her."

I do my best to nod and ignore the mom guilt crashing in. My stomach's already worse for wear because the conversation I need to have with Meg is still looming. I need to tell her about James, and soon—we don't have much of our walk left. I have to proceed with caution, though, especially after everything she just said about Brooklyn and Lily. "Uh, Meg...I...I also have something to tell you, and you may not be too thrilled."

Everything looks like it's moving in slow motion as she looks over. It's so quiet, I think I can hear my heart echo through my thick winter coat.

I gulp down the nerves in my throat and proceed, "I was at Kayli's team dinner this weekend, and a couple of moms mentioned that James might have a crush on Liz."

"What?" Meg's tone and crinkled face are the epitome of

annoyance. "Who said that? Nikki? Ugh…she's such a gossip. I can't believe her. James and Liz are just friends."

I hesitate, trying to decide how to respond. I don't want to fight with Meg over this, and she's right—Nikki definitely likes to be in the know. But I've never known her to make stuff up. "I'm sorry. It's only what I heard, and I thought you should know."

"No… I'm glad you told me." Meg slows her voice back down to a normal pace. "At least I know there's a rumor out there. Now I simply have to figure out a way to put an end to it." Meg pauses and looks across me to Naomi. "Have you heard this, too?"

Naomi cringes, pulling her scarf up over her chin and looking like she might want some ice crystal body armor as well. "Worse even…I'm so sorry. I was skeptical of it being true, so I didn't know how to bring it up."

"Oh my God," Meg sighs, running her hands over her hat as she looks up at the sky, looking like she's lost all her patience. "Out with it. What'd you hear?"

Naomi opens her mouth but then pauses, closing her eyes for a minute before she calmly responds, "About a week ago, I started hearing stories about Liz being involved somehow with the Sienna-Stacy debacle. At first, I thought it was because she was friends with both of them, and she was caught in the middle or something like that. But then I heard it was because she had a crush on James too—"

"So, Liz has a crush on James," Meg cuts her off. "That doesn't mean he likes her too."

"Well…" Naomi's word lingers as she rocks her head side to side. "Then last week, I guess James picked Liz to go to the nurse's office with him when he got hurt at recess. And yesterday, I heard Liz had written the letter J on her wrist."

I look back over to Meg, who starts to say something but

then stops herself. Clearly, what Naomi said has made an impact.

"Fabulous," Meg groans after a minute of recovery, raising her hands to her temples. "He's already struggling with school, he barely has time to fit in his extra soccer training with his basketball schedule, and now he wants to add a crush on a girl to his to-do list."

"Maybe it's not that bad," Naomi reasons, giving me a quick side-eye before continuing. "It's usually pretty innocent at this age."

"That's not the point," Meg counters. "It's his concentration, his focus, what he should be worrying about…he shouldn't be thinking about a girl and whether or not she called him, forgot to look at him in the hall, or likes him anymore. Ugh! This drives me nuts. And perfect timing too. Right before Valentine's Day. I suppose he'll want to buy her some lovey-dovey present."

"That's right." I grasp for anything to get us off this contentious topic. "Isn't that Service Day at school for the kids?" I'm impressed I even remember this. But it's just because it's one of the only school events I truly love.

"Oh my gosh, yes," Meg groans, rubbing her forehead. "Which, I totally forgot to ask you guys…I need a few more volunteers for the stations that day. Can either of you help out?"

"Wait, what? I didn't realize you were helping with that," I reply.

"I'm not." Meg shakes her head. "But the mom who's in charge hasn't been able to round up enough volunteers, so she asked if I could help."

"Got it," I say. Of course, Meg can't help but be involved. "I could help out if it's only for a couple of hours."

"Thanks. It should be pretty simple. They've already nailed down all the different volunteer stations and have all the supplies. Just come to the cafeteria after the girls get on the bus, and we should be wrapped up by eleven thirty."

"I wish I could help you out." Naomi sounds sincerely disappointed as we near the parking lot. "But I'm already committed to help out with Leo's class."

"No problem. I'm sure I can round up someone else." Meg shakes her head as her pace slows. "Sorry, guys, I still can't get over what's going on with James. And, I apologize. I didn't mean to take out my frustration on you. It's just that…ugh… and now, I have to deal with it in front of all these gossipy moms' eyes during Service Day."

"Maybe it's like Naomi said, and it won't be as bad as you think," I say, but now I wonder if I should be worrying about this same issue in terms of Kayli's situation with Gavin. I carefully tread over the slippery surface back to my car. "My fingers are crossed for you." I wave goodbye, and then I cross them for myself.

* * *

It's impossible to sit still waiting on the stair landing for the bus to come. For the past two days, Kayli's body language after school has been my primary source of information on how her day went. The bounce in her step and ginormous grin on her face on Monday clearly indicated a good day, even as she kept a straight face brushing past me toward the kitchen. Yesterday was the complete opposite, though, with her scowling face and the stomping up to her room before grabbing a snack being dead giveaways. I'm hoping day three will be better.

Scree-eeech! The bus jerks to a halt in front of the entrance to our cul-de-sac. I don't understand why the driver hasn't learned to approach the stop more gradually by now. At this stage, I almost wonder if he does it intentionally, so he can watch the kids rattle around a bit.

Ryn's first off the bus, but in a rare move, she waits at the bottom of the steps for Kayli, who follows close behind. I don't even need to see Ryn put her arm around Kayli to understand it's been a horrible day. Kayli's puffy red face and watery eyes are a dead giveaway.

Ryn cringes at me as I meet them in the mudroom and help her with her coat.

"Rough day?" I ask Kayli, setting aside Ryn's boots as she heads off to the kitchen.

Kayli can't even get words out, shedding her backpack, coat, and boots as tears stream down her face.

I put my arms around her, and she buries her face in my chest. Her warm tears begin to soak through my shirt. "Oh, honey. I'm so sorry." We hug in silence for what seems like hours as guesses as to what could have possibly happened whirl through my head. I know she isn't physically hurt. Several years ago, I learned to distinguish Kayli's different cries. This cry is definitely the someone-did-something-mean-to-me type.

At least I know whatever happened doesn't have to be solved immediately. We have plenty of time to sort it out, so I can stand here hugging her as long as she needs. It's best not to rush it. I need her to be the one to pull away. After a few more minutes, she finally does.

"I hate my life." She looks up at me for a brief second, but then the tears start to pour out even faster, and her head crashes back into my chest.

"Oh, hon." My mind races through a million more scenarios. "I'm so sorry you're hurting." I keep holding her and rubbing her back. It has to be something with Gavin. Things with her schoolwork, friends, and basketball have been going so well. I can't imagine anything else causing so many tears.

I run my hand over the back of her head. I'm so sick of how he's been manipulating her. First getting her to change who she is, hiding their relationship, and then treating her poorly in front of everyone to bolster his lie. I don't care if his mom's been busy or out of town or whatever, the way he's been exploiting Kayli disgusts me. There has to be a way we can talk through these things without her shutting me out.

After a few more minutes, she pulls away again, looking at me but not saying anything.

"What can I do?" I search her eyes for an answer.

She only shakes her head and slowly starts moving into the kitchen. At least it's not to her room. This is a good sign. Some food might help, and being in the kitchen always provides a good distraction. Usually, Kayli opens up more if it looks like I'm busy with something else.

I follow her in as Ryn's finishing her snack. Maybe it will help even more if I take the focus off Kayli. "Did you have an okay day, hon?" I ask Ryn.

Ryn tilts her head back and forth. "So-so. Ethan acted like a know-it-all when we got our math quizzes back. He's so annoying lately. But then, a couple of the third-grade players said hi to me when I saw them in the hallway on the way to the library."

"I'm so glad," I reply, preferring to focus on the positive as she slides off her stool and starts toward the stairs. She did a pretty amazing job at their tournament this past weekend, and the coach asked Ben if she could finish out the season with them. Thank goodness Ben was on board after watching her play.

I wipe up Ryn's crumbs and take her plate over to the sink as Kayli grabs a snack.

"Gavin and I are over," Kayli grunts, snapping off a huge chunk of her granola bar as she shakes her head. Chomping on the large piece in her mouth, she doesn't even bother to sit.

"Oh?" I grab onto the counter for balance as I pull out a stool. Shrapnel of relief and concern hit me all at once. This is good news, right? She finally saw through him and recognized what's been going on. I knew she'd see it. My warnings and hints finally must have clicked. She just needed time. But wait, why was she crying, then? Oh man, that little punk…if he—

"He treated me like crap again today." She proceeds to tear off another huge bite with her teeth, gnawing at her snack like it's her prey as she continues shaking her head. "In front of everyone, too. I was so sick of it. So, I finally told him it's over…in front of everyone." She polishes off her granola, dusts off her hands, and leaves me with my mouth hanging open as she turns to go upstairs.

"Wait, honey," I call after her. "Please come back. Talk to me. What happened?"

When she turns around, every part of her body droops toward the ground. Except for her eyes. They look right at me as she groans, "What?"

"Please. Sit down," I plead. At least she's responding. I roll the dice. "What'd he do?"

She stays in her spot, but her posture straightens as she crosses her arms. She shakes her head as the words hiss out, "He and Brody started a rumor. About me. They're—they're so stupid."

"What was the rumor?" Each word is cautious, tiptoeing out of my mouth.

Her lower lip quivers, but then it disappears, folding in under the cover of her upper lip. Her grip on her arms tightens. She inhales, holds her breath, and then blurts, "That I kissed Gavin." She tosses her arms to her side, her voice growing louder as she continues, "It's not true! And I didn't want the whole school thinking it was. So, I told Gavin he was a jerk and a liar."

A tornado of emotions whips through me as I think of something to say. Proud of Kayli, infuriated at this boy, grateful my strategy of waiting until she figured this out worked. She hit her limit and stood up to him. Their crush is finally over, and it's because she decided…not me. I release my breath, slowly, as if I'm blowing it through a straw.

I start with the most important thing first. "Honey, I'm so, so proud of you. What you did…standing up to him…I hope you realize how amazing that is…how amazing you are."

A smile slowly creeps across her face as she gives the tiniest of nods.

Then I can't help myself. I ask, "But, why would he do that?"

Any hint of a smile vanishes as her face shifts and her volume increases. "I don't know…He—he and Brody…they're just so—I don't want to talk about it!" She barely gets the words out, trembling as she spins around, quickening her pace as she walks away.

Watching the back of her head quiver, I know she's started crying again, and I need to wait. She needs time. She'll tell me later.

FRIDAY, FEB 14

"Honey?" I compel my voice to be its kindest as I press my cheek against Kayli's door. Waiting for a response, I stare at the skinny crack separating the door from the trim molding. Maybe if I inch a bit closer to this tiny crevice, she'll be able to hear my urgency more clearly. I close my eyes and gradually exhale. I don't want to sound too panicked making my second attempt. "Sweetie? The bus will be here in a few minutes."

"I'm not going," she retorts matter-of-factly. I strain my ears, picturing her tensed face and crossed arms. Nothing. Wait…was that her moving? Maybe she's getting up.

"Mommy?" Ryn calls from downstairs. "Is Kayli coming?"

"She needs a few more minutes," I reply to her, but the message is intended for both of them. "Why don't you start getting your coat and boots on?"

I lean my head against Kayli's door. I was so praying this wouldn't be her response. The struggle to get her to school yesterday isn't one I wanted to repeat. Sure, her breakup with Gavin may have been more like an explosion. And, yeah, it was in front of everyone. But how Gavin and Brody can convince everyone to take Gavin's side is beyond me. How do these other kids not see through their tactics and manipulation?

As my wait continues, the prickliness under my skin intensifies. But I need to stay calm. If I overreact, even in the slightest way, she'll respond at ten times the strength. "I know this is hard, hon, but you have to go to school. What can I do to help?"

Silence. How long do I wait…how hard can I press without accidentally igniting her fuse? She really does only have a couple more minutes. I'm probably a horrible mom, but even in these circumstances, I refuse to drive her to school. Besides, if any sort of battle is going to erupt between Kayli and me, it's way better if it occurs on our own property versus in front of the school and peering eyes from the queue of cars unloading.

It's not like I don't feel for her. I truly do. Every muscle in my body wants to strangle those boys for what they did— spreading a rumor around school that Kayli kissed Gavin. What kind of creep is Gavin for not setting the record straight? And who does Brody think he is, convincing all the other kids that Gavin is this innocent victim? I want to shake both of them.

I know it's not my fault, but it's been increasingly impossible to keep my mom guilt at bay. Could I have warned Kayli that something like this could happen? Maybe I should've prepared her for what she could do if it did. Feelings for someone can switch on a dime, especially at their age. Even though she detests whenever I try to help or give advice, I still could've…

"Sweetie, you have to go to school." I inch even closer to the space between the door and the trim, hoping this time she'll listen. I'm doing everything in my power to stop myself from opening the door. I made that mistake yesterday, and it didn't end well. Not only did it make Kayli's emotions skyrocket, but it turned her anger away from those boys and instead toward me. I need Kayli to know I'm on her side. And I am. I'll do everything I can to help her, but there are a few obligations in life she still has to fulfill, even when she doesn't want to. "The bus is going to be here any minute."

Dealing with Kayli's roller coaster of moods these past couple of days has been a lesson in restraint, patience, and sympathy I never knew I could muster. The sulking, moping, and the slamming of doors. Waves of tears followed by eruptions of anger. And I can't blame her. Here she was, trying to protect Gavin and help him maintain his friendship with Brody, and he throws her under the bus. He could have ended the rumor immediately, but he didn't. What a coward, and such a betrayal. And then, when kids started taking his side… of course Kayli's devastated and mortified. Of course she doesn't want to go to school.

Finally the door is yanked open. Kayli brushes past me without even a passing glance. She stomps down the stairs, yanks her backpack and coat off the hook, and storms out the door, completely ignoring me and her sister, who was waiting for her by the door.

"Is Kayli going to be okay?" Ryn asks, looking up at me from the bottom of the steps.

"I hope so." I'm surprised by how much I need to focus steadying my legs as I go down to meet her. "Thank you for being so sweet, patient, and understanding with her. I know she hasn't been the easiest person to be around these past couple of days." I reach the bottom and give Ryn a huge hug, just as much for me as for her, and then grab the door as I hear the bus rumbling down the hill.

As she walks through, she says, "I put a Valentine in her bag. I wanted to cheer her up."

That's right. I totally spaced…it's Valentine's Day, aka Service Day. I try to turn my look of shock into one of more like a pleasant surprise. "Oh, hon. That's so thoughtful. Kayli will love it." But my stomach sinks as I imagine myself now having to confront all the stares and potential questions—I'm sure the other moms volunteering have heard all about the rumor too. And I'm supposed to be at their school in only a few minutes. As I give Ryn one last pat on the back goodbye, my words come out even less steady. "And it's Service Day, remember? I'll see you at school later this morning."

* * *

After surviving what feels like a minefield of prying eyes from the moms milling around the cafeteria, I finally reach the safety of Meg's presence and tap her shoulder. "Need any help?" I try to play it cool as my eyes dart back and forth between her table and the nine other lunch tables encircling the room, covered with supplies. These scenes are like shark-infested waters to me: lots of moms, divvied up into small groups, and already submerged in a task or conversation. With my unshakable fear of accidentally interrupting an inappropriate group, finding a safe spot to linger feels like a heroic feat.

"Oh, hi." Meg smiles, looking up from a box containing stacks of plain white cards. "Please." She pushes the box of cards between us, immediately providing a much-needed sense of purpose. "We need to put a stack of cards and a set of markers in front of each seat at these two tables. The first round of kids will be coming in a few minutes."

I eagerly grab the box of markers and work my way around the tables as Meg follows closely behind with the cards. I'm a little surprised, but relieved, she isn't bringing up the issue with Kayli. "So, how does this work?" I ask as I finish up, right as the kindergarten classes start pouring in.

"Hi, guys!" Meg indicates she'll answer my question later and then directs the little ones to find their seats. "Thanks so much for helping us today. This station is our *gratitude* station.

Here, we'd like you to write thank-you cards to our local police, fire, and ambulance workers. Each of you can take one card, use the markers in front of you to draw a picture and write 'thank you' on it. You can also add anything else to your card to show your appreciation for these very important people and what they do to keep us safe."

The kids are adorable as they happily get to work. I'd forgotten how little kids are at this age. It's only been a couple of years since Ryn was in kindergarten, but I can't believe how much older she looks and acts now in comparison. The teacher, Meg, and I go around to help the kids stay on task, give ideas for drawings, and spell words. In no time, a bell rings, indicating their time is up. Meg thanks everyone and instructs the kids to put their completed cards in one of the boxes. Then they move on to the next station, and a new class joins our table.

"So, there are five stations?" I ask after Meg quickly goes through her spiel again, noticing the ten tables are separated off into groups of two.

"Yeah, but each class only has time to go through three. We tried to space them out, so the kids get exposed to at least a couple of different types of services."

I scan the room again, discreetly pointing to the two tables to our right, where kids are loading supplies into plastic freezer bags. "So, this one next to us is the care package station?"

"Yep." Meg moves in closer to me as she shows me around the room. "They're putting together socks, snacks, and toiletries for the homeless. After that, there's the birthday card station for the elderly in long-term care facilities, then cat toys for the animal rescue center, and the tied fleece blankets for a women's shelter is the one on the other side."

"So cool." I glance back at the kids, who appear to be having a great time. "I love that they do this every year."

The bell rings again, and Meg gives her rundown to the

last group of kindergarteners. The morning continues to fly by as the different grades parade through like clockwork. We briefly say hello to Naomi when she comes through with Leo and the other first-graders. I sit with Ryn when she comes by with her second-grade class. And Meg gets to help Brooklyn when the third-graders pass through. I love that we're so busy, Meg doesn't even mention Kayli. Plus, it's always fun to get an insider view of the kids and their class dynamics.

But as the clock inches closer to ten forty-five, which is when the fifth-graders are supposed to come through, my blood pressure ticks upward. Who will Kayli sit next to? How will Brody and Gavin act? Will anyone be whispering about *The Rumor?*

As the last group of fourth-graders plops down at our table, I notice the delivery of the speech Meg's been giving all morning is unusually unsteady. It's only now I remember James and realize Meg might be just as nervous about him as I am about Kayli. Maybe that's what's been occupying her thoughts all morning. I look over and try to give my most reassuring smile.

After the bell rings one more time, the fourth-grade classes filter out and the fifth-grade classes stream in. The first class contains a few of the girls from Kayli's tennis team, including Liz. They're pulling their teacher towards the blanket station to the left of us. Mr. Slater's class, which includes Poppy and James, follows close behind and sits down at the cat toy station. Ms. Andreen's class chooses the birthday card station, and the fourth class selects the care packages. That leaves Mrs. Putnam's class heading straight toward us.

I busy myself straightening cards as I sense the single-file line trailing Mrs. Putnam getting closer. *Calm thoughts*, I tell myself as I wipe the moisture from my hairline. It'll be fine. What's the worst that could happen anyway?

"Where's Kayli?" Meg whispers, leaning over to me.

My eyes zip back and forth between the two tables as the kids sit down. Meg's right. Kayli's not here. I scan the tables once more, now aware that the boys are totally separated from the girls. At the far end, my focus is immediately drawn to Gavin and Brody, who are already messing with each other's cards, even as Mrs. Putnam hovers right above them. I catch her eye, and she gives me a wink. But what's that supposed to mean? I pray it's to signal everything with Kayli is fine.

As Meg starts in with the instructions, I'm surprised to see Sienna and Stacy sitting next to each other. Whispering back and forth, giggling, it seems like their friendship's been repaired. After Meg finishes, I debate whether to go talk to Mrs. Putnam about Kayli. I don't want to make a big deal about it in front of her class, and I assume if it were serious, she'd approach me. But my impatience around not knowing continues to grow.

After the kids start working on their cards, I slowly make my way over to the other end of the table. Mrs. Putnam sees me coming and takes a couple of steps away from Brody and Gavin but gives them a look that indicates she's not going far.

"Is everything okay?" I whisper when I finally get close enough.

Mrs. Putnam bows her head in a slow nod. "I needed some help correcting papers this morning, and Kayli seemed like she needed some alone time."

"Thank you," I say, not knowing how else to respond. Warmth creeps up my neck. I'm sure Mrs. Putnam has likely heard all about the rumor too.

"Things like this happen," she says. "Kids get through it. It simply takes a little time for another scandal du jour to take its place."

"Right," I say, but I struggle with believing Mrs. Putnam sometimes. She tends to be extremely laid-back until all of a sudden, she's not. Yeah, yeah, everything's fine and normal, and all fifth-graders go through this, and then sound the alarm, fire drill, your kid's in trouble.

"Let's keep in touch, though," she says. Maybe she could read my face.

"Of course," I say as the bell rings to signal times up.

As Mrs. Putnam's class leaves and the next class sits down, the sound of Mrs. Putnam's voice echoes through my head. *Scandal du jour.* She actually called it a *scandal.* That's a pretty strong word. I knew the rumor was a big deal, especially to Kayli, but a scandal? Maybe Mrs. Putnam was using the word sarcastically. She does have a dry sense of humor.

The bell rings again, and now it's Ms. Andreen who's heading our way. Recognizing me from my help with the fall retreat, she gives me a smile as she directs her class to sit down.

"Hi, Mrs. Munsen." Emily and Mandi smile and give me a tiny wave as they find their spots before Meg presents the instructions for the final time. Some kids this age might act embarrassed or pretend they don't notice a friend's parent at an activity like this. It's nice to see that's not the case with these girls.

Glancing around the table to see who else I know from their class, I notice Meg's preoccupied with something going on at the tables next to ours. I follow her gaze to Lily, who seems to be having a great time, sharing ideas and giggling with the other girls. I smile, looking back at Meg, but she doesn't smile back. Instead, her lips are pressed together, and her eyes are narrowed. It's as if she's firing off a heat-seeking missile to someone...and it's not Lily. I follow her gaze once again. This time, I get it. She's watching James talk to Mr. Slater.

Mr. Slater's arms are crossed as he glares at James. Finally, he puts his arms down and shakes his head as James takes off toward the doors. I look over to Meg to check her facial expression once again, only to see she's eyeing up something else.

Now what? I look back over to the entrance. Whoa…is Liz waiting for James by the door? I can't tell for sure—she's only there for a split second—and now they're both gone.

Meg's neck reddens as the bell rings for the last time. The teachers gather their students and lead them out of the cafeteria. Time for us to clean up.

"Did you see that?" Meg hisses.

I cringe and weakly nod.

"He wasn't paying attention at any of the stations. His whole focus was entirely on her. Watching what she's doing… making faces or gestures to her to get her attention. It was ridiculous."

"I'm sorry." I rub her back, hoping she calms down.

"Dawn!" A familiar voice comes from behind us.

I turn to see Nikki carrying a box with a bunch of sticks streaming with feathers, ribbon, and tiny bells poking out, clanking with each step. "Hey," I say. "You remember Meg, right?"

"Of course," she replies as Meg graces her with one of her notoriously fake smiles. "I didn't realize you'd be helping today. You should've joined me at the cat toy station."

"It was pretty last-minute." I can't help but notice Meg's eye roll as I scramble for a way to diplomatically dodge the snide invitation Nikki just extended. It's impossible for me to miss Meg's irritation with Nikki's insinuation of me working with her instead of Meg. "I'm glad I was able to help. It's such a great activity for the kids."

Nikki looks around and then leans in closer to me, basically cutting off Meg, before whispering, "I didn't see Kayli, though. Is she still having a pretty tough time?"

"I think she'll be okay." I shift in my stance, crossing my arms to keep them from shaking. I don't know why Nikki's discussing this now…with all these other moms around.

"Oh good!" She clutches her hands together in relief, but

seems to be oblivious to my discomfort as she keeps going. "From what Mandi said, it seemed like a pretty big deal. It's too bad Kayli had to go berserk on those boys. I mean, clearly what they did was wrong, but it's unfortunate her response was so over-the-top. I think it turned off some kids, so they had a harder time seeing her side." Her box of cat toys clangs as she adjusts her grip. "When I didn't see her come through, I wondered if it had gotten worse."

I feel my face warm as my heart rate accelerates. All I can do is shrug. I try to think of something, anything to change the subject, but I'm at a loss for words. All I know is I'd do about anything to be done with this conversation.

"We better get this cleaned up, Dawn." Meg swoops in to save me. "The kids will start coming in for lunch any minute."

"Oh, of course," Nikki says as I silently thank Meg for the rescue. "I should get these cat toys turned in, anyway."

After she turns to leave, Meg puts her arm around me. This time, it's her turn to rub my back. I lean my head on her shoulder, but I don't dare to look at her. I don't want to start crying.

"Bet you're glad there's no basketball this weekend." She pulls away to grab one of the boxes with the finished cards. After handing it over, she picks up the other box filled with the leftover supplies. "I know I am."

"Could you imagine?" I shake my head as we head to the office to drop everything off. I've never looked more forward to an empty calendar box. "And I'm guessing Kayli's more than elated there's no school on Monday."

"Isn't that funny? James is probably bummed." Her voice drips with sarcasm.

When we get to the office, Meg says hello to a couple of the other moms in there, but I'm surprised by the speed with which she drops our stuff off and wants to leave. As we exit the building, she indicates her car is parked in the opposite direction of mine.

"Thanks for your help today." She holds her arms out for another hug.

"You too," I barely get out before getting choked up again.

"We'll get through this." She stands up straighter as she lets go.

"I hope so." I wave and then quickly turn toward my car before she can see me wipe my eyes. Over the course of the morning, the weight of what's going on with Kayli has finally caught up with me.

I knew she was mopey at home, and things were hard for her at school. But it wasn't until I saw her teacher and heard her description—*scandal*—that it sank in. And then what Nikki said…kids turning on Kayli because she went *berserk on those boys*, and Kayli's *response was so over-the-top*. Now I have a much better sense of what Kayli's been going through.

And to think, this was only in a period of two hours—two hours of feeling the discomfort of prying eyes and assuming people were talking about me. After only two hours, I could barely make it through without crying. Kayli's school day is six hours—day after day.

As I pull out of the parking lot, I try to think of something I can do for Kayli. I rack my brain for things that typically cheer her up. Treats, love stories…and then I remember…it's Valentine's Day. It's perfect. We can make fondue for dinner tonight. I can grab some sort of decadent chocolate dessert, and we can watch one of Kayli's favorite cheesy romantic comedies. It will be great…well, maybe not great, but it'll be something.

WEDNESDAY, FEB 19

When I get out of my car, it definitely takes more effort than usual to wave to Meg and Naomi. I pull on my hat and make my way over. I need to snap out of this. But this past week has been brutal with Kayli, making me seriously question if I have enough strength to go traipsing through the snow. This is the first morning I've ever contemplated bailing on one of our walks. Finally, I convinced myself I needed to get out of the house, though, thinking maybe a little fresh air and venting would help me feel better. But now that I'm here, I'm not sure I made the right choice.

The gray, slushy snow's downright depressing, and seeing the mud poking through it only reminds me of Kayli. As her sullenness melts away, I've been taken aback by how much anger there is lurking underneath. It's going to take more than a few warm days for her mood to get back to a more content, let alone cheerful, place.

"You hanging in there?" Naomi asks, wrapping her arm around my waist as Meg pats my shoulder and the three of us get on our way. "Are things with Kayli improving at all?"

I focus on the trail ahead: straight, predictable. I leverage its stability to keep my emotions in check. Everything with Kayli still feels so raw. I should be elated her crush is now over, but it's impossible. The heartbreak—compounded by Gavin's betrayal and public embarrassment—has taken a toll on her, and it's been gut-wrenching to watch her deal with so much hurt. And with each lingering day, I increasingly question my role in her inability to overcome it. "Unfortunately, things aren't improving a ton. The stomping and the slamming of doors has subsided, but she's still spending most of her time holed up in her room."

I can sense the looks of concern by my friends, but I don't dare turn to face them. Instead, I look up over the treetops, trying not to blink, so the cool air can halt any tear even thinking of forming. The separation of her pain from mine feels nonexistent at this point. The only difference is that I'm motivated to try to get through it, whereas she's as pleased as can be, languishing in grief and self-pity. "I'm trying every-thing…making her favorite meals, picking up fun treats and desserts, offering up the movies she loves, and asking if she wants to go on walks or have friends over. But she turns it all down. She can't seem to crawl out of this funk."

"I'm sure it takes time," Naomi says. "It's only been a week."

"But this week has felt like an eternity." I'm borderline whining now. "Even the extra day off of school didn't help. And based on the few words she said this morning, she's still getting heckled at school."

"Not that it helps"—Naomi's tone sounds more exasper-ated than anything—"but I've heard the teachers are watching those boys like hawks, and it's going to be even more so now, considering what they discovered yesterday."

"What happened yesterday?" My eyes widen as I look over. "And how do you guys find out all this stuff?" It's like there's a secret newsletter recapping the kids' days, and I got omitted from the distribution list. At least I have the two of them to fill me in.

Naomi avoids my questions, cringing as she looks across me to Meg. "James isn't implicated, is he?"

"Not yet," Meg sighs. "I feel like I'm still waiting for that shoe to drop, though. He swears he's not involved. But considering the number of boys he knows who are—half his friends are implicated. Not to mention how he's been hiding stuff from me about Liz. The confidence I have in him telling me the truth is about slim to none."

"Wait, so what's going on?" I try one more time. "This is about the boys, but not Kayli?"

Meg looks down, shaking her head, and then motions to Naomi to fill me in. Wow, things must not be going well for her. It's extremely unusual for Meg to be this quiet. It makes me wonder if anything else happened with James since I saw her on Friday.

After getting the go-ahead, Naomi finally responds. "You know how the kids can create those documents to share with each other so they can work on assignments together?"

"Yeah." I forget the name of them, but Kayli's used them for a few of her group projects.

Naomi continues, "Well, I guess a group of fifth-grade boys created some sort of master *chat* document. They used it to evade the teachers as they wrote messages back and forth, basically using the shared document to text each other during class."

"Whoa…" I don't know what else to say. My brain struggles to process what this even means as we cross over my favorite bridge. Even the vast sheet of ice looks messy now. Covered with pawprints, snowmobile tracks, and snowplowed trails to reach the icehouses, the wintery magic is long gone.

"Right?" Naomi replies. "Which is bad enough, of course, but then they started using it to post, and comment on, pictures of girls in bikinis. Apparently, one of the teachers busted a boy looking at it yesterday morning. And since then, additional details have been trickling out."

My mouth opens, but only a tiny sliver of nothingness comes out as I wait for the wires in my brain to uncross. I don't know how these kids even come up with these ideas. I mean, it's actually pretty ingenious when you think about it, but it's also terrifying to predict where it'll lead. What other schemes will they employ to outmaneuver us over the coming years? It's going to be impossible to keep up with them, especially when it comes to exploiting technology.

I turn to Meg. "So, you don't know if James was involved?"

Meg shakes her head. "The teachers are still trying to figure out who had access to the document. Hopefully they'll nail that down by the end of today. But it's looking like they won't ever be able to figure out who posted the pictures. The kids themselves, at least the innocent ones, don't even know. The software doesn't track who posts what."

"That's crazy…" The words come out of my mouth, but they linger in my head, suddenly stopping me in my tracks. What if there's an inappropriate picture of Kayli? I look first to Meg and then to Naomi. "What about the pictures? They're not of anyone we know, right?"

"No, thank God," Naomi replies. "The rumor is when some of the kids were researching Mexico for their social studies project, they started seeing beach shots. Then they got the idea to use similar keywords to find more photos. This way, they were able to get around the school's security measures that were supposed to prevent them from stumbling on inappropriate sites."

"It's like one your prophecies came true," I say to Naomi.

"Don't get me started," she replies. "Boys objectifying women already? It could spiral downhill so quickly. It completely messes with their heads on what normal female bodies, or relationships with them, look like. And it fosters such unrealistic expectations. Involved or not, I hope all the parents are talking to their fifth-grade boys about this."

Yikes…if this isn't one of Naomi's more passive-aggressive hints to Meg.

"The whole thing makes me sick," Meg says, thankfully not seeming to take Naomi's dig personally. "It's like James and these boys can't think of anything else except girls these days. Ugh—did I tell you he was late to practice yesterday?"

I glance over at Meg as her volume increases. Ah-ha. So, this must be the something else that happened. Her facial expression confirms my hunch. The pulsing vein on the side of her temple is unmistakable. I knew it. It's best if I keep looking ahead, though. Straight and predictable, even if it is gloomy.

"And it's not hard to guess why either." Meg's really on a tear, throwing up her hands. "Liz, of course! First, it's skipping out on Service Day, so he can give her his little lovey-dovey card. Which, by the way, he probably wrote when he was supposed to be doing his homework. And then yesterday, I come to find out he was supposed to be watching game film with his teammates after school, and he was a total no-show. One of them had to track him down, and he found James talking to Liz outside her locker. I don't get it. I just don't get it."

"Oh, Meg." I scramble to come up with anything to make her feel better. "I'm sorry."

"And then there's Brooklyn," Meg keeps going. "She isn't doing any better. Did you see her during Service Day? Following that little boy around, trying to sit next to him at each station. I swear, I saw her try to hold his hand once…"

"And you've spoken to James about this, right?" Naomi asks as we pivot around at our usual spot on the trail and start retracing our steps back to our cars.

"Until I'm blue in the face." Meg tilts her head back,

covering her eyes, and then tosses her arms down to her side. "But do you think he listens? I try to reason with him: how the relationships at this age will never amount to anything except take his focus off things that are much more important. A girl-friend isn't going to get him better grades or improve his jump shot. She isn't going to get him into a good college. I tell him he'll have plenty of time to worry about girls, but when he's older…much older…when he has everything else figured out. All he says is 'Yeah, yeah, Mom' and then disappears into his room."

"Ugh…these kids and their rooms," I groan. "Before this year, I can't remember a time when Kayli ever closed her door. Now, it's a miracle if it's open. It's like one day, a switch flipped and a wall was built."

"Exactly." Meg tips her head back in disgust again before turning to Naomi. "What about Lily? How are you guys handling her crush situation?"

Naomi shakes her head. "I don't know…I feel kind of guilty talking about it. What you guys are going through sounds so hard, but things with Lily are actually pretty good."

"Do not feel guilty." I grab her coat sleeve and make eye contact with her. "Please share your good news. I need it," I beg.

Naomi laughs and then looks across at Meg to get an okay from her too before she continues. "Jared's just really nice. He came over to help set up the website for Leo's STEM blueprint business this weekend. He's polite, super helpful, and so sweet to Lily. He even encouraged her to talk to the school counselor about the gym teacher."

"You're so lucky," I say. "Hopefully it stays that way. We need a promising example."

"So you're not worried at all?" Meg asks. "Even with Lily's anxiety?"

"I'll always worry a little," Naomi replies. "But things with

Lily's anxiety are actually going well. We've even been planning how to taper off our visits with Dr. Brinks. Lily's so much better at handling her worries, her phobia seems to be contained, and she even seems to be okay with our upcoming road trip. We're going to do one more visit before spring break and another right after we come back. If all goes well, Dr. Brinks says we can be done for a while."

"That's amazing." I stop in my tracks and give her a hug. "I bet that feels so good."

"It does." Naomi pulls away, discreetly wiping a tear from her eye as we start moving again. "I mean, it could always flare up again, or there could be other hiccups down the road. For now, though, it's like I have my old Lily back. Oh, and did I tell you she's writing the cutest little love story for that writing contest?"

"That's right. I'd totally forgotten about that," I say. "It's due at the end of the month, isn't it? I can't imagine Kayli taking part, but I'm so glad Lily is."

"Same for James." Meg shakes her head, sarcastically adding, "I'm sure he's way too preoccupied with girls to have time for anything else."

"What about the dance?" Naomi asks. "Are you thinking James will take Liz? Lily actually wanted me to ask you if she could bring Jared...since he goes to a different school."

"That's right. The dance," Meg groans, rubbing her forehead. "I've barely thought about it. I mean, I've thought about getting all the logistics taken care of, but in terms of James... wow, I guess. And I can ask about Jared when I meet with Principal Jacobson and Cynthia tomorrow. Which reminds me," Meg says as the parking lot comes into view, "I've been meaning to ask you guys if you wouldn't mind helping with chaperoning. It'll be Cynthia and me, but then we need two or three other parents."

"You can count me in," I reply as Naomi nods. "I've no

idea if Kayli will even go, but I'm still happy to help you out. So, are things going better between you and Cynthia now?"

"Actually, yeah," Meg smirks. "That's one positive thing coming out of James's crush on Liz. Sienna and Stacy are back to being friends, so Cynthia's removed the heat from me."

"I've heard Sienna and Stacy have been pretty horrible to Liz, though," Naomi sighs.

"That's terrible," I say. "Why do those girls have to be like that?"

"I don't get it either," Naomi replies. "Has Kayli said anything about Emily? I've heard things may have gotten a bit rocky between the two of them too."

"Wait, what? With Emily and Kayli?" My legs feel stuck again.

Naomi looks back, slowing to wait for me to catch back up. "Mm-hmm. Because of Emily and Brody. From what I hear, it's been going on for a while but has been kept top secret. I heard since Kayli's split with Gavin, it's starting to create some friction between her and Emily."

"Brody…? Gavin's Brody? Are you serious? But he can be so mean." I'm at a standstill. My body literally can't move forward. Brody. Brody and Emily…

"Yep," Naomi says. "And I guess Emily's dad is furious about it. He can't stand him."

"It's too bad. I know she's a little boy-crazy, but Brody?" Meg shakes her head as I finally start walking again. "More casualties from these worthless crushes. These kids don't realize what they're throwing away. These friendships are so valuable, especially when—not if—the relationship ends."

I can't even form words. I'm legitimately stunned as we reach the parking lot and wave goodbye. Emily and Brody… when did this start? Of course, that makes things more awkward for Kayli. Brody's been the catalyst for so many of Gavin's misdeeds, and now Emily has a crush on him…unbelievable. My heart shatters as it sinks in. The worst part is Kayli didn't even tell me.

* * *

I'm pulling my famous triple chip cookies out of the oven when the girls come home.

"Oh...what smells so good?" Ryn bounces into the kitchen with a huge smile on her face and heads straight for the cookie sheet. "Can I have one?"

"Where'd Kayli go?"

Ryn shrugs. "I dunno. Upstairs?"

"Let's wait, then. Do you have any homework you need to work on?"

"Just math, but I'm going to wait until Daddy can help," Ryn says, heading over to the snack drawer.

"Got it," I reply, grateful it's still going well for Ben to help her. "I'll be right back, hon."

I know Kayli loves her alone time, but I can't stop myself from checking on her. I want to keep reminding her I'm here if she needs anything, and I'm also dying to see if she'll say anything about Emily and Brody. As I tiptoe upstairs, I tell myself: stay calm, whatever she says isn't personal, this is not going to last forever, and it won't affect our whole life.

"Kay?" I say after tapping a few times on her door. I take a deep breath, open the door, and peek my head in. She's at her desk, holding a pen with a notebook in front of her.

"Hi, sweetie, how are you?" Crap, I should've asked her a more open-ended question that would get her to talk more.

"Fine."

"What are you working on?" A little better, but not much. I should've prepared more.

"Nothing."

Even though it's still a one-word answer, I take it as a positive sign that she's responding at all. Plus, her face is back to its normal shade of cream: no signs of red or puffiness. Maybe today went better. I decide to press my luck and enter her room, something I haven't done in days. I slowly walk over to her bed to sit down. It might be better if I start off doing the talking, beginning with the least-threatening topic first. "So, Meg and Naomi were telling me a pretty crazy story about the boys in your grade today."

"What?" She turns to face me, looking genuinely interested.

It's still only one word, but this is good. She's not yelling for me to leave. She actually looks curious and seems like she wants me to continue. "About how they were secretly sharing notes and pictures on this shared document. Sounds like they caused quite an uproar. Do you know anything about it?"

She turns back to her notebook, mumbling, "Not really."

Dang it. Here we go again. She's starting to close down. I need to think of something quick. "I made your favorite cookies for after dinner tonight."

"Okay." She doesn't look up as she starts to write something down.

"Maybe later tonight we could go for a walk or watch a movie or something?"

"Nah."

Ugh. I'm not getting anywhere. "What about Friday night? It's mentor night for basketball, right? That should be fun."

"Mom, can I have some alone time, please?"

Got it. Loud and clear. Time to leave. At least she's being polite. Emily and Brody will have to wait. I get up slowly. "Okay, yeah, sure. I should get dinner going anyway."

"Shut my door, please."

Got it, yep. Shutting the door.

* * *

I've been staring at my computer screen for over five minutes trying to summarize these negative results in the most constructive way possible. How can I phrase "the investment made in your latest marketing campaign appears to have had no effect at all" any better? I keep strumming my fingers across the keys, but no letters are typed. I need to focus.

"Hey, hon." Ben pops his head in. Thank God he's brought a glass of wine with him.

"Thanks." I accept the glass and spin my chair around to face him as he takes his rare but recognizable coaching position on the couch. This is one of Ben's signature moves. Whenever he leans forward, rests his elbows on his knees, and folds his hands, he clearly has news. "Girls in bed?" I ask.

He runs his hands through his hair before he nods. Uh-oh…he's not leaning back into the couch or resting his feet on the coffee table. I brace myself as he starts to talk. "Things with Kayli were a little rough, though. Don't you think she should be over this whole breakup thing by now? I mean, it's been a week, right? Seems a little much for a fifth-grader to me."

"Yeah, I don't know," I sigh. Similar to me, when Ben first found out things with Kayli and Gavin were over, he was beyond ecstatic. But I don't think either of us could have guessed how hard she'd take the breakup. "Sometimes these things can take longer than we want."

"But why is she making it such a big deal? I don't know if letting her blow it so out of proportion is the greatest thing. Even when I picked her up from basketball yesterday, she seemed angry. She was so loud, and she had *quite* the attitude when Coach Brad was giving her pointers. It was inappropriate, actually, and I could tell some of the other parents noticed it too."

I take a big sip of wine, hoping it reaches my nerve endings quickly. I'm sure Ben's well intentioned, and in certain circumstances, he may be right. But I also don't think girls should always be expected to be quiet and polite. If something is upsetting her, she should have every right to be sad or gloomy. Kayli obviously has strong feelings about what happened, and she should be allowed to feel and process them. "It's hard to watch, I get it. But she has a right to feel sad or angry or whatever. We can talk to her about her behavior at practice and discuss other ways she can work through these feelings, but we can't just tell her not to feel what she's feeling. We have to let some of this play out...and on her own timeline."

Ben shakes his head, pursing his lips. "She's in fifth grade, though. This makes no sense. She doesn't need to be stomping around the house and hiding out for hours on end in her room."

Now I shake my head. "Sorry, but I disagree. Our home should be a safe place. This is the one place I want her to feel she can vent, stomp around, and hide away in. It won't last forever. She just needs more time and grace from—"

"Whatever...I guess." Ben shakes his head, quietly agreeing to disagree for now. He gets up to leave, stopping to give me a quick kiss on his way out. His parents' fights when he was younger definitely left a scar—he truly detests conflict.

I turn back to my screen. There's no way I'm going to be able to finish this report now. I lean back in my chair and close my eyes, thinking back to that summer at the golf course and the kiss with my manager. It's obviously a completely different level, but getting over something that traumatic takes time. And Kayli's perception of how deeply this hurts is very real. I don't want to negate her feelings or make her think they aren't important. In my experience, that only shatters a person's confidence.

FRIDAY, FEB 21

"You guys have everything?" I ask before locking the car. Ryn clutches her basketball as she takes off for the Activity Center. "Ryn, wait for us please, sweetie!"

"Fine," she groans, slowing down. "But come on, then!" She stops and waves for us to join her. Her patience only lasts a few seconds, though, until she can't stop herself from continuing to proceed ahead and test the length at which she can distance herself from us.

"You loved mentor night last year, remember?" I rub Kayli's back as we slowly make our way across the parking lot. Tonight, I struggled to even get her to come. *No one's going to talk to me* was her excuse, which I knew was an exaggeration. Even though things between her and Emily may be a little strained, her whole team's going to be there. She'll have plenty of girls to talk to. "And last year, they kept the boys separated from the girls."

We finally catch up to Ryn at the entrance and head in together. As soon as we're through the doors, though, Ryn races ahead once again. This time straight for the spectators' window, which spans above the four courts below. She presses her forehead against the glass. "Mommy, there's Mollie and Josie." She points to the nearest corner. "Can I go down there? Please?"

"Just a minute, hon," I say as Kayli and I go over to get a peek too. "Let's go down together and figure out where to put your stuff." I'm relieved to see the boys are a couple of courts down from where the girls are. I'm also elated that even though Ryn continues to play up on the third-grade basketball team, she hasn't forgotten about her second-grade friends.

We head downstairs and find a line of duffle bags and coats along the wall. "Let's put your and Kayli's stuff together," I say, holding their balls while they take off their coats and then giving Ryn a quick hug. "Be good, have fun, and I'll be back at eight to pick you up."

Ryn takes off before I'm even done speaking, but Kayli remains by my side. "Do you see your teammates?" I scan the packed, noisy room. "Mandi should already be here if Mollie is."

Kayli points to Emily and Mandi shooting at a hoop a few feet from Cori and Nikki, who are standing off to the side chatting.

"How about I walk you over? I want to say hi to Cori and Nikki anyway." Obviously, I don't say this to Kayli, but I'm dying to get their perspective. Since Kayli's breakup with Gavin, she's been radio silent with me, and I still have no clue how Emily's crush on Brody has affected her.

Kayli doesn't say anything, so I push the envelope and start walking over. She reluctantly follows, so I take it as a good sign she's still willing to shoot hoops with them.

"Hey, guys," I say to Cori and Nikki as Kayli heads over to their girls. I keep it casual. Potential friend drama isn't something I want to delve right into. "Everyone gets a couple hours off tonight, huh? Anything fun planned?"

"Hi, yeah." Nikki's eyes light up. "We're going to Randy's Pizza for a bite if you want to join us."

"That'd be great, thanks." This is perfect. Alone time with these two moms at Randy's...I'm sure I'll be able to get a full download of what they know.

As the whistle blows and the girls head to center court, I follow Cori and Nikki back toward the entrance. Even among this large group of girls, it's hard to miss Kayli lagging behind Emily and Mandi. She keeps her head down while her sister breezes past, skipping arm in arm with Mollie and Josie. The contrast is jarring and makes me even more curious about what's going on with Kayli and her friends. I know the kids at school aren't going out of their way to be kind to her, but I haven't heard of anything specifically mean in the past few days either. And although she hasn't wanted to hang out with her friends, she hasn't said anything negative about them either.

"See you in a bit," I call to Cori and Nikki as they chitchat on the way over to their car. I've never been so eager to get to Randy's in my life.

* * *

Nikki and Cori are already in line when I enter the dough-scented restaurant. The place's packed, so instead of joining them, I grab the last open table. As I'm taking off my coat, I feel a hand on my back.

"Small world." Meg grins.

"Oh my gosh, hi." I turn all the way around, give her a quick hug, and then motion for her to join me. "Want to sit with us? Nikki and Cori are still in line."

"Nikki, huh?"

"Yeah..." I notice the tinge of disdain in her tone. I know Nikki can be gossipy, but Meg's persistent uneasy attitude toward her makes me wonder if that's all there is. Either way, I know it's better if I downplay why I'm with them. "We bumped into each other at the mentor night. It was very spur-of-the-moment."

"Ah…well, have fun. But just, you know, be careful about what you say around Nikki."

"For sure." I give my most reassuring nod before she goes back to her table. Yikes.

As I sit down, I check the line and see it's Nikki and Cori's turn to order. I text Ben to tell him my plans. He sends me a picture of his feet up on the coffee table next to a beer with the television on in the background. He doesn't seem to mind one bit.

"Here we are." Nikki sets down three glasses of beer before taking off her coat and sliding in across from me. "A recommended pairing from the chef."

"Thank you." I smile and then take a drink. "It's perfect."

"And a small pepperoni with extra cheese is on the way," Cori adds, scooching in next to Nikki after scanning the room. "This place's really hopping. I guess a lot of people shared our great idea…is that Meg over there?"

"Yeah." I keep my focus on the two of them. There's no way I'm turning to look. "She stopped over here while you guys were ordering."

"Oh good. We got to see her when she was dropping off James," Nikki replies. She takes a sip of her beer before continuing, "How are things with James and Liz, by the way? I heard he skipped practice for her or something like that this week."

"Oh…I…I don't know." I take another sip as Meg's advice echoes through my head: *Be careful about what you say*. I can't believe I need to be on guard already. I'm also torn on how to reply. Do I correct Nikki and tell her James was only a little bit late, or do I play dumb and avoid feeding the rumor mill? Playing dumb has to be better. I look across to Cori, who actually might know the answer if she's been substituting in the school at all this week. "You'd probably know more about that than me."

"Actually, I've been pretty out of the loop lately." She shakes her head. "Between substituting at the middle school and carting Brandon and all his friends around, I haven't had much time to focus on Emily's social circle."

"Well, that's the word on the street," Nikki says, looking back at me. "Or hallway."

"Yeah, I don't know." My arms feel itchy all of a sudden, so I pull my sleeves down. I don't want to show them I'm anything close to being bothered. I need to make this all seem like it's no big deal. "She hasn't said much about it. I think she's been pretty busy getting things set for the dance." There, that should help. Let's get off James and onto another topic. I take another sip of my beer.

"That's right...the dance." Nikki turns to Cori as our pizza finally arrives. "I wonder if they'll figure out the whole picture thing before then. Have you heard anything more on that?"

"No, but that's a good question," Cori replies, distributing the plates and napkins. "I can't get over the fact they still don't know who posted them. It's putting Principal Jacobson in such an awkward position. With this and the outstanding issue of the body spray, more than a few parents are starting to give him a little heat."

"There's still an issue with the body spray?" I ask as I grab a slice.

"Can you believe it?" Cori shakes her head in disgust. "I guess some kids have figured out how to rig the caps, or spouts, or whatever, so they keep spewing odor. The overpowering scent basically serves as a continuous stink bomb. They've been set off in bathrooms, lockers, and I heard one was even set off on a bus. They have no clue who's doing it."

"All fingers point toward fifth-grade boys, but nobody knows for sure who," Nikki adds.

"That group of boys...," Cori huffs. "They're totally wreaking havoc this year. It was nothing like this when Brandon was this age."

"And what's amazing is no one has turned anyone else in," Nikki says. "It has to be more than one kid. And not to turn on one another or rat each other out...it takes a lot of trust and shows a ton of loyalty. Mandi told me she thinks they made some sort of pact. If one goes down, they all go down."

"I've heard that too," Cori says. "Even Brandon and his buddies are in awe. They can't believe none of the boys have caved."

"Friendships at this age are so important," Nikki replies, looking straight into my eyes. "You don't want to jeopardize them."

Whoa...is Nikki purposely luring me into talking about Kayli? Even if she isn't, I decide to take the bait. I'd rather have this be out in the open and know more about what's going on. "By the way, is everything still okay with Kayli and your girls?" I ask. "Ever since that blowup with Gavin happened, Kayli's pretty much shut me out."

Cori's eyebrows go up as she looks over to Nikki. Nikki wipes her mouth with her napkin as I force myself to be patient. But with each additional second, I grow more positive that what I'm about to hear isn't going to be good. If things were all fine and dandy, there'd be no hesitation. "I think it's so tricky," she finally says.

I nod and wait some more, trying my best to keep my expression plain. I don't want to influence her response in any way. She has to feel comfortable saying it...

"I think Emily and Mandi are both trying to be under-standing." Nikki's words come out slowly as she looks over at Cori for reassurance. "But as time passes, they might be having a hard time understanding why she's not back to her old self yet."

Back to her old self? Hmm...I try to read between the lines. They want her back to her old self? So, Emily and Mandi aren't mad at her—even with what Brody's been saying?

Cori finishes her bite. "That's my understanding too. I think they've been trying to cheer her up and going out of their way to include her in stuff, but I don't think Kayli's been super receptive to it. They say she wants to be by herself."

My brain struggles to process what's being said. So, these girls are going out of their way to be friendly to Kayli, but Kayli's the one who's making it hard? I'm so confused.

"Yeah, I think they're trying very hard," Nikki says, cringing. "But it's almost as if they're starting to take offense to being blown off so much."

"So, Emily and Mandi aren't mad at Kayli?" I'm finally brave enough to confirm. "Even though Kayli freaked out on Gavin, and Brody is Gavin's best friend, and Emily has a crush on Brody?" There it is. I said it. It's all out in the open. There's no going back now.

"Oh heavens, no." Cori's surprise appears genuine as she shakes her head. "Emily would never pick a boy over a friend. She knows better than that. Besides, Brad's totally put the kibosh on her and that boy. He's nothing but trouble. Brad can't stand him."

Nikki's face softens, and she reaches across the table for my hand. "The girls really have tried to be there for Kayli."

"Oh my goodness, you guys..." I feel absolutely horrible right now. Here it's my daughter who's causing all the awkwardness, not theirs. I'm so embarrassed. I understand her shutting me out—kind of—but her friends? That makes zero sense. "I'm so sorry if your girls are feeling hurt. I totally get it, and I appreciate how hard they're trying. I'm actually surprised, too, how long it's taking Kayli to get out of this funk. I've been trying to give her space and be understanding, but obviously, I need to do more. I'll definitely talk to her about this."

"Don't beat yourself up." Nikki looks at her watch and then stacks up our empty plates. "I'm so glad everything is out in the open now. And sometimes, these issues with kids take more time than you think. We should probably get going, though. The girls will be finishing up soon."

* * *

I look back at the girls as I pull out of the parking lot, trying to get a better gauge on Kayli's mood. She looks exhausted. And with her tournament tomorrow, I feel a sense of urgency to get her back home…and alone, so I can ask her about her friends. "So how was it?"

"I won Lightning, and Mollie, Josie, and I got first place in the second-grade three-on-three tournament. It was so much fun." Ryn bounces in her seat and then turns to Kayli. "How many slices of pizza did you eat?"

"I don't know," Kayli sneers, but then she seems to realize how much her careless response deflated her sister's excitement and tries to redeem herself. "Two, maybe?"

"Mollie and I each had three…and an ice cream sandwich." Ryn's excitement appears rejuvenated as she scooches up in her seat and grabs the back of mine. "And, Mommy, we had two varsity players as our coaches. It was so cool. They kept telling me I was such a good dribbler."

"That's great," I say, pulling into our driveway. "I'm glad you had a good time. It's pretty late, though. We should probably get ready for bed soon." I turn to look at Kayli. "Especially since you have a tournament tomorrow."

After the car comes to a stop, Ryn grabs her stuff, jumps

out, and heads inside to find Ben. Lately, she's been preferring the nights when it's his turn to tuck them in.

"How'd it go for you?" I turn to Kayli as she slowly collects her stuff.

"Fine." She shrugs and slides out of the car.

I hold the door open for her as she comes inside. Although her depleted posture tells me it might be better to wait to bring up her friends, I don't have the patience or the time. She has another basketball tournament with these girls tomorrow. I need to buck up and say something. Maybe I can work my way into it if I make it seem like I'm sticking to basketball. "Were any of your teammates on your three-on-three team?"

"Harper and Greta." She rests her head on her arms as she takes a seat at the island. She looks tired, but not upset. If she was upset, she would've retreated to her room.

"Ah…" I act like this is totally normal and grab a couple glasses of water. Maybe a drink will give her a reason to stay in the kitchen longer. "I bet you did well with their height."

"I guess."

"And how were your coaches? Did you have a couple of varsity players too?"

"Yeah, they were cool." She sits up and takes a drink. "I actually sat by them when we were eating pizza too."

"Oh?" I try hard to hide my concern. That means she probably wasn't sitting by her normal friends or teammates. "Were they giving you some extra tips?"

"Yeah, they were super helpful." She pushes her glass away as she gets up. "They had some cool stories about the things they went through with boys when they were my age."

Okay, now I'm intrigued. Keep a straight face, keep her talking…no big deal. "That's nice of them to share that with you. Did they have some good advice?"

"Actually, they had some *really* good advice." She rubs her eyes as she starts making her way out of the kitchen. "I can't wait to try it on Monday."

"Just a minute, hon." I can't let her walk away yet. "I need to talk to you about something."

"What?" She turns back around all slumped over, rolling her eyes.

Clearly this isn't the best time, but I have to get it out. "It's about Mandi and Emily."

"Mom…," she groans. "I don't want to talk about it." She slumps over even more.

"Honey…," I sigh. "It's fine if you're mopey or get your frustration out here at home, but you need your friends. And they're trying to be there for you."

This makes her straighten up, but she doesn't say anything. She stands there, in silence, glaring at me. I try to read her face, but I'm at a loss. I try to think of something else I can say. "They're your teammates. Good teammates support each other and count on one another."

"You don't…" She runs her hands through her hair, hesitating for a minute before her eyes fixate on the ceiling. "Fine," she exhales and then quickly turns to head back upstairs.

"Love you," I call after her, knowing full well how much I irritated her. I need to give her space right now, but at least I got something through. And I can't help but smile a little. It's not a huge victory, but it counts as a tiny win, and even tiny wins start to add up.

TUESDAY, FEB 25

My phone buzzes, interrupting my train of thought. I glance down at my watch. Now I'll never finish this report before the girls get home from school. I flip my phone over. The school? My heart rate climbs. I rarely get a call from them…usually it's only when one of the girls is sick or hurt. But wait, I glance at the clock again. Shouldn't they be on the bus already? I wipe my palm and push Accept. "Hi, this is Dawn."

"Hello, Dawn. This is Mrs. Putnam. I was hoping to catch you before Kayli got home this afternoon. I need to update you on an incident she was involved in today."

Mrs. Putnam is calling about Kayli and an *incident*? Oh man, now what? I wipe my palms again, trying to focus on my breath. I need to be able to pay attention to what she says… and her tone. My voice wavers as I clarify, "Incident?"

"Yes. Are you aware of an improperly shared document some fifth-grade boys created?"

The *shared document*…the one with the pictures of girls in bikinis? Oh, dear heavens, maybe Naomi was wrong…maybe there were actually pictures of someone we know—Kayli. My heart pounds against my chest. So much so, I swear it makes contact with my shirt. Focusing on my breath is completely useless. But wait, what was Mrs. Putnam's tone…it didn't sound upset, did it? Normal volume, steady—monotone really —just higher at the end, so I know she asked a question.

"Dawn? Do you know about this document?"

Oh jeez, she's still waiting for my response. "I um…I—I think so."

"Okay. Well, the specifics don't matter. You only need to know it was completely against school policy. And the fifth-grade teachers have been working with Principal Jacobson for the past week, trying to determine who added the inappropriate content. Well, yesterday, Kayli turned in some evidence that we were able to use to identify the culprits."

So, she isn't calling about pictures of Kayli? What a relief…Kayli only turned in the evidence. Hold on. Kayli turned in evidence that got several boys in trouble…yesterday? And she didn't tell me…and what evidence, how'd she get it, and who'd she turn in? And why would she hide this from me? My head spins, trying to determine which question to ask Mrs. Putnam first. "Can you provide a little more detail?"

"I'm sorry, but not much." She sounds genuinely disappointed. "Only that Kayli informed us that while she was practicing her social studies presentation with the school's new video app early last week, she captured some boys in the background uploading the inappropriate content. For privacy reasons, all I'm allowed to tell you is that the evidence is indisputable, and the teachers and the administrators are very grateful she was able to help us figure this out. You'll have to talk to Kayli to learn the rest."

"Oh, okay. I guess that makes sense." My stomach sinks as I glance at the clock. Of course, the only boys that come to mind are Gavin and Brody. Would she really do that, though? I guess I'll know for sure in a few minutes. "Well, thank you for letting me know what happened. I appreciate it."

"Dawn—one more thing."

This time her voice lowers at the end. It's not a question. It's bad news.

"Somehow, the kids figured out who turned in the boys…I believe she faced some significant backlash today from her classmates. I want you to know the teachers and Principal Jacobson are extremely proud of Kayli's bravery for doing the right thing. We are doing everything we can to discourage this backlash, including counseling any kids we find taking part in it. We think it'll be resolved quickly."

My stomach sinks. Of course she's facing backlash. Especially if Gavin and Brody are involved. Oh man…

The familiar scuffles entering the mudroom tell me I need to wrap this up. "Okay. Thanks, Mrs. Putnam. I appreciate the call and everything else you're doing to help Kayli through this."

I take my phone with me, stepping out of my office and forcing a smile as Ryn comes into the kitchen. But my attention is instantly diverted over to the footsteps thundering upstairs and the thud of a slamming door that follows.

"Not at all. Please reach out to me anytime if you have questions or need anything else."

"Will do…okay. Yep. Thanks. Bye." I reach for the counter, using it to catch my balance. I can't believe this is happening.

"What's a traitor?" Ryn looks up, pausing her excavation of the snack drawer.

It's hard to breathe, let alone think straight. Oh, dear Lord. I roll my neck. "Where did you hear that word, sweetie?" Please say on television or some video you watched at school.

"Everyone was chanting it on the bus. They were shouting it at Kayli. Something about what she did to Gavin and Brody."

My phone nearly slips through my fingers. It *was* Gavin and Brody. And now they're getting all the kids to call Kayli a traitor? I need to sit down. No. I should go talk to Kayli. No. I need to sit down. Ugh…why can't I do this? I should be able to handle stuff like this without falling to pieces. I should be able to watch her struggle. Allowing her to handle things like this is supposed to send the message she's capable and competent. But my internal alarms won't shut off. The tug of being a first responder is too great. "I'll be right back, sweetie."

At least Mrs. Putnam gave me a heads-up. Technically, Kayli was *helping*. And what she did wasn't wrong…regardless of her history with them. What the boys did was wrong. And that's how Mrs. Putnam and Principal Jacobson are seeing it. But knowing Kayli's underlying intentions were likely somewhat malicious, I can understand why so many kids at her school are upset with her. So, even though what she did wasn't wrong, I honestly don't know how long it's going to take for this to blow over.

It's actually pretty hard to believe Kayli *accidentally* captured Brody and Gavin posting inappropriate pictures to the shared document using the school's new video app last week, had the intuition to save the recording, and then determined she could use it to get back at them by showing it to Mrs. Putnam yesterday. Wait, yesterday was *Monday*—oh man…the high school mentors and their *really good advice* she couldn't wait to try. Perfect. These girls provided the inspiration for this conviction, but now they're nowhere to be seen to help with any resulting blowback.

Over and over again, I remind myself to stay calm as I head upstairs. Pausing in front of her door, I say it to myself one more time before I proceed with my customary three light taps. "Kayli? Mrs. Putnam just called. I think we should talk." Knowing how unlikely it is for her to respond, I slowly open the door. "Oh, hon." I walk over to her heaving body that's faceplanted in her pillows, sit down, and start rubbing her back. "I'm so sorry."

She cranks her neck toward me, tears streaming down her face, only long enough to say, "Everyone's calling me a traitor!" before flinging her face back down.

I continue rubbing her back, but the circular motions become less steady. "I know this is hard, but it won't last forever. Your teacher and principal believe you did the right thing. And I do too."

She scooches herself up into a sitting position, pressing her lips together. The lines in her forehead deepen as her attitude hardens. "Why does anyone even care about Gavin and Brody? They're such jerks. Especially to girls. They act like they rule the school, walking around proclaiming who's worthy or not. It's so rude." Then she tucks herself under my arm as her voice softens. "I thought at least my friends would be on my side... and we have practice tonight too." She looks up, her wide eyes searching for comfort, reassurance, acceptance...the typical magical powers of a parent who can fix everything.

"I bet they'll come around." I blink back tears as I hug her closer. Unfortunately, that's the best I can do right now. Maybe after basketball practice tonight she'll feel a little better. She can see her friends and work off some of this steam. I've never had much success with magic. "Sometimes it just takes a little more time."

* * *

Unfortunately, things aren't any better by the time I tuck Kayli into bed later that night. My heart aches as her body stiffens and quickly pulls away from my hug. But her averted eyes and curt goodnight signal any more of my questions will have to wait. And now, it's not only Kayli who's upset, it's also Ben. I gently close her door, lingering on the landing before going back downstairs. Heaven only knows what he's going to say now that Kayli's out of earshot. When he brought Kayli home from basketball practice—where he apparently got a firsthand glimpse of things not going well—his telltale huffs and under-the-breath muttering clearly indicated he was holding something back.

I do my best to smile at him as I pass behind the couch on my way to the kitchen. I knew it. There it is. The readied wine-glass, waiting patiently for me on the counter. I take a sip before heading over to join him. At least he's got his feet up on the coffee table and a beer in his hand. He actually looks relaxed. Maybe it's all good now.

I plop down next to him and smile. "Hi." There's no way I'm going first. I need to see what kind of headspace he's in before I say any more.

"Hi," he plainly replies, with no noticeable change in expression.

Ah…okay. I see how it is. No problem. I can play this game too. Pretending to be totally engrossed in the television gives me time to sort out how I feel about all of this anyway. I'm pretty sure I'm proud of Kayli. No…I know I am. Standing up to those boys was huge. Sure, there's a tiny part of me that wishes she would have done it a little differently. But what else could she have done? It's not like—

"So…" Ben pats my leg as he shifts into his coaching posi-tion. "I'm thinking we need to start using a slightly different strategy with Kayli."

"You do." I purposely frame my response as a statement as I turn to face him, resting my arm on the back of the couch.

"I mean, what is all this teaching her?" He lowers his chin and shakes his head. "What's good about us being okay with her stirring up all this controversy? Creating all this commotion? You should've seen the looks her teammates gave her when I picked her up tonight. I don't think any of them thought she did the right thing. She can't lash out like that to get revenge on a boy. She needs to keep her head down and get over him."

Who is this man? I know he hates conflict, but doesn't he see what's really going on here? I set my wineglass down and cross my arms. I struggle not to sound patronizing. "Ben, she turned in boys who were sharing pictures of women in bikinis at school. They were the ones clearly breaking the rules. And they were objectifying women. Our daughter stood up for all the girls in her grade and hopefully taught these boys a good lesson." I straighten my posture, holding my chin high, but not too high—I don't want to seem prissy.

"Honey..." He sets his beer down and turns to me, rolling his eyes. "These are fifth-grade boys. Of course they're going to be looking at girls in bikinis. So what? Now we want Kayli to be the feminist police? I mean, seriously, she's not going to have any friends...it's not worth it to create all these waves."

Triggers go off all over my body. *Don't make waves.* That's exactly what my coworker at the golf course told me too. I wasn't handling the aftermath of the kiss with my manager well at all, and she could tell something was up. When I finally confided in her, her repeated response was that I should stay quiet. *Everyone loves him. He's worked here forever. He has a family. It was only a kiss. It didn't mean anything. It's not worth it. Just keep your distance and keep quiet.*

The triggers spark a fire in me, and every fiber of my being tells me Ben's wrong. "I can't believe you're saying that. You have two daughters!" I can't remember the last time my voice with this loud, and the words keep pouring out. "You want them to grow up thinking not only that it's okay for boys to objectify them but also that they should be quiet when they see something they believe is wrong solely to maintain social harmony? That's not right!"

"Hang on. That's not what I'm saying...," he starts, but I can't even look at him anymore. This isn't a conversation I can have right now. I'm too hot. I can't think straight. I leave my wineglass on the table, and I go upstairs.

WEDNESDAY, FEB 26

"I'm not going!" Kayli ducks under her quilted navy-blue comforter as I peek my head in.

Ironically, above her buried head hangs a large watercolor print of a girl taking a jump shot with the letters *GRL PWR* down the side. She used some of her Christmas money to buy it only a couple of months ago. I figured this would happen, though. That's why I'm up here early. With what happened at school yesterday, almost anyone could've guessed she wouldn't want to return today. I couldn't risk waiting until the last minute. "Honey, I know this day's going to be really hard for you, but you have to go to school. What can I do to make it easier?"

"I'm not going." Her voice is more muted as she scooches under the covers even further.

"How about I make some French toast?" If anything can get Kayli out of bed, it's French toast. "How about you take a shower, get dressed in some comfy clothes, and when you come down, your French toast will be ready?"

This time, all I get is silence. No movement either.

"I know you can do this, hon. It's going to be a tough day,

but you've gotten through so many tough days already. I know you can get through this one too."

More silence.

"Okay, I'm going to go start the French toast. You should get in the shower soon—"

"French toast?" Ryn interrupts from behind me in the hall-way. "You're making French toast? You never make French toast on school days. Oh, oh…will you please make the kind that you fill with peanut butter? Please?"

Normally, I'd warn Ryn about appreciating what she has rather than complaining about not having something else she wants. But this is actually brilliant. It'll entice Kayli even more. She loves that version, and I rarely make it. "Yep. Today's your lucky day," I say loud and clear.

Ryn cheers, and we head downstairs to start getting out the ingredients. Thank goodness she's still her bubbly, cheerful self. I can't imagine having two despondent children at the same time. Her positive and lighthearted outlook on the day gives me hope things will improve with Kayli eventually.

More relief washes over me as I hear the shower turn on upstairs.

"Is Kayli in trouble?" Ryn asks as she spreads the peanut butter on the bread while I mix up the eggs, milk, and vanilla.

I want to choose my words carefully. We still haven't explained to Ryn exactly what's going on. She obviously knows something's up, but I also don't think she needs all the details. Besides, I'd rather avoid putting her in the position of feeling like she needs to explain things to the nosy kids on the bus. "No, but some of the kids at school are pretty mad at her."

She finishes up the last sandwich and sets down the knife. "So, what *is* a traitor?"

I keep my eyes on the egg mixture as I hand it over. Unfor-tunately, it's not only the word the kids were chanting on the bus yesterday—it's also the word her friends were whispering behind her back at practice last night. Practice was the real knife through the heart. I make up a definition that's simple enough for Ryn to understand. "It's when someone purposely tries to get a friend in trouble."

"Is that what Kayli did?" She dips the peanut butter sandwiches in egg wash and then stacks them up for me so I can place them in the pan.

"Kind of." Once I have all the French toast in the pan, frying, I put the ingredients and dirty dishes away and get out a couple of plates and silverware.

"And that's why everyone's mad at her?"

I nod as I flip the sandwiches. "So maybe this morning, we should try to be extra nice and supportive of Kayli since she's going to have a pretty rough day at school."

As I slide the French toast on to a couple of plates, Kayli drags herself into the kitchen and hoists herself onto the stool next to Ryn. Her unbrushed hair is still dripping wet, and she's wearing black from head to toe. I try to keep the focus off her for now. There's no need to push her morning further into a tailspin. "How's math coming along these days?" I ask Ryn.

"Ugh," she groans, grabbing for the syrup. "I hate math."

"Really? Dad says you're doing great."

"Yeah. When he helps, it's fine. At school, it's the worst."

"Is Ethan still acting like a know-it-all?" I recall what upset her a few weeks ago.

"I'm done with him." She shakes her head before stuffing a huge bite into her mouth.

"Why? What'd he do?" Kayli suddenly looks concerned for her sister.

"He's a backstabber. He told Mr. Kane that Daddy does my homework for me."

Wait, what? Ben would never do that…would he? Then I remember his sheepish face as he handed me my coffee this morning and apologized for our dispute last night. He definitely has a knack for finding the easy way out.

"Figures." Kayli swipes her last bite over the remaining syrup on her plate. "You have to be so careful. One minute someone's your friend, and a minute later, they turn on you." She stuffs the bite into her mouth, pushes away her plate, and heads to the mudroom to grab her stuff.

"Yeah." Ryn mimics Kayli's tone and follows her lead, shoving her plate away and stomping into the mudroom.

Yikes. What am I even listening to? Is Kayli talking about Gavin…or Emily? Or maybe she's referring to her entire grade, all of whom Kayli thinks have turned against her. I meet the girls in the foyer and watch for the bus to come. I hope it's late today. I need more time. More time to give advice —or tell them something encouraging. Unfortunately, no such luck. I see the top of the yellow roof peeking over the hill.

"I'm sorry you guys are having such a tough time with your friends. Hopefully, with time, things will get better. Love you." It's all I can get out as they walk under my arm that's propping the door open. Anything I can say that's even close to being helpful will have to wait.

* * *

My drive to the trail is a blur of mud and dirty snow. Each year around this time, I have the same internal debate. Do I want it to snow one more time to cover up all this mud, or do I want the sun to shine more and help turn the mud into green grass? The debate in my head is pointless, though. In Minnesota, it always snows again—always—usually several times. Mother Nature likes to push me to my limit…until I reach the point where I'm on my knees begging for spring.

I try to get a read on Naomi and Meg as I get out of my car, taking a minute before I walk over. I stretch my arms above my head and arch my back. I can do this. I drop my arms and bend forward as I exhale. My muscles still feel tight. It's like my defense system's on high alert. I go through the motions one more time. I'm pretty sure they'll be on my side. What Kayli did clearly wasn't wrong. She might not have carried it out in the best way, but by no means should she be facing this much heat. Meg and Naomi will understand, though. They're my allies…

I straighten my back and roll out my shoulders. As I walk over, their arms open.

"How're you doing?" Naomi wraps her arms around me.

"Hanging in there." I move to Meg's arms next. I don't know why I even questioned it. I knew they'd be here for me, but their hugs are reassuring.

"How's Kayli?" Meg asks as we get on our way. "I seriously can't believe she did that. Did you know about it ahead of time?"

I shake my head. "I wish. Although maybe it's better I didn't. I don't know what I would've said anyway."

"Yeah, that's a tough one," Naomi says. "I mean, what those boys did was undeniably wrong, but I don't know…I wish there was a way she could've done it so she wasn't facing so much crossfire. It doesn't seem fair."

"Maybe she could've done it anonymously?" Meg offers. "Or, she could've had you do it. Or, she could've said she didn't want to turn the boys in, but you made her."

I struggle to keep my head up as I listen to her suggestions. I know they're well intentioned, but they only make me feel more pathetic. "Yeah…I probably should've asked more questions." I shake my head. "I actually had a tiny opening, but I waved it off since I needed to talk to her about something else. Then, unfortunately, I forgot all about it."

"What do you mean you had an opening?" Meg asks.

"After the mentor night, she told me these older girls gave

her some *really good advice*, and she couldn't wait to try it on Monday."

"After your dinner with Nikki and Cori?" Meg asks.

"Yep." I do my best to shrug off the fact that she had to drag Nikki into this, noticing a large tree that's fallen and blocking the trail up ahead. "I'm a total mom failure."

"Don't be so hard on yourself." Naomi's voice soothes. "The boys are the ones who did something wrong. The parents and teachers know that. The other kids will come around."

The insides of my stomach start to cave in. I feel like I'm about to throw up. "So, now what do I do?" I feel inept in all parenting capacities.

"I wish I had better advice," Naomi replies. "I can talk to Lily and make sure she understands why this backlash at Kayli is unwarranted. I'll also tell my other mom friends to do the same with their kids. And maybe the teachers will say something similar."

"Same," Meg says. "This is tough. Hopefully things die down soon as the kids get a better understanding of why Kayli wasn't in the wrong."

I rack my brain for a silver lining to the situation as the rhythm of our boots clunk around my head, but it's futile. My guilt only increases with each step. I can't come up with a good excuse for not asking more questions earlier. Kayli's been in such a fragile state, I should've been more tuned in. I've gotten too much in the habit of letting her handle everything on her own. I need to step in more.

Meg finally breaks the ice. "You know, this whole situation further underlines why these relationships are so not beneficial for kids this age. It creates all this unnecessary drama and steers the kids off track from other things that are actually beneficial—schoolwork, sports…"

Here we go again. I can't help but smile, though. Meg's relentless.

"Did I tell you James is going to ask Liz to the dance?" Meg shakes her head. "And he wants to do it in this *special* way. Make some catchy poem on a sign with candy bars on it or something—he wants me to buy the candy for him! He got the idea online somewhere. Like he doesn't have better things to do than make some mushy love sign."

A few birds chirp off in the distance. I'm guessing they're getting sick of winter by now too. Similar to James, though, I don't know if Mother Nature is listening.

"Oh, and Lily can ask Jared." Meg finally ends the silence. "Principal Jacobson said as long as the dates are in fifth grade, it's fine. He actually thought it was a nice idea to invite some kids from Park Academy since most of those fifth-graders will attend Valleybrook next year."

"Oh, thanks." Naomi's voice is unusually flat. "Lily will be so happy."

"You don't sound super excited." I slow down as we approach the large tree that seems to have been ripped from the ground and strewn across our path. The horizontal trunk is almost up to our waists. I don't even know if it's possible to proceed. "What do you guys want to do? Try to climb over this or turn around?"

Meg's eyes pan down the trunk until they reach the clump of roots torn from the ground, taking most of the surrounding dirt with it. "Let's turn back. We've faced enough hurdles lately."

"I hear you," I say. Although I'm slightly bummed our walk will be cut short—no favorite bridge or picturesque view for me today—I can actually use the extra work time. We turn around and begin to retrace our steps. "So, back to Lily…are things still going okay with her and Jared?"

"Maybe too well," Naomi replies. "Don't get me wrong, Jared's a great kid, but now Lily wants to be able to hang out with him in her room, and it makes me so nervous."

"Whoa…yeah." Meg takes a quick look back at the fallen tree before saying, "I think that would make almost any parent nervous. You're not going to allow it, are you?"

"I don't know," Naomi sighs. "I understand her point. Our house is so tiny, and when they're in the living room, Leo's basically on top of them—he idolizes Jared."

I don't have words. I can't imagine leaving Kayli alone in her room with a boy right now.

"And they're in fifth grade," Naomi continues. "It's not as if they'll do anything. They need a quiet place to work, and her room is right off the living room. I told her the door has to stay open the whole time, and I can check in on them whenever I want."

It still seems risky to me, but maybe no matter what Naomi's rules are, the kids will find a way to do what they want. It's so hard to know how our involvement or rules affect these kids. I'm literally tongue-tied on the matter. And knowing Meg's opinion, it's probably best to change the subject. "How's Leo's website doing these days?"

"Really good." Naomi's eyes brighten as she starts to smile. Maybe everyone's a little relieved to move onto a less controversial topic. "He's only gotten a few sales, but he loves it. He wants me to sign him up for a bunch of STEM camps this summer. I can't believe registration is on Tuesday—that seems so early. Which reminds me, are either of you attending the band meeting on Monday night? Lily wants to do choir, but I've heard most kids are doing band."

"James is doing choir, too, thank God," Meg says. "His plate full enough already. He doesn't need to add summer band lessons or band camp. Choir is so much simpler."

I nod, grateful Kayli wanted to avoid band too. "Same with Kayli."

"At least those camps are during the day," Naomi says.

"Lily's begging me to let her go to this three-day coding camp where she stays overnight."

"Whoa…that's huge," I say. "But I love that she's so into coding. I wish I could find a class or camp that'd get Ryn more excited about math. She detests it right now, and her class-mates aren't making it any easier. Oh, and get this—this morn-ing, Kayli was there when Ryn was telling me about it, and she warned Ryn to beware of friends turning on her."

"You think that's about Gavin?" Meg asks, pausing before she looks over. "Or Emily?"

"Who knows…" As I focus on the trail ahead, the mud and snow off to the side blur into one tan, muddy mess. "When I spoke with Nikki and Cori about the girls during mentor night, they said Emily and Mandi were trying to be friends with Kayli, and *she* was the one turning them away."

"That doesn't line up at all with what I've heard," Naomi says. "And with Emily and Brody still together…"

I rarely question the information Meg or Naomi share, especially when it comes to what's going on with the kids at school, but this time, I have to. "Really? When I was with Cori on Friday, she said Brad put the kibosh on Brody, and things with Brody and Emily were over."

"That's not what I hear," Naomi says. "Someone even mentioned it last night. They thought Emily might have some-thing to do with the fallout on Kayli, too. Apparently, Brody convinced her to take his side."

I press my lips together to keep my jaw from dropping to the ground. All I can picture is a wooden wheel churning around this town's rumor mill. Emily's contributing to the fallout because of Brody—how does Cori not know this? Her best friend, Nikki, is usually in the center of the rumor mill, turning the crank. "Cori's normally clued in, though, with Nikki…," I reply. "Wouldn't she know?"

"Yeah…I don't know," Naomi says. "Sometime Cori's

focus is a lot more on Brandon. Or maybe she has heard stuff, but Emily's denying it. I only know what I've heard."

"And I've heard the same," Meg adds as we reach our cars. "Naomi has better sources on this than I do, but I've definitely heard the same rumblings. I'm sure we can help, though. I'll keep talking to my network and reiterate that Kayli shouldn't be the one being punished. I think parents will reinforce this message with their kids once they know more about what's going on."

"I agree," Naomi says. "It may not work for everyone, but it'll help for sure."

I hesitate, briefly questioning the repercussions of getting more involved. I suppose it could make things worse, but I can't imagine how. And maybe accepting their offer will actually help. I quickly relent. The message they want the kids to hear is the right one, and if no one speaks up, it's hard to see how they'd come up with it on their own. "Thanks, you guys. I truly don't know what I'd do without you. Oh, and save me a spot in yoga tomorrow, Nay. I'm going to need it."

MONDAY, MAR 2

The bus door opens, and Kayli's the first one out—Kayli? She's never out the door before Ryn. And she has a smile on her face...and a bounce in her step. She actually looks happy. As the two of them race toward the garage door, I feel a bounce in my own step, heading into the mudroom to meet them.

The door bursts open, and they tumble through together, out of breath.

"Hey guys!" I smile, helping them with their stuff. "Good day at school?"

"Yep," Ryn answers, turning on her autopilot and heading straight to the snack drawer.

"And I have exciting news." Kayli nudges past her sister, silently teasing her to another race—the first to grab a snack and get back to a stool at the island.

Exciting news...it's been ages since Kayli came home this cheerful, and with *exciting* news no less. Meg and Naomi assured me their plan to get the parents—and their kids—on Kayli's side has been working. But prior to this very second, Kayli had yet to crawl out of her social doldrums. What sort of magical turn of events could have resulted in this about-face in mood? "What is it, hon?"

"I decided I'm going to be in band." She scooches up in her seat, breaks off a piece of granola bar, and pops it into her mouth. Still chomping away, she adds, "The trumpet was seriously so fun."

"Band…are you serious? And you're telling me this now? The band meeting's tonight, isn't it?" The exasperated words fall out of my mouth too quickly to stop them. I take a deep breath as I grab a stool and sit down. So what if the band meeting's in a few hours, a huge time commitment, and a significant chunk of money? If band's making Kayli this happy…

"How was I supposed to know?" Kayli plays the innocent victim card. "They just let us try the instruments today."

"What?" I can't help but gasp. "They didn't let you try the instruments until today? Why in the world would they wait until the last minute? They can't expect parents to drop everything and make a huge decision like this in point five seconds." Again, my mouth acts like a spigot that won't turn off. I don't know why I care so much about this. It's band. Sure, it'll be a little more of an investment, and it'll take up more time than choir—especially this summer—but it's nothing insurmountable.

Ryn teasingly pats my back as Kayli shrugs, shifting in her seat but maintaining eye contact. She must really want this, holding her ground while I stare her down. And I guess it's not her fault if they waited until the last minute. Besides, this could be a good thing. She's finally excited about something, and it's something that forces her to be with other people. It'll get her out of her room and back into human civilization.

"So, now you want to be in band?" I relax my shoulders, but I can't resist rubbing my forehead. I had planned for her to be in choir. It's what she's been telling me she wanted to do for the past several months. Ever since we were made aware the fifth-graders had to choose between band and choir the spring before middle school. I was so relieved she picked choir. It seemed so simple—no instrument to be responsible for, no lessons, no camps—not to mention it's free.

"Yes." She straightens up, her eyes remaining laser-focused on mine as she gives one more adamant nod.

"And you want to play trumpet?"

"Yes. It was so fun to play. And I was really good at it…the instructor said so."

Mm-hmm. I'm sure he did…anything to entice these kids. "You're sure?"

"Positive."

"So, now you want me to figure out how to get you a trumpet, sign you up for band camp, organize summer lessons, and pay for all the related expenses…and do all this at tonight's band meeting?"

Kayli's face drops. Maybe the unexpected burden of her *exciting news* is finally sinking in. Probably not, but maybe she now understands why I wasn't initially jumping for joy.

"Yes…," she stammers out, actually looking quite apologetic. "I really want to do band."

I look over at Ryn, who's now giving me her signature puppy dog face. Ugh…these two. Less than twenty-four hours ago, Kayli and I were basically in these exact spots. Except then, she was rolling, literally rolling, on the floor. Apparently, that's a normal way for an almost eleven-year-old girl to communicate she doesn't know which summer activities she wants me to sign her up for. I look at her face one more time, and I feel myself relent. "If you sign up, then you're signing up for the whole year."

"I know."

"So, no bailing. And you're in charge of taking care of

your trumpet. And remembering to practice. And anything else that comes with it. No reminders or nagging from me."

She nods, more steadfast this time. "I promise."

I pause, but it's more for dramatic effect. I never had any real rationale for not letting her do it. It was more the last-minute surprise of it all that threw me. "Fine. I guess you can do trumpet."

She leaps off her stool and throws her arms around me. "Thank you, thank you!"

Seeing her smile and the warmth of her hug feels good. The last time I hugged her, her tears soaked through my shirt. This is a million times better. Not sure it's enough to get me through the anxiety-inducing parent band meeting tonight, but still...I'll take it.

* * *

The parent chatter spills from the packed gym and echoes into the hallway, acting like Pavlov's bell. My stomach instinctively clenches as my social anxiety sets in. I inhale through my nose and exhale through the tiniest opening between my lips, racking my brain for something to help me relax. Unfortunately, Meg and Naomi aren't going to be here—unless, of course, Lily or Jake pulled a last-minute about-face like Kayli. But maybe a few other parents I know will be. "Who else is doing band, sweetie?" I look back at Kayli, who's somehow lost all her excitement and now looks as anxious as I feel, dropping several steps behind me.

"Mandi and Emily, and I'm pretty sure Liz," she mumbles, dragging her finger along the wall as we inch toward the gym doors.

"Are you sure you want to do this?" I stop and look back to face her. I don't want to be the one driving this ship. And if she's having second thoughts, I'm more than happy to turn back at any time. "You can still change your mind, you know."

"No." She straightens her back and catches up to me. "I want to do band."

"Let's go, then." I duplicate her posture.

Passing through the gym doors feels like entering a stadium concert mid-song. It's super loud, and there's an overwhelming sense of urgency to figure out where we are supposed to be. I look for someone familiar, but my vision fails me as I scan the room with my nerves on high alert…too high. The sea of faces is overwhelming, all blending into a blur of color.

"Do you see any of your friends?" I hope her younger eyes allow her to distinguish someone recognizable.

Thankfully, Kayli points to Mandi and Emily, who are sitting next to their moms in a row by themselves. Although Kayli's kept her lips sealed on how things have been going with Emily, they can't be too bad if Kayli's okay sitting with her.

"Great." I can't handle standing in purgatory another minute.

When we get to their row, Mandi scooches down, happily making room for Kayli, and the two of them start chatting about who else is playing which instrument. This is perfect. There's no indication whatsoever that Mandi's bothered by Kayli's tattletale controversy. Hopefully the same goes for Nikki. But that reminds me—either way, I need to be careful sitting next to the rumor mill operator.

"Hi." Nikki grins but looks noticeably surprised. "I didn't know Kayli was doing band."

"Neither did I." I don't hide my sarcasm as I say hello to Cori, take off my coat, and sit down. This is good. Let's keep the discussion on band. "It's a very last-minute thing. Apparently, she was very inspired by trying out the instruments today at school."

Nikki's look turns confused. "I thought the kids tried all the instruments last week."

Huh? I look over at Kayli, who quickly turns away from me, busying herself with her friends. I can't help but shake my head. She totally lied…but why? I channel my best poker face. "Oh, right. Well, then, something else must have inspired her today." Then I glance around the room, feeling the need to dig myself out of this hole as well as safeguard myself from any sort of traitor-gate interrogation. "It's crazy how many people are here. How many kids in their grade are doing band?"

"A lot." Cori leans forward to see me. "Each year the number goes up. They got a new band instructor when Brandon was in fifth grade, and he's fabulous. The kids absolutely rave about him. Every year, more and more kids pick band instead of choir. Last year, so many sixth-graders were in band they had to separate it into two sections because they couldn't all fit into the same band room. I'm guessing this year will be the same."

"Impressive. So, what instruments did your girls pick?"

"Mandi and Emily are both doing clarinet," Nikki replies. "They've been planning it since second grade. Mandi was so worried she wouldn't score well, but she did fine."

"Score well?"

Cori leans forward again to explain. "Last week, when the kids tried the instruments, the band instructors ranked them on a scale of one to five. The kids had to score a four or a five in order to be able to pick that instrument."

"Ah…got it," I get out right before a drumroll starts. So the kids didn't simply try the instruments last week, they got scored on them too. Doesn't seem like a thing that would slip Kayli's mind. I guess she *was* a wreck last week, but still, she clearly lied…

A drumbeat begins to whirr from the podium up at the front as a stout man, not much older than me, snares away. You can see the joy in his eyes through his wire-rimmed glasses as beads of sweat start to drip from his hairless head.

"Ta-da!" his voice booms after he taps his last note, drops the drumsticks, and jumps into jazz hands. "Thank you so much for coming and allowing your children to join me on this amazing adventure of learning an instrument. It's going to be a magnificent journey, one that has the opportunity to teach responsibility, perseverance, and the love of music."

The audience is clearly entranced as this uber-engaging fellow distributes packets and continues to describe all the wonderful opportunities that can be had by our children this summer in his cruise-director voice. "In the last week of July, your child's odyssey will begin at our critically acclaimed band camp, where they'll learn the fundamentals of their instrument and begin to be exposed to the glorious sounds it can make. Then in August, the fun and learning will continue with weekly band lessons where they'll share in the delight of playing their instrument with a small group of classmates."

After providing a few animated examples of the musical growth he's witnessed among former students, his over-the-top presentation winds down, and Nikki starts packing up her stuff.

"Before you leave," the band director calls out, "make sure to turn in the two forms in your packet and get your name on the sign-up sheet for preferred lesson times. Instrument rental information is also in the back, and I'll be up here for any additional questions."

Nikki looks over as we get up. "Unfortunately, we're not sticking around. Since Brandon did all this band stuff a few years ago, Cori knew it was better to get here early, rather than wait in the lines after the presentation."

"Lucky you." I glance over at the long lines of parents forming at each of the tables and say goodbye. As they grab the rest of their stuff and make their way out of the room, I realize I made it. No awkward questioning from Nikki, and things with Kayli's friends seemed amicable. Way better than I thought. Meg and Naomi's plan seems to be working. I finally feel like I can breathe normally again.

I turn to Kayli. "Which table first...preferred lesson times or instrument rental?"

"Preferred lesson times."

I grab my coat, and we start weaving our way over to the table.

"Hey, stranger!" a loud, syrupy voice calls from behind. I recognize it immediately.

"Hey." I turn to Natalie and quickly try to cover my surprise. Although I got used to seeing her in her high-end tennis attire at tennis pickup this fall—here, at a band meeting...in February? I force myself to focus on her face. "This sure seems like the place to be tonight."

"Yeah." Natalie towers over me, beaming as Liz and Kayli move off to the side to start their own conversation. Although I'm never super comfortable around Natalie, or the country club moms she spends all her time with, I feel myself relax a little at another indication that Naomi and Meg's plan worked. "I was hoping to get here earlier since I knew the lines would be crazy, but Liz had tennis. Thank God we have the instrument figured out and can skip the one for rentals."

"You're lucky." I glance over the next line awaiting us. "Which instrument is she doing?"

"Flute," she says. "She wanted to do the same instrument as Sienna and Stacy."

"Really?" I make sure to quickly close my mouth. Last I heard, they were feuding over James. That was a couple of weeks ago, though. Things can change so quickly in fifth grade.

"I know." She rolls her eyes, brushing off my surprise like a pro. "It's still a little rocky, but things should get back to normal soon. With golf starting in a few weeks and tennis ramping up, Liz's other *distractions* will soon have to fall by the wayside."

I can only nod. She has to be referring to James, but I'm not brave enough to clarify.

"Speaking of tennis…" Her voice grows excited again as we near the front of the line. "Kayli *has* to enroll in Coach Brian's lessons this summer. Oh, and his league, too—sign-up starts tomorrow. Liz would love it if another friend joined. And with Julia and her teammates moving on to high school next year, there'll be a few spots open on the middle school team. If Kayli keeps practicing, she could have a real shot."

Obviously, I'm not going to admit Kayli wanted to do absolutely nothing as of yesterday, so I just say, "Oh, that sounds great. I'll talk to her about it tonight." Then I say goodbye and proceed to take my turn filling out the sign-up sheet. What a relief…another parent, another conversation not mentioning the Gavin-Brody incident…another win. After selecting our lesson time slots, Kayli and I move on to the next queue of parents.

As we get in the line for instrument rentals, I recognize one more familiar face ahead of us. I haven't seen her since we chaperoned the fifth-grade retreat together this fall, but since things have been going so well with the other moms, I decide to press my luck. "Amy?"

"Oh, hey." She turns back and smiles. "How are you?"

"Good…a little overwhelmed, maybe." I motion to the chaos surrounding us and notice Kayli starting to chat with Tommy off to the side. "But good."

She laughs. "I know, right? This night's so hectic. What instrument is Kayli doing?"

"Trumpet."

"Same as Tommy…for now, at least."

"What do you mean?"

"I wasn't expecting it to be a tough decision for him. He's been planning to play trumpet since forever. But a couple of his buddies decided to do choir at the last minute, so then he

wasn't sure what he wanted to do. The lunchtimes in middle
school are dependent on if the kids do band or choir, so he had
to pick whether he still wanted to play trumpet or be with his
friends during lunch."

"That is tough…I didn't realize how this affected lunch."

"Yeah…" She tilts her head side to side like she's still
mulling it over. "That can be huge for these kids, but I'm actually relieved he stuck with band. It'll be good for him to have a
break from some of his *buddies.*" She lowers her voice. "I'm
sure you're well aware that Gavin and Brody haven't been
model citizens this year."

Whoa, wait…what…Tommy is buddies with Gavin and
Brody? I guess that makes sense since they all play basketball
together. But let me get this straight, they were supposed to be
in band, but Gavin and Brody changed their mind last-minute?
That has to be why Kayli changed her mind too. The pieces
start falling into place. Of course.

Amy's still waiting for me to respond—I need to address
the Gavin and Brody issue. But what do I say? Although it
seems she knows they're troublemakers, her son *is* friends with
them, so I'm sure she knows their moms. "Yeah, it's been a
little challenging these past few weeks."

"You know Gavin's mom, Lisa, right? Have you had a
chance to speak to her about it?"

Unfortunately, I can't tell a whole lot from her tone, but it
doesn't seem accusatory. I discreetly roll my neck as I look over
to check on Kayli and Tommy assessing the different trumpets.
Do I dare admit the thought never crossed my mind? In the
beginning, I truly believed Kayli could handle it. I thought
staying in my lane would be better. And when Gavin spread
that rumor, I figured Lisa would find out from the school.
Same with the inappropriate pictures. Besides, what would I
have even said? "No, I haven't seen her much."

Amy sighs. "I know it's been tough with her trying to figure out all this stuff for her dad. She's been out of town a bunch trying to find the right care for him."

"I can't imagine." My neck relaxes. I'm off the hook. I couldn't have spoken to Lisa even if I was *supposed* to.

"I'm sure her absence has played a part in Gavin's issues. She's always been the rock of their little crew, and with her gone so much…but still, it's no excuse for his behavior." She shakes her head. "When I heard what those boys did to Kayli —turning her into the villain even though she did the right thing—I felt awful. So did Tommy. I urged him to stick up for her, but I'm not sure if he ever said anything."

"That's okay." I feel a smile start to form. Amy's on our side, too. And when I see it's her turn to sign up for rentals, more relief washes over me. I gesture to the table, indicating she's next.

"It was great running into you." She smiles goodbye. Another success. Three for three.

A few minutes later, I feel Kayli next to me as I make the final signature promising to pay thirty dollars a month for the next year, plus fifteen more for insurance, a hundred for summer lessons, and seventy-five for band camp. In total, I'll be forking over five hundred and fifty dollars so my daughter can avoid eating lunch at the same time as two unruly boys.

It's actually sickening, now that I have time to think about it. It's basically a settlement in reverse. Kayli is switching her entire life path to avoid something—someone—who should be the one getting out of her way.

I know this strategy all too well, too. Probably so well, I don't even know when I'm doing it myself. It's definitely how I handled things with my manager at the golf course after the kissing *incident*. Finding excuses to leave the room if we were even close to being alone. Asking other girls to cover for me when I was scheduled to close with him. I thought about quitting, but I needed the money too badly. Instead, I reverted to wearing the tank tops and shorts with more coverage and took different shifts. I listened to my coworker's advice, never said anything, and kept my job. What if I had, though? How would that have changed things?

"Hey, hon," I say as we walk out to the car. I can't not say anything now. But I try to make my voice sound easygoing... only curious. "Nikki and Cori mentioned that all the fifth-graders tried the instruments last week. It made me wonder if there was another reason you may have switched to band so last-minute."

She shrugs and then mutters, "No."

"So, you're sure this is what you want to do? It's a huge commitment. You should really love it. You shouldn't be doing it just to, say, get a different lunchtime or something."

"Mom..." Her chin tilts down as her eyes roll up. "I'm not."

"You're sure?"

"Yes," she groans. "I'm sure."

The crunch of her boots is the only sound for the rest of the way through the parking lot. I don't know what else to say. How hard do I press her on this? I mean, it's fifth-grade band. It's not like it's a huge deal. Besides, it's not like playing the trumpet is a bad thing. And she'll have the same lunchtime as her friends. It could actually be good.

I open the door for her. "You know, Liz's mom mentioned doing tennis lessons this summer and maybe a league. She thought if you kept practicing, you could have a shot at one of the spots on the middle school team since Julia and her friends are moving up to high school."

More silence as she slides in.

"Do you think you'd be interested in that?"

She shrugs.

"Honey, I don't want to put a ton of pressure on you, but

sign-ups are tomorrow, and a lot of this stuff fills up so quickly. I'd hate for you to miss out on stuff and regret it later."

I still don't get a response. I get in and start the car.

"Remember basketball tryouts this fall, and how you wished you would've done more over the summer?" I check on her through the rearview mirror. It's almost as if she didn't hear me. Her expression is blank as she stares out the window.

I wish I knew what was going on in her head. Everything seemed to be going so well tonight. "Sweetie, is something wrong?"

"No! Gosh, Mom…," she groans even louder.

Okay, then…she's frustrated with me, got it. But I can't seem to drop it. Whatever, Naomi and Meg step in every once in a while with their kids, and it seems to work out okay for them. "How about I sign you up, and then we can cancel if you decide you don't want to do it?"

"Fine," she huffs. The hum of the engine is the only sound the rest of the way home.

Fine. I smile. I don't let her see it, though. Sometimes, she simply needs a little nudge—guidance—it's definitely not the same as overstepping.

WEDNESDAY, MAR 4

It would be really good if you could stop by. The words in Ms. Andreen's email reverberate through my head as I get out of my car this morning. I'm embarrassed to admit I didn't even know Kayli submitted a story for the writers' workshop contest. But apparently, she did, Ms. Andreen reviewed it, and now there seems to be a cause for concern. Possibilities of what the problem could be swirl through my head, with each idea spinning by worse than the last. There's nothing I can do about it now, though. I just have to wait until my meeting at eleven thirty. I'm praying this morning's walk will take my mind off of it for a while.

"Morning, guys." I push my thoughts aside as I make my way across the brown, matted grass to Naomi and Meg. The dormant ground reignites my excitement for the snow that's supposed to come tomorrow. Everything looks so blah. A fresh layer of pristine white snow will do a world of good, especially since it's not supposed to start to warm up for a couple of weeks. The kids are excited too. The forecast calls for eight to thirteen inches, so they'll likely get dismissed early. Or, if they're lucky, school might even be canceled. "Did everyone survive the chaos of activity sign-ups?"

"I'm still recovering," Naomi replies as we get on our way. "I've never realized how stressful that is. And why they make you go through it this early in March is beyond me."

"Welcome to the world of organized summer activities." Meg laughs, looking over to Naomi. "Did your kids get into everything they wanted?"

"For the most part," Naomi sighs. "What a scramble, though. At the last minute, I tried switching Leo to a different STEM camp because Lily couldn't get into the overnight coding camp during the week she wanted. It ended up being the one thing I couldn't get to work."

"That's so frustrating." I think about how that happens to me almost every year. "Especially when it means one kid is busy one week while the other sits around bored."

"Yeah…maybe it's meant to be, though," Naomi says. "I think I'll enjoy some quality one-on-one time with each of them."

"So, Lily's doing the overnight coding camp, then?" Meg asks. "Is Jared doing it too?"

"Oh my gosh!" Naomi raises her hand to her forehead, slowing her pace as she turns to us. "You guys, how did I not think of that? I was so busy creating a list of websites, logins, class codes, and schedules. Ugh. I can't believe I didn't ask Lily. She never said anything about it, and in the chaos of planning and scheduling, it never crossed my mind. What if he is?"

I try to look as positive as I can. "Maybe he isn't, though. You said she didn't get the week she wanted. That could be the difference. Either way, I'm guessing if you talk to her about it before she goes, it'll be okay."

"I don't know…" Naomi covers her face as she shakes her head. "Things have been a little too heavy with the two of them lately. It's happening way too fast." She looks up at us.

"Did I tell you I walked by her room while he was over on Saturday? The door wasn't open all the way, but I saw him resting his hand on her leg."

"No way," I can't help but gasp. Lily? Sweet, innocent Lily? That's unbelievable.

"So, what'd you do?" Meg asks as we cautiously cross a large patch of ice. Its thin surface, littered with cracks, is the only thing protecting us from the water lurking underneath. With each step, the creaking sound and oozing bubbles warn us to tread with caution.

"I tapped on her door, which made him yank his hand away, and then I went in to ask if they needed anything. When I left, I made sure the door was open as wide as possible."

I exhale, wondering what I would've done in that situation. I keep thinking these kids are only in fifth grade, so nothing can really happen, but maybe it can. Although we shouldn't be ever-present and ever-rescuing, they still need our guidance and oversight. We can't step back so far that we completely sideline ourselves. "So, then did you talk to her about it?"

"Of course. Right after Jared left, I spoke to her," Naomi says confidently. "I told her what I saw, and how it's natural to want to show your affection for someone you care about, but then also about the importance of trusting that person and making sure you're ready. I couldn't believe how curious she was about kissing, though. She was asking all these questions about how old I was when I got my first kiss and how I knew I was ready."

Gosh, Naomi's so good. She always knows the right thing to say—and then she gets all this information, too. Fifth-graders…curious about kissing. It seems so young. Then, all of a sudden, it hits me, and my mind can't organize any of my thoughts. What if the rumor of Kayli and Gavin kissing wasn't just a *rumor*? When I heard what happened, I focused solely on how devastating the rumor was for Kayli. I never contemplated the kiss could have actually occurred. I assumed it didn't, but what if it did? I look down to make sure my legs are still there. My eyes confirm I'm walking, but I literally don't understand how.

Naomi continues, "So, I know it's coming. And now, knowing there could be an overnight with the two of them… that's a whole other level."

"Definitely," Meg says. "Liz is already a distraction for James, but thinking about kissing and what that could add to the mix…it makes it so much more complicated."

Naomi raises her eyebrows at me as Meg starts searching for something in her pocket. I wonder if she's thinking what I'm thinking: Meg seems way too calm as she says this. Shouldn't steam be coming out of her ears by now? Something's up. After pulling her phone out of her pocket and taking a look at the screen, she motions for us to hold up. "Sorry, it's the school."

I gaze off into the trees as Meg answers her phone, involuntarily pulled back to thinking about Kayli and Gavin. If my hunch is correct, and they really did kiss, it would explain so much. No wonder Kayli's been a walking zombie. An actual kiss changes everything. Gavin's betrayal is a million times worse. She must have been devastated. I glance down at my legs again. Still there. But why? Why didn't I think to ask her about this from the beginning?

"No problem. I'll be right there." Meg wraps up her call and puts her phone away. "Sorry, guys. I have to go pick up Brooklyn. She isn't feeling well and has a fever. You can keep walking, though. I'll just turn around."

"No…," Naomi says, then hesitates, looking over at me as Meg picks up the pace. "If it's okay, I'll head back too. I'm dying to see whether Lily's and Jared's camp schedules align."

"Works for me," I add. Maybe turning around will help stop my head from spinning.

"How'd registration go for you guys?" Naomi throws the question out to both of us once we find our new rhythm. Apparently, she wants to take the conversation in another direction too.

"Mine was pretty simple," Meg says. "Having everything settled with James's AAU and soccer teams ahead of time made it easy. I only had to sign him up for a few other basketball camps. And Brooklyn's signed up for soccer and dance. They'll probably do a little golf and tennis at the club too, but those sign-ups aren't a problem." Then she turns to me.

My mouth stalls. I need to get a grip. I don't even know if my hunch about Kayli and Gavin is correct. And I definitely don't need to add more rumors to the mix. I just need to continue putting one foot in front of the other. Finally, I'm able to compel some words to come out. "Ryn was pretty easy too. She's doing a volleyball camp, the basketball skills session the varsity coach puts on, and the park program that's near our house. Kayli was a little trickier since she wasn't sure what she wanted to do. I ended up signing her up for stuff and told her we could back out later."

"Smart," Naomi replies. "These things fill up so fast. Is she doing basketball and tennis?"

I nod, pushing myself to stay on track and keep my mind off of her and Gavin. "Some of it even starts after spring break. And she might try this babysitting class, and then, of course, there's band camp and trumpet lessons."

"I thought she was doing choir." Meg doesn't hide the surprise in her voice.

"So did I." I keep my eyes straight ahead. It's probably best to keep things simple. "But Monday, she came home and said she wanted to play the trumpet. I was a little rattled, but everything worked out. There are a lot of kids doing band, so I think she'll have fun."

"Definitely," Meg says. "Liz's doing band too. When James

figured this out, he actually wanted to switch out of choir. I guess being in band would've guaranteed they'd have lunch together next year. Eventually, though, he realized how time-consuming it'd be."

I keep my mom guilt to myself as my sense that something's changed about Meg solidifies. "How are things going for them? It seems like you're getting to be more okay with it."

"I guess," Meg sighs. "Kevin thought I was being unreasonable with the whole thing, and that if it's going to happen, we couldn't pick a better girl. We warned James that his sports and school still need to come first, and he agreed. They don't spend a ton of time together. Just texting here and there. I can check his phone anytime, and their messages have been super innocent. Mostly, they share strings of emojis or take turns saying hi."

"Wow—that's…good," Naomi says.

I keep my mouth shut, relying on Naomi's diplomacy. But it's crazy how Meg changed her mind. Just like that, too. Kevin thought she was being unreasonable, so she flipped a switch.

"Oh, and he asked her to the dance on Friday too." Meg grows more excited. "His sign actually turned out really cute. I brought it when I picked him up from school, and Natalie was there for Liz. I'd given her a heads-up to park in the lot rather than in the drop-off lane, so we could get a couple of pictures. Liz seemed thrilled."

"So, are you guys picking up Liz, then, and taking them together?" Naomi asks.

"Yeah, Kevin's taking them both," Meg replies, then turns to me. "Is Kayli going?"

"I honestly don't have a clue." I can finally be completely honest again. "There have been glimpses of her coming back to join the real world, but it's still a coin toss. She actually did pretty well at the band meeting. She was still a little quiet, but she sat next to Emily and Mandi and then spoke with Liz and Tommy while we were waiting in lines."

"But everyone's being nicer to her?" Naomi asks.

"Yep." I still almost can't believe it. "It seems like your plan to help everyone understand it was Gavin and Brody who were in the wrong worked. So, thank you. Even Amy Platts was nice about it."

We walk in silence for a few minutes as our cars come back into sight. "Last weekend of basketball, huh?" I turn to Meg.

"Yeah," she replies. "The state tournament is always fun. James loves how huge the trophies are. Is Kayli excited?"

"She hasn't said much," I say. "But Ryn's pretty pumped. Which reminds me, how are things with Leo's STEM club? Did that little girl ever get to compete?"

"They're officially done," Naomi says. "Their last competition was this weekend, and two of the boys were sick, so they were super grateful she could fill in. The little girl and her mom were ecstatic they were able to make something work. And next year, the STEM club is planning to have two teams and do a much better job at getting the word out ahead of time."

We finally reach the parking lot and quickly say goodbye, so Meg can pick up Brooklyn. At least the walk helped take my mind off of my meeting with Ms. Andreen this morning. Only forty-five more minutes left to kill.

I triple-check my blind spot, backing out of my space. Why in the heck am I so nervous? I mean, what's the worst that can happen—another issue related to Gavin? Whatever it is, Ms. Andreen is great. She was a tremendous help with the Kayli and Sienna ordeal this fall. Maybe she'll have some words of wisdom for this too.

* * *

I pour myself a glass of wine and grab a few chocolates before heading over to the couch. I usually love it when it's Ben's turn to put the girls to bed. But tonight, it only gives my nerves more time to fester as I run through the ways to start my conversation with him. *Kayli's teacher thinks she's depressed.* No, that's too dramatic. *A story Kayli wrote has her teacher concerned.* That sounds better. And then of course there's the issue with Ryn...

The weight of Ben's footsteps coming down the stairs begins the countdown. He grabs a beer from the fridge as I shift my position on the couch. I try to replicate the coaching position he's always doing. Maybe it'll signal to him I want to talk.

He sets his beer on the table, plops down next to me, and pats my leg. "What's up?"

My posture seems surprisingly helpful. I feel sturdier, stronger, and the pressure of my elbows on my legs calms any jitters trying to push their way through. "I went to see one of Kayli's teachers today. She emailed me yesterday about a writing contest Kayli participated in."

"Oh?" On a worry scale of zero to ten, Ben seems to be about a one.

"She was a little concerned about what Kayli wrote for her story."

"Why? What'd she write?" His voice grows higher, almost testy.

Is he mocking me? This is serious. "It was about a girl who was accidentally locked in her school alone over a weekend. She tried using the school phones, but they didn't work. There were some other people outside the windows laughing at her, but no one would respond to her call for help. It was pretty dark."

"But it's only a story, right? And didn't she write it a while ago?" He seems way too prepared...almost as if Kayli forewarned him of my impending concern. *Mom, it's just a story*, she asserted after school today with her obligatory eye roll, effectively snapping a rubber band on the pit of my stomach.

"Yeah, but the teacher thinks Kayli's been pretty down and out in real life lately too. I mean, we've both noticed that."

"I thought she was being a dramatic teen." He winks, taking a swig of beer. "Don't kids this age tend to blow stuff out of proportion and think everybody's judging them all the time?"

Now he's being a wise guy? This isn't making sense. Why is he treating this so lightly? "This teacher sees it a little differently. She thinks Kayli's faced a lot of rejection lately, from Gavin—even her friends. She thinks Kayli's blaming herself and is holding on to a lot of anger from these betrayals."

Ben tilts his head and gives me his best *you've got to be kidding me* look.

"What? I agree with her." Why is he being so insensitive? Kayli must have gotten to him. When Ms. Andreen told me, I was nearly in tears. "Kayli's confidence has clearly plummeted. She's been afraid to say or do anything to rock the boat. She hasn't been herself at all."

"Honey...come on." He draws out his last two words. "She's finally starting to come out of it. She seems so much better lately. She even wants to be in band. Please don't do any sort of crazy postmortem and stir everything up again."

I don't know what to say. Ben may think Kayli's getting back to normal...or maybe she convinced him she is. Either way, I don't see it. She still acts like a recluse and gives me radio silence most days. It's been impossible to get her to open up about anything. And her body's been in an almost permanent state of wilt. Doesn't Ben see this?

"I don't know." I lean back into the couch. "I think we need to do more. Ms. Andreen said we need to be empathetic, validate her feelings, and help her find ways to move on."

"See? That makes sense." Ben beams, patting my leg again. "We should get her to move forward. Not rehash the past." He nods for extra affirmation.

I keep my mouth closed as Ben looks like he just solved world hunger. I don't know what else to say. It doesn't feel right —it feels like we're sweeping something under the rug. We can't empathize or validate her feelings if she can't even express them. I look up at the ceiling. Maybe things have gotten a tiny bit better, but something's still off. I don't know whether it's because she and Gavin really kissed, or if it's Emily, or something else. When she refuses to talk to me about it, I don't know what else to do.

Ben smiles as he studies my face. "We're going to figure this out, honey. Now we know. It'll be okay. We haven't scarred her for life."

I appreciate the *we* and know he's trying to reassure me, but my guilt won't subside. I just don't know if we're doing enough…I still feel like I'm missing something.

"How about the tournament this weekend? Aren't you excited to watch Ryn?" He changes the subject. Apparently, this is solved, and he's onto the next.

That's right. I still need to talk to him about Ryn. "About Ryn…"

I'm sure he can tell from my tone that what I'm about to say isn't good. "Uh-oh," he groans in disbelief. "We never have issues with both kids, do we?"

"Yeah, it's a first," I sigh as the pit in my stomach expands. "Mr. Kane stopped me in the hallway after my meeting with Ms. Andreen."

"What are the odds?" He laughs. "Not your lucky day, hon."

I pause to figure out the best way to break the news. It's not helping that Ben's already making light of it—he should be bracing himself.

His smile fades as he rubs my back, indicating he's ready to take it more seriously.

"So, the good news is that Ryn's math homework has seen an improvement over the past several weeks." I keep an eye on Ben's reaction, but he still seems to be cool as a cat. "The bad news is that her test and quiz scores are still well below average."

"Oh man…" He slaps his knee. "And here I thought Ryn and I were making progress. Shoot! What did Mr. Kane say to do?"

"Well…" I try to think of the best way to phrase it. "Mr. Kane thought the problem might be from how we are *helping* Ryn. He actually suspected that perhaps someone might be providing the answers rather than helping her to figure them out."

"Come on…" He throws his head back. "I help her."

I decide not to say any more. I want it to really sink in.

"What? I do…" He shakes his head and then tips it back to stare at the ceiling for a minute. "Okay, maybe I could do a better job of getting her to come up with the answer. But it takes her so long sometimes, and there are so many problems to finish." He closes his eyes, and his inhale seems to go on forever. When he finally turns to look at me, I actually see a tinge of guilt spread across his face. This is good. Maybe now he'll listen to Mr. Kane's suggestions.

"Mr. Kane said he'd be okay with Ryn not finishing all the questions on her homework if, for the ones she actually finishes, she comes up with the answers on her own."

Ben pauses, tilting his head from side to side like he actually gets to decide if he likes this idea or not. "I can work with that."

"Good." I can't help but roll my eyes. "He also suggested that if she has a question about a problem, you should ask her about the ways she could potentially solve it first and maybe why one method might be better or easier than another. Or even better, she could try to do the problem both ways and see if the answers check out."

"Got it." He smiles and settles back into the couch. "See, honey? Saving the world one child at a time. Now, we just need to conquer the state tournament."

Okay then…in typical Ben fashion, he's onto the next thing yet again. I don't know if I'll ever get over how easygoing he can be with this stuff. "Yep. I have Ryn, and you've got Kayli."

"Can't wait." Ben picks up the remote and starts flipping through channels.

According to Ben, all our problems are now solved. I guess we're done here.

SUNDAY, MAR 8

"There she is, there she is!" Ryn grabs at my arm and points over to Kayli, who's taking off her shooting shirt. Perfect. We've found the right gym, and her game hasn't even started yet. I scan the bleachers and spot Ben sitting next to Mandi and Poppy's dads. With Mollie sick and Cori at Emily's older brother's game, it seems I'm still free from having to deal with Nikki and Cori's gossip du jour this weekend.

"Hey, buddy." Ben high-fives Ryn as she sits down. "How'd your games go?"

"We got third." She grins, holding up the medal around her neck. "But next year, our team's going to be in the finals like Kayli's." She looks over to me for affirmation.

I nod and smile. I'd never mention how grateful I am that they didn't make it this year. If they'd won, there's no way we would've made it to see Kayli's game.

"How's she been doing?" I gesture to Kayli on the court.

"Really good," Ben replies. "As good as I've seen, probably. All tournament, she's been making most of her shots, playing great defense, and hasn't had a turnover that I can remember."

"Awesome," I reply as the buzzer blares. It's time to start.

I sit up in my seat as Kayli and her teammates take their places around center court and get ready for the tip. The ref tosses up the ball and Harper swats it to Mandi, who quickly dribbles it up the court and passes it to Kayli. Kayli's wide open, so she drives to the basket for an easy layup. Right at the last second, though, a girl from the opposing team catches up to her and recklessly flings her body into Kayli to try to stop the shot. The whistle blows immediately, and Kayli heads to the line for free throws.

"Better make it!" someone over by the gym entrance yells. I trace the sound to see where it came from just in time to see Amy Platts giving Brody a stern look while he, Gavin, and Tommy cover their laughs.

I glance back at Kayli, who's obviously now realized she has some special fans in the gym. Great. I hope this doesn't affect her confidence. She shakes her head as she goes through her free-throw routine, taking two dribbles, spinning the ball back into her hands, and then shooting. The ball ping-pongs around the rim, but it doesn't go in. A few moments later, her second shot's also a miss.

Ben looks at me in disbelief as the other team gets the rebound and brings the action to the other end of the gym. "She never misses two in a row."

I can only nod. I'm guessing Ben has no clue about the extra distraction that's come into play. But as Amy and the boys scurry over to us, I don't have time to point it out now.

"Hey," Amy whispers after climbing up the bleachers while the coast is clear. "I'm so sorry about Brody. The boys promised me they'd behave from now on." She plops down next to me, giving the boys another stern look as they take off their coats before sitting down a few rows below us. "They finished their last game a few courts down, and Tommy really wanted to see the girls play. It's so awesome they made it to the finals."

"I'm sure it'll be fine," I lie through my teeth as Kayli throws the ball away after she misreads which direction Harper was cutting. "How'd Tommy's team do?"

"What's going on?" Ben mutters, rubbing his forehead.

"They got fifth," Amy replies, not appearing to hear Ben. "The refs in the first game called everything, so we lost that one but then won the rest—"

"Come on, Kayli!" Ryn cheers, hopefully reminding Ben to stay positive. "You got this."

I glance up at the scoreboard after Coach Brad calls a timeout. We're down by six. There's a steady hum of chatter from the bleachers, but it isn't quite loud enough to cover up Brad's disappointment with his team. "Get your head in the game!" he shouts right in Kayli's face before whipping out his clipboard and scribbling a bunch of X's and O's for the girls to see.

"Whoa…" Amy looks around and then leans in closer. "Brad's getting intense."

"Right?" My stomach curls up in knots. "He makes me so nervous sometimes."

"It looks that way for Kayli, too." Amy discreetly points over to the bench.

I see what she's saying. I totally recognize that look on Kayli's face. It's the same look she has when she breaks or loses something expensive. My gut wrenches seeing someone else inflict that same distress on her.

The whistle blows as the girls pile their hands in. "Together!" they yell before heading back onto the court. As Mandi pats Kayli's back before she goes over to the ref to inbound the ball, Kayli throws a look of daggers to the boys seated below us.

I can't imagine what's going through her head with Coach Brad's yelling and Brody and Gavin's heckling. And even though I have no control over any of it, every muscle in my body tenses, silently pulling for her to do her best and not make any other egregious mistakes that'd result in her coach's wrath or the boys' mockery.

My neck starts to ache from the strain as the game continues to be a nail-biter. Kayli isn't playing her best, but she looks like she's doing everything she can to hang in there. The other team's putting on a lot of pressure. They're causing all the girls on Kayli's team to make errors, including a few turnovers from Kayli. Her team is trying so hard, though. It's obvious to everyone, with the sweat dripping down their flushed faces.

Thankfully, with a couple of minutes left in the game, things start to look more positive. Amy squeezes my arm as Kayli steals the ball and goes in for an easy layup, bringing the score within two. "Let's go, Valleybrook!" she shouts as Coach Brad calls another timeout. Now there's less than a minute left on the clock.

The crowd's louder this time around as Coach Brad instructs the girls, but I can still make out most of what he's shouting. "We need another steal!" He locks eyes with Kayli, grabs her shoulders, and shouts, "But no fouls!"

"She already has four," Ben says, looking across Ryn to me. "Why isn't he telling someone else to go for the steal, someone who can risk being more aggressive?"

I can only shrug. Even though I've been to what seems like a million games by now, the strategies used during these last-minute close calls are still beyond my comprehension. It does seem like Brad continues to put a disproportionate amount of pressure on Kayli, though.

I cram my sweaty hands between my clenched knees as the girls head back out onto the court. Thank goodness no one can see what my heart's doing right now. They'd probably rush me to the hospital. *Come on, honey*, I plead in my head as the other team inbounds the ball, but it's no use. Almost as soon as the ball is released, Kayli lunges at the recipient, which results in a quick whistle. Crap. My heart sinks. That's five.

Even from across the gym, I know that look. The look of Kayli using every muscle in her face to hold back her tears. I'm pretty sure I have that exact same look on my own face.

"What did I tell you?" Coach Brad shouts as he whips his clipboard to the ground and shoves Poppy to sub in for Kayli.

"I can't do everything!" Kayli screams back, loud enough that even those two gyms down could hear. She snatches up her water bottle below Coach Brad's feet and huffs off to the end of the bench without another word.

My head sinks into my neck, flooding with emotions as I try to comprehend what just happened. My first thought is *good for her*—for standing up for herself. But then my chest starts to tighten with anger. Brad shouldn't be able to shout at her like that...it's not right. And my stomach begins swirling with nerves—still, she shouldn't scream back at her coach, right? In this case, though...yeah...she should. He was treating her like crap, and she shouldn't stand for it. My chest relaxes, filling with pride.

Kayli only looks defeated, though. Not proud. I try to fathom what's running through her head as the clock runs down and her team loses by two. I take a deep breath and keep my eyes on her as Ben, Ryn, and I make our way down the bleachers.

"Tough loss," Amy says, following close behind.

"Yeah. Thanks for coming." I muster a smile as I look back to see her meeting up with Tommy, Gavin, and Brody at the bottom of the bleachers while Kayli meanders toward us.

"Way to go," Tommy says to Kayli as she gets within earshot. "I'm sorry you guys lost, but you played really well."

"Yeah, way to make your team lose," Brody taunts her right before Tommy elbows him.

"Enough!" Amy says to Brody as she mouths *sorry* to me

before yanking on Brody's arm and leading the boys out of the gym.

"Don't you need to meet with your team?" Ben rubs Kayli's back, apparently oblivious to the steam coming out of her ears.

"Do I have to?" she groans, looking up at him as her eyes plead for him to say no.

"If your team is meeting, then yes," Ben replies.

Kayli mopes over to the far corner of the gym. Even from this distance, I can tell Coach Brad's giving her another earful as she sits down. I wish he wouldn't do this. It can't be helpful to the girls in any way.

"I don't understand how he thinks talking to the girls like that is effective," Ben says as if he's reading my mind. "Kayli played well. She led their team in scoring, and she held the other team's best player to only four points. All the girls worked their butts off. This was a really good team. Why doesn't he focus on the positive?"

My heart shatters into a million pieces as the team meeting ends and a shell of my daughter returns to us, her eyes filled with tears. "Do I have to go out with the team for pizza?"

"No," Ben replies, clearly reaching his limit with Brad's lectures. "We can go home."

Kayli doesn't look back at her coach or her team as we leave the gym. She leans into Ben's side, and he takes her bag, wrapping his arm around her.

"Great job, kiddo. We're so proud of you." I give her a quick hug before heading to my car with Ryn. If only Coach Brad would say something like that. The game's over. There's nothing the kids can do about it now. They probably know what they did wrong and feel bad enough about it already. Screaming at them even more isn't going to help.

"Why is Emily's dad so mean?" Ryn asks as we make our way across the parking lot.

"I don't know, hon," I sigh. "I guess he gets frustrated. Or maybe that's how he was coached when he was a kid." I don't tell her it's not actually super uncommon.

"I sure hope I don't have a coach like that."

I put my arm around her. "Me too, sweetie. Me too."

* * *

Shutting the door behind us with my hip, I slip off my shoes no-handed, carry the three grocery bags into the kitchen, and hoist them up onto the island. "Thanks for your help, hon," I call after to Ryn, who's already on her way downstairs.

"Where's Kayli?" I ask as Ben comes over from the couch to help.

"Where else?" He motions upstairs as he starts unloading the bags.

"How'd the car ride go?" I now feel a pang of regret over Kayli not riding with me.

"Not great." He accidentally tears the paper bag, yanking out a box of cereal.

"What do you mean?"

"I don't know," he groans. "She got into the car all huffy, complaining about Brad. I get it, but I also think she needs to get past it. The game's over. The whole season's over. There's nothing she can do about it now."

I try not to cringe, picturing Ben's nonchalant reaction to Kayli's passionate call of injustice. "So, I'm guessing you weren't super empathetic."

"I don't even know what that means." He shoves the gallon of milk into the fridge a little too forcefully. "I only said it's not a big deal, and it doesn't even matter now, which it doesn't."

Great. He's not only negating Kayli's feelings, he basically said the exact opposite of what Ms. Andreen told us would be helpful. I know Ben's well intentioned, and he loves Kayli. He's just blind as a bat when it comes to seeing the cruelty his daughter's facing. I cross my arms, but it fails to quell the frustration surging up my throat. "Honey, Brad was way out of line…totally inappropriate. He owes Kayli an apology."

"You can't be serious." His head falls back, caught by his interlaced hands. He stares up at the ceiling, almost as if he's asking it for help.

"One hundred percent." I stand my ground. "How he treated her…how he yelled at her. He needs to take a good look in the mirror."

"He's her coach. Sorry to say, hon, but coaches yell sometimes. It's what happens."

"These are fifth-grade girls!" I can't help myself. My frustration has completely boiled over. My skin feels like it's on fire. I inhale, count to five, and exhale. I need to collect myself. "It's not right. It makes her think people—men—can talk to her like that…treat her like that. I don't want our daughter to be a doormat and get walked all over. We can't simply brush this off. I need to go talk to her."

"Ugh…," he groans, running his hands through his hair. "Okay. Go talk to Kayli. But please be careful of what you say about Brad. This is a small community. She and Ryn are going to be playing basketball for many years. Brad's on the board…"

"I'm putting our daughter's needs first." I fold up the last of the grocery bags and glare at him. "That's all I can promise."

"Fine." Ben holds up his hands in surrender, shaking his head as he retreats to his spot on the couch.

I take several deep breaths as I head upstairs. I can't stop thinking about what would've happened if I'd had someone who supported me in sharing my story back in the day. How would things have been different if someone had encouraged me to speak up after the kiss with my manager at the golf course...how would I be different? I can't help but believe being quieted back then impacted my ability to speak up on other things going forward.

After reaching the top of the stairs, I stare at Kayli's door for a few seconds while I think about the roller-coaster ride she's been on. Riding through the high of giddiness when someone starts paying special attention to her, followed by the ups and downs of mixed messages and manipulation, and then jerking to a stop with a devastating betrayal. She needs to regain her footing—her confidence—and start working toward some sort of new normal. And she can't do this alone. She needs support. She needs encouragement.

"Honey?" I ask after tapping on her door a few times.

Silence.

"Honey," I call out again. "Can I talk to you for a second?"

"What?" It's more of a shout now, but it's muffled.

I take that as a yes and slowly open the door. Kayli's sprawled out in her sweaty uniform, facedown on her bed. Her blackout shade is pulled, and all the lights are off.

"Sorry about the game, sweetheart." I take a seat next to her and rub her back.

More silence.

"How are you feeling?"

"How do you think?" She cranks her tear-stained face and glares at me. "My life sucks. I lost the game for my team, and all the girls hate me."

"Why on earth would they hate you?" As the words come out of my mouth, I instantly question whether it was the right thing to say. I need to be empathetic.

"Because my turnovers and foul lost us the game," she groans. "And I yelled at my team that no one else was doing anything."

"What? I didn't hear that...and your turnovers and foul didn't lose the game. There were lots of things that contributed to your loss. This is a team sport. It's not just you." Okay, now I'm completely off-track. This is clearly not empathizing or validating. I need to turn this around.

"That's not what Coach Brad said." She starts to sit up.

"What'd Brad say?" Saying his name is like a match lighting my mouth on fire.

She folds her knees in front of her and wraps her arms around them. Her voice shakes as she says, "That my selfishness and lack of leadership lost us the tournament. That's what he said after the game. In front of the entire team, too."

And then there's the explosion, and my mind is detonated into tiny little fragments. Are you kidding me…who is this guy? Why would he ever say something like that to a fifth-grade girl? He has a daughter for Pete's sake. How does he not know this?

She drops her arms, her tone borders on snarky, "And, of course, Emily's right there next to him, smirking like Miss Smarty Pants the whole time. I'm sure she was loving it."

I scramble to put the pieces back together. I need to be supportive, empathetic. I rub her back again. "Oh, hon. I'm so sorry he said that to you. That'd make anyone feel horrible. But it's not right, it's not appropriate, and it's not true. If you want, we can—"

"Whatever." She grabs her pillow and buries her face in it, mumbling, "Everyone at school already hates me anyway. It's not like it can get any worse."

"What do you mean?" My head spins as I try to keep up. "What else is going on at school? I thought the kids now understood why you turned in Brody and Gavin."

"Some do…" She pauses and then looks up. "But some don't. Especially the ones who have a boyfriend who got in big trouble and thinks their dad favors me over them."

Ah…I got it now. Things with Emily *are* still a problem. "Emily, huh?"

"Her and her stupid boyfriend," she groans. "And then

Mandi feels all caught in the middle. I don't want her to feel like that. Dumb Brody. Why'd he have to come to the game and make all those idiot comments? Ugh...I hate him so much." She punches down on her pillow. "I don't know why Emily likes him. He and Gavin ruin everything."

I look around her room, searching for the right words to say. As each second passes without a response, I grow more uncertain. I have to start somewhere, though. "You know, the way those boys are treating you isn't right. And same with Coach Brad. You have every right to be this upset. You have every right to speak up, to stand up for yourself. If you want, we could talk to someone. Someone at school. Someone on the basketball board. I could go with you."

"I don't know," she sighs, hesitates for a minute, and then says, "No...I'll figure it out."

"Are you sure?" I rub her back one more time. I want to support her, but this needs to be her decision. I don't want to be just another person pushing her into doing something she doesn't want to do. "I know it can be hard to speak up, but how they're treating you isn't right. We have every right to say something...to make them aware that how they're treating you is wrong."

She shrugs, looking down as she fiddles with the pillowcase. "I just don't want to make things worse. I guess I'll think about it." She's quiet for another minute and then looks up at me. "Thanks, Mom."

WEDNESDAY, MAR 11

As I get out of my car, a sudden gust of wind pretty much shuts the door for me. At least it's sunny. This time of year, I hope each day is the last coldest day until next fall. And looking at the forecast for next week, my wish may actually come true. On Wednesday, it's supposed to be in the low fifties, which is basically shorts weather for kids around here.

I steady myself through more intermittent gusts as I make my way over to Meg and Naomi. Each step bringing me closer to Meg's exponentially louder voice. For more than one reason, I'm grateful I doubled up and wore my fleece ear band underneath my stocking hat today. Meg doesn't pause her rant for even a second as I join them and we get on our way.

"She's driving me crazy! When we first met, we made a list of all the things that needed to get done and then divvied up the tasks. We've been meeting every other week for nearly two months. The fact that she hasn't done any of the things on her list never came up. Not once."

"What can we do to help?" Naomi asks as I'm still playing catch-up with what's going on.

I nod to show my support. I'm pretty sure this is about

Cynthia and the dance, but whatever the debacle, I'm willing
to chip in to help Meg. This is pretty rare form for her. She's
usually fine juggling a million things at once, even with
extremely tight deadlines. If she's this frustrated, things must
be pretty bad.

"Thanks, you guys." Meg drops her voice back to a more
normal range as she starts to calm down. "It's so late, though,
it's probably easier if I do it myself. It's really only making a
few phone calls, and I know most of the vendors anyway from
other events I've helped with. I'm just so annoyed with
Cynthia. I mean, when you volunteer, you should do what you
signed up to do—and James is so excited too. It's these kids'
first dance, so I want everything to be perfect, you know?" She
tilts her head back, exhales, and then brings it back down as
she adjusts her jacket. "What about Lily? Are you guys all set?
Does she have something fun to wear?"

"She does." Naomi's words creep out, almost as if to make
sure the coast is clear. "She has a yellow dress from last Easter
that still fits her, so probably that…if she goes." Naomi looks
down, pausing for a minute as branches crackle around us.
"Jared's been avoiding her."

"Avoiding her?" Meg's eyebrows scrunch together until
they're one as she leans across me to get a better view of
Naomi. "How is that possible? I thought he was Mr. Perfect.
Why would he do that?"

"I don't know." Now it's Naomi's turn to focus on her
jacket, unable to hide the disappointment in her voice. "But he
didn't attend their coding class the last two times. It's been a
week since Lily's heard from him. She's tried calling and email-
ing, but he won't respond. She thinks it's over."

"That's awful. Poor Lily," I say as the wind howls above us.
"How's she handling it?"

"Better than me for some reason." Naomi stretches her
arms over her head and then brings them down to the back of

her hips as she arches her back. "But I can't tell if she's fully processed it. They got to be so close and got along so well, and he was so nice and polite. It doesn't make any sense. He was such a good kid. And they were spending so much time together. It's hard to believe she could get over him this fast."

"Well, you're super lucky if she bounces back this quickly." I focus on the bright side. "Maybe some of Lily's resilience can rub off on Kayli when we get together over spring break."

"That, or Kayli can teach her to survive the aftermath of a breakup—how's she doing, by the way?" Naomi reaches for a tissue from her coat pocket. "I heard Brody and Gavin are still tormenting her quite a bit. What was it this time...stealing her lunch tray? And then something about her being unable to steal it back and losing the game."

I feel myself grow warm. How awful...why do these boys have to suck so much? And why doesn't she mention this stuff to me? Right when I feel like we're growing closer, I find out something else she's withheld. What else is she keeping from me?

"I heard that too." Meg's words have an unusual sadness to them. "That has to be so hard. You think she'll go to the dance?"

"I can't imagine." I shake my head, thinking back to the past few mornings and how hard it's been simply getting her to go to school. "After what happened at the tournament this weekend, it's been a challenge to even get her out of her room. She thinks everything is all her fault and everyone's mad at her again."

"Why would everyone be mad at her?" Meg asks as we reach the bridge and face the unprotected blasts of wind. We cling onto each other as we stagger across. It's hard to even talk.

"Everything with Kayli feels so complicated," I get out after we're more protected by the trees and Meg releases her death grip on my arm. I take a deep breath before continuing, "Her coach said some pretty inappropriate things to her during and after their last game. He essentially blamed the loss on her. Ben didn't want to create any sort of issue, so we didn't say anything. But it was pretty intense."

"Well, if it makes you feel better, you wouldn't be the first one to let that cat out of the bag," Meg says. "When Brandon was that age, Brad was a huge problem. They even contemplated removing him from the board. I guess since he and Cori have been so *financially supportive* of the program, they've kept him on."

"That's so frustrating," I sigh. The weight on my chest makes it harder to get words out. "I know these are volunteer roles, and they take a ton of time and are not enviable positions by any means, so I hate to complain. But he's so hard on Kayli and puts a ton of pressure on her. I think she reached her limit on Sunday, and she blurted out some things she regrets now."

"What'd she say?" Naomi asks as we finally hit our turn-around mark, thankfully putting the wind at our backs now.

I do my best to recap what happened at the tournament: how Emily's crush on Brody is putting their friends in the middle, how Brad's attention to Kayli is making Emily jealous, and how Kayli feels guilty about both of these things and believes avoiding everyone is the best course of action. Thank goodness the wind is blowing in a more favorable direction when we hit the bridge this time. My legs definitely need the extra push to get across.

"That's a lot for a fifth-grade girl to shoulder," Naomi says. "What are you telling her?"

I cross my fingers for another boost of wind. I get so drained when my parenting skills are placed under the microscope. "It's still a work in progress since I've only started putting the pieces together over the last few days." I purposely omit the part about Kayli's depressing writing piece and Ms. Andreen's advice on helping to get her to take tiny steps forward. "Kayli's been a bit of a hermit, and it's such a delicate balance of trying to get her to open up more without pushing so hard she shuts me out."

"Sounds awful. Poor Kayli," Meg says. "If we can be more helpful, let us know."

"Thanks. I will." I turn to Meg as the parking lot comes into view. I really don't want to end our walk on such a depressing note. "How's everything else these days? What's everyone doing with their free time, now that basketball is over?"

"Free time...I wish." Meg shakes her head, chuckling. "James and Brooklyn have already started indoor preseason soccer workouts. Two soccer players, you guys. Each with a totally different schedule. I don't know how I'm going to get this to work."

"If anyone can figure it out, it's you," I tease, feeling lighter with the change in topic. "How's Brooklyn doing so far? This is her first time playing, right?"

"So good." Meg cheers up, even adding a little bounce to her step. I love this version of Meg. I feel like it's been missing lately. "And her coach is my dream come true. It's one of her teammate's moms, and she's out-of-this-world fabulous. She's all about empowering the girls and wanting them to be supportive of each other. After the initial team meeting, one of the other moms mentioned she thought the coach might be a little too competitive and focused on winning, but Kevin and I love how invested she seems."

Naomi gives me a nudge, and we're both grinning when we reach our cars and say goodbye. Yep. This is the friend we both know and love.

* * *

I bring my wine into my office as Ben heads upstairs to put the girls to bed. Even though it's technically my turn, he's taking one for the team so I can get caught up on work. I can't believe how behind I've gotten lately. I take another sip before I flip my laptop open and start scrolling through my inbox. This could take hours. As I begin to sort through the madness, my phone interrupts me. I turn it over. It's Naomi.

"Hey, Nay, what's up?"

"Umm, well…" She sounds nervous, scared even. "I just got off the phone with Meg, and we think…there's a possibility…Kayli may have done something."

"Done something? Kayli?" I get up from my desk chair and move over to the couch as my head spins with possibilities. The last couple of months *have* been a little rough for her. First, she goes berserk on Gavin on the playground, then she busts him and Brody with the school's video app, and last weekend, she exploded at her coach in front of everyone. Even though her reactions are somewhat justified, her heat-of-the-moment decisions haven't been resulting in the most positive outcomes.

Naomi continues, "Sorry, yeah. I think she started this rumor. And um…and it's going to create quite a mess if it's not true."

Oh man, I can't believe this. I lean my head back for a moment before grabbing for the blanket. I suddenly feel the urge to cover my eyes. "What's the rumor?"

"That Gavin and Brody are the ones behind the body spray."

"Oh…" This actually seems plausible to me. "But wait, you don't think it's true?"

"There's no proof. And if it's not true, and Kayli's only spreading it to get back at them, it could cause some real problems…for Kayli." Naomi pauses for a couple of seconds before she continues. "It's just…I, um…you know, considering her history with these boys…well, it's a serious accusation. We should make certain it's true before it gets too far down the road."

"No. You're so right. Of course. I'm so glad you told me. I'll go talk to her right now."

"Okay. Good," she sighs. "Good luck."

As I put my phone away and head upstairs, the past few days race through my head. What is going on with her? I've tried to be understanding, give her room, and be there for her, but it's clearly not enough. She needs more guidance. I know getting too involved with her social world strained things between us before, but I need to get over it. I can't stand by as she tries to navigate this craziness on her own. Having her continue to problem-solve these issues in too much of a vacuum is producing a damaging aftermath, and I need to intervene.

I pass behind Ben, who's settled in on the couch, on my way to the stairs. I don't even contemplate telling him what's going on. Not yet. All he ever wants to do is immediately stifle any sign of conflict or turmoil. I need time and space to really understand what's going on. And if the problem requires an uncomfortable confrontation, then so be it.

Outside Kayli's door, I remember what Ms. Andreen said: empathize, validate, and help her take steps to move on. It's the *help* in taking these steps to move on where I've failed. Because of what happened with this fall, I've been too reluctant to offer Kayli help. I didn't want to swoop in and rescue. I wanted her to problem-solve on her own. But without enough outside advice or insight, Kayli's rash decisions are resulting in some very negative consequences. I need to help her think through other ways to solve these problems.

I tap on Kayli's door. This time, I don't wait for her to respond. I march right in and sit down on her bed next to her. "I need to talk to you about a rumor that's being spread."

Her face immediately reddens as she slouches down, trying to cover it with the book she was reading.

With this response, I don't need to bother clarifying what the rumor is or her involvement in it. "Do you know if it's true?"

"Am I in trouble?" She peeks out from behind her book.

"Honestly, you could be. But can you tell me what's going on first?"

She uses the book to conceal her face again. "I'm sorry. I don't know why I did it. It's...ugh...Brody and Gavin. They don't leave me alone. They're always teasing me about some stupid thing I did, and I...I get so mad."

"So, the rumor's not true, then?" I take a stab at reading between the lines.

"I don't know..." She finally puts the book down and begins to plead her case. "I mean, it could be. I've seen that body spray in Gavin's and Brody's lockers before. But I guess, no, I don't have proof it's them."

"Honey, this is a big deal. That's a serious accusation, and you could get in a ton of trouble for lying about it. You can't go spreading rumors about people. For goodness' sake, don't you know how wrong that is? Think about when they did that to you."

"I know, I know, and I'm sorry." This time, she scooches way down. She's almost lying flat as she pulls a pillow over her face. "You can tell everyone it's my fault, *again*."

The pit in my stomach hits a new low as I listen to her voice fading and watch her shrink away. I can't keep allowing her to slip into this less-than version of herself. I glance around her room. I look at the GRL PWR poster, her shelf of basketball medals and trophies, and the team photo with her and Emily holding the ball in the center. Their smiles and their posture—they were trying to see who was taller as they sat up as straight as they could.

"Honey, this seems so unlike you. So much of what's been going on lately seems unlike you. How you're handling things on the playground, with your friends, and with basketball. It makes me wonder if there's something more behind this."

"Like what?" She squirms under the blanket.

"Like...did something else ever happen between you and Gavin?"

"What do you mean?" She pulls the pillow off her face, hugging it into her chest as she scooches up to sit. I can sense the change in her energy immediately. She wants to tell me.

I do my best to make it easier for her to open up. "I don't know. It feels like you're not telling me something. Sometimes, when you bury your feelings or hide something that happened, it festers and builds until it erupts...usually in a negative way. Some of your behaviors have been quite the eruptions lately." I give her a little nudge and a smile. I want to signal that if she tells me, she won't get in trouble.

Her face tightens ever so slightly. It looks like she has something to say, but she won't—she can't.

Resting my hand on her leg, I soften my voice as much as I possibly can. "Honey, did Gavin ever kiss you?"

Her eyes widen as she clenches her pillow even tighter to her chest and slowly shakes her head no. She's silent for a minute or so, but then with huge puppy dog eyes, she adds, "But he wanted to. He tried."

I have trouble finding words. The pressure in my head mounts. *He tried* can only mean she didn't want him to. And she didn't let him. I tilt my head and nod, trying to telepath to her that I understand. She's not in trouble. As my thoughts get more organized, I finally put words together. "I'm so proud of you, honey." I wrap my arms around her. "I love that you trusted your gut and didn't do something you weren't ready to do. That's incredibly brave."

I feel her heart pounding as she looks up at me and says, "I pushed him down when he tried. That's why he got so mad. That's why he didn't end the kissing rumor." She pulls away. "That's when everything started going wrong." She sinks back into her bed.

The shame on her face levels me. She has it all wrong. This isn't about her. Gavin's the one who's in the wrong here. He's the one that didn't listen to her or see this wasn't something she wanted to do. He's the one who needed to be pushed away because he took things too far. Oh no…this is not her fault. I feel my blood heating up as it races through me.

"Honey, you did the right thing." I look her straight in the eye, fighting the urge to grab onto her to get her to understand this. "This is not your fault. You have every right to say no to anyone who wants to kiss you or touch your body in any way, no matter how innocent. If you don't feel right about it, it's okay. This is your body and you're in charge."

She doesn't look convinced. She still looks scared, like she did something wrong.

"And it's completely okay to push them away—or down— if you have to." My energy surges. Every fiber of my being is pushing me to get her to understand this. "Punch them in the face, even, if they don't listen…or kick. Do whatever you ne—"

"What is going on in here?" Ben gasps from the doorway, startling both of us. "Why would you be telling Kayli to punch someone in the face? We're not punching anyone in the face."

"Yes, we are." My fists clench Kayli's bedspread as I try to keep my voice steady, turning to face him. "If that's what our daughters need to do to prevent a boy who is trying to kiss them when they don't want him to."

"Come on." He sighs, rolling his eyes as he steps into her room. Shaking his head, he takes his favorite seated coaching position at Kayli's desk chair. "You can't be serious. We're not teaching our kids to *punch* a boy in the face. That isn't how you solve problems."

"No. You come on." My voice loses its balance a little as my volume increases. I forget about Kayli. I turn all the way around and move to the end of the bed, mirroring his position as I face him. "That's exactly what I want Kayli and Ryn to do. They shouldn't let a boy, no matter what their age, get them to do something they don't want to do, especially pertaining to their bodies. Maybe give him a warning first—like you get any closer, and I'll punch you in the face—but then yes. Kick, punch, fight. I don't care if the boy is in kindergarten."

Ben huffs through his nose, mocking me. "You honestly can't feel that way. Punching? These kids are ten. There isn't some other nonviolent way to resolve it? That's ridiculous."

I can't help it. His condescending expression and patronizing tone are infuriating. I'm so fired up. I don't even know if I actually believe what I just said, but I don't care. It's the point of it all. "You can't do that! You can't tell me what I can and can't feel, or if what I'm feeling is ridiculous! These are my feelings. I get to feel them!"

I follow Ben's glance back to Kayli. She's basically hiding under her covers like a scared puppy. In her ten and a half years of life, I can't remember a time Ben and I have ever fought like this in front of her. She's probably worried we're getting a divorce now.

"Listen, honey." I rest my hand on her leg and wait for her to peek out of her covers. "I'm sorry I'm getting so upset at Dad. It's just...there was a time in my life, before him, that something like this happened to me." I glance over at Ben, who's now sinking back into his chair. "I didn't stand up for myself. I didn't speak up, and I think it's affected me ever since. I don't want that to happen to you. I don't want you to lose your voice."

She sits up straighter in her bed. Her puppy dog eyes are

still there, but they're slowly transforming. First, they look more protective, and then they appear almost aggressive.

I continue, "If you want, I'd be happy to go with you to talk to someone at your school and tell them everything that happened. I'm betting if they knew what happened, they'd want to talk to Gavin and let his parents know what's going on."

I follow her glance over to Ben, who's squirming a bit in his chair, but he stays silent. I'm sure he's wondering what the heck I even just referred to.

"But what will it even do?" She slumps over, bringing her eyes back to mine but seeming to lose some of the fight she just had. "What if nothing changes? What if it makes it worse?"

"That's a possibility." I caress her head. "Some people may not like it when you speak your mind or get mad when you stand up for something you believe in. But this isn't about them. This is about you. Even if telling someone what happened doesn't change anything about the situation, Gavin, or any of the other people involved, it will change you."

She takes a deep breath as she looks me in the eye. "And you'll go with me?"

"Of course." I discreetly wipe a tear away as my eyes well with pride. "I'll be there with you the whole time."

Walking into the gym is like walking into a country wedding scene. There are hay bales, huge wine barrels, and tables with checked tablecloths scattered around the perimeter, and twinkle lights zigzagging across the ceiling. A couple of teachers are setting daisy-filled vases on the tables, and Naomi's busy helping another one hang up the photo booth sign across the barn door prop. It's truly the scene right out of Meg's head. Everything looks perfect.

I stroll over to Meg, who's off in the corner, digging through a huge stack of containers, and gently rest my hand on her back. "This place looks amazing. What else is even left to do?"

"Oh, hi!" She whips around with a pencil still between her teeth. "Thanks so much for getting here a little early. This has been complete madness. The kids will be here in less than thirty minutes, and I still haven't set up the food or drinks. Cynthia's a total no-show, too. Apparently, another catering gig came up for her tonight."

"No problem. Show me the way," I say as confidently as I can.

She hurries me over to a couple of long tables where there about twenty or so plastic-covered platters of fruit and cookies. As she fights with the seal on the first cover, her voice grows eager. "So, fill me in. I heard Gavin and Brody got in a heap of trouble."

"Here, let me help." I take the container, slide my finger between the tape, and just like that the cover pops off. "I don't know anything about that." I keep popping open lids as Meg scurries around the table, arranging it all. "But Kayli and I met with Mrs. Putnam, Principal Jacobson, and the school coun-selor on Thursday. Kayli told them everything from the attempted kiss to the name-calling and tormenting. And she confessed to starting the body spray rumor."

She stops moving for a second to look up. "And you were there the whole time?"

"I was, but Kayli did all the talking." I keep my focus on the containers, swallowing the lump of admiration creeping up my throat. I don't want to gloat, but she was incredible. "We had practiced a little that morning on what she was going to say, and she carried it out beautifully. She wasn't emotional. She didn't whine or complain. She simply told them what happened in a very stick-to-the facts way. They were all so understanding and encouraging. And, they said Kayli wouldn't get in trouble for starting the rumor since she cleared it up so quickly."

"That's great." Meg hands me some waters to start stacking in the beverage tub that she pulled out from underneath the table. "I heard Brody and Gavin's parents met with Principal Jacobson yesterday. I don't know who else was there, but I know neither one of them can come to the dance tonight. Kayli's coming, though, right?"

I nod. "With Mandi and Emily."

"Really?" Meg's eyebrows say it all.

"I know." I shrug but smile. "Kayli wants to give Emily

another shot. After Mrs. Putnam made both the boys apologize and admit what they did was wrong, Emily must have realized the error in her ways too. She called Kayli last night to say she was sorry and invited her to go with her and Mandi tonight. I'm glad, though. It's good. All these kids are still learning."

"That's for sure. Some adults are still learning, too. Did you ever get Brad to apologize?"

"Yeah, right." I roll my eyes as she hands me the last bottle and then takes a few steps back to admire her work. "Ben gave him a call, and all he got was a bunch of excuses. So, I'm not holding my breath on that one."

Meg glances at her watch. "Yikes! Kids are going to start coming soon. Do you mind manning the check-in tables out in the hall? I'll send Mr. Slater to help, too, but everyone else wants to be in the gym, so they can see more of the action."

"Not a problem," I say as she hands me her clipboard and walks me out to the entrance. Her mouth moves a mile a minute, explaining the check-in process. Then she hurries off to find Mr. Slater.

Not even two minutes go by before kids begin to trickle in, and it doesn't take much longer for the trickle to turn into a steady stream. It's fun to see Kayli's classmates. Some seem so excited while others have a lot more hesitation on their faces. And some, like Sienna, Stacy, and Liz, act like they own the place. When Kayli, Emily, and Mandi come through, they beeline it to Mr. Slater. Kayli's obviously too embarrassed to be checked in by her mom. No biggie. I can handle it. I'm just happy she's having fun.

Once all the kids have arrived, I help Mr. Slater clean up the entryway decorations and put away the registration tables. After everything is back to normal, I finally get a minute to poke my head into the gym. The screaming kids and blaring music make me glad I was assigned to check-in duty. It's almost impossible to see in the darkened room. As my eyes adjust to the lack of light, I try to make out some of the faces.

I finally recognize Lily dancing with a couple of girls off in the corner. She has a huge grin on her face as she and the other two girls twirl around, singing along to the music. James and some other boys hover over the snack table, not paying one iota of attention to a large group of girls trying to flaunt their dance moves nearby. Not far away, I see Kayli dancing…with a boy. Who is it, though? No matter how hard I strain my eyes, I can't tell.

Overhead, the music slowly fades as the DJ's voice comes on. He tells everyone thanks and to have a great night. The lights come on just in time for me to see Kayli letting go of Tommy's hand as she says goodbye.

Behind me, parents start coming in to pick up their kids. It's not until now that I realize I've been on my feet for the last two and a half hours. I'm exhausted and ready to go home.

"Hi." Kayli hops in front of me, beaming.

"Hey, sweetie." I put my arm around her. "Did you have a good time?"

"The best! Did you see who I was dancing with?"

"I think I did. Tommy, right?"

"Yep!" She holds out her hand. "And he said I had the softest hands."

"Tommy's pretty nice, huh?"

"He is…" She pauses. "A pretty nice *friend*."

"Gotcha," I say right as I see Nikki, Mandi, and Emily waving down Kayli from the entrance. "You better get going, though, sweetie. Nikki and the girls are waiting."

"Okay." She gives me one last huge smile and then runs off to meet her friends.

After making sure everyone has rides and saying our good-byes, Naomi, Meg, and I start to clear off the vases and fold up the tablecloths while the teachers tackle the garbage and pack up whatever is left of the food to take home. Thankfully, the vendors will grab everything else tomorrow.

"Well, we survived, ladies." I move to the next table and grab the vase, while Meg helps Naomi fold the tablecloth. "And it seemed like all the kids were having a great time. Lily was dancing up a storm, that's for sure." I look over at Naomi, lacing my voice with some friendly sarcasm. "She definitely doesn't seem fazed by any little breakup."

"I don't know," she sighs. "I still can't believe it's this easy for her to get over Jared."

"She's going to be fine." I give Naomi a wink. "He may have even unintentionally prepared her for the breakup… always telling her how great she was just as she is."

"Maybe." Naomi exhales as she nods slightly. "Her confidence does seem to be pretty incredible lately. Did I tell you she decided to back out of the coding camp and wants to do a couple of theater camps this summer instead?"

"See?" I reply. "And I love that he set the bar so high. The next boy Lily has a crush on is going to have to be really stellar." I look over to Meg next. "James looked like he was having fun too. Although, I didn't see him with Liz."

Meg doesn't look up as she yanks the tablecloth off the next table. "Apparently, he's also great at handling breakups. Liz dumped him yesterday."

Whoa. The vases clang as I come to a stop. I don't have any words.

"At least he can get back to keeping his head focused on school and sports," Meg continues. "The thing that bothers me, though, is he wasn't even the one to tell me. Cynthia told me when she called to bail on tonight. When I asked him about it, he just mumbled, 'Who cares?' I swear, he doesn't talk to me about anything lately. I'm so envious of how you've managed to keep that with Kayli. I saw her rushing right over to you after her dance with Tommy ended. It was adorable."

I can't help but smile a little. I loved that too. "Yeah, it's great to see her so happy, and I love that she told me he's just a friend. I'm sure she'll be a little more hesitant to jump into anything this time around. But you're right, I'm so relieved she's being open with me again."

"You're getting to be quite the parenting guru this year," Naomi teases, giving me a little ribbing as we finish stacking up the tablecloths and vases by the door. "Now you're officially an expert in handling both boy and girl drama."

"Totally." I pile on the facetiousness. "Squashing rumors, repairing friendships, I'm your everyday relationship super-hero." But then I grow a little more serious. "Now I just need to find the right balance of stepping in versus letting them figure it out on their own."

"Same." Meg scans the room one last time, then switches off the lights before we head out to our cars. "I was just reading this book that said you need to act like an assistant manager or something like that. Not a micromanager, an assistant manager."

"I love that," Naomi says. "I definitely need to keep reminding myself of things like that. It's going to be tough to keep letting them handle more and more as they get older. I'm so glad we have each other to keep us in check."

Meg and I agree as we all get into our cars, but I wait to start mine until they drive away. This is the first minute of silence I've had in several hours. I glance out the window as if I'm waiting for a sign. The moon is bright, and the sky is full of stars. It's so quiet. Too quiet. No noticeable signs, but I know I'm ready. I turn on my car, not even needing to wait for it to warm up before I take off. I turn up the volume on the radio and sing along the whole drive home.

THANKS FOR YOUR SUPPORT!

If you enjoyed this book, I'd really appreciate it if you'd leave a review on the website on which you purchased it. Also, please check out the other books that complete the series:

Mom Walks: Starting in 5th (September 2020)

Mom Walks: Catching Up (September 2021)

Mom Walks: Sharing Failure (February 2022)